It Was a Light Kiss,

so brief it might not have been there at all. Pat was almost unaware of the new sensation starting deep within her.

"We have a lot in common," Santos commented as he got up to leave. "But sometimes those who are closest do not get along. The stakes are too great."

Then he pulled her up beside him and enveloped her in a fierce embrace before leaving her for the night.

Her mind and body in total turmoil, Pat undressed and crawled under the covers. Santos was in that bed with her, although he was not in the room. By dawn she was irrevocably in love.

ANTONIA SAXON
is a former actress whose first contact with publishing came as an editor. She now writes full-time, often making use of her travels to provide the backgrounds for her novels.

Dear Reader:

Silhouette has always tried to give you exactly what you want. When you asked for increased realism, deeper characterization and greater length, we brought you Silhouette Special Editions. When you asked for increased sensuality, we brought you Silhouette Desire. Now you ask for books with the length and depth of Special Editions, the sensuality of Desire, but with something else besides, something that no one else offers. Now we bring you SILHOUETTE INTIMATE MOMENTS, true romance novels, longer than the usual, with all the depth that length requires. More sensuous than the usual, with characters whose maturity matches that sensuality. Books with the ingredient no one else has tapped: excitement.

There is an electricity between two people in love that makes everything they do magic, larger than life—and this is what we bring you in SILHOUETTE INTIMATE MOMENTS. Look for them this May, wherever you buy books.

These books are for the woman who wants more than she has ever had before. These books are for you. As always, we look forward to your comments and suggestions. You can write to me at the address below:

Karen Solem
Editor-in-Chief
Silhouette Books
P.O. Box 769
New York, N.Y. 10019

ANTONIA SAXON
Paradiso

Silhouette Special Edition
Published by Silhouette Books New York
America's Publisher of Contemporary Romance

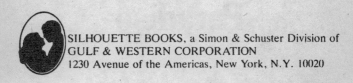SILHOUETTE BOOKS, a Simon & Schuster Division of
GULF & WESTERN CORPORATION
1230 Avenue of the Americas, New York, N.Y. 10020

ISBN: 0-671-53588-9

First Silhouette Books printing April, 1983

10 9 8 7 6 5 4 3 2 1

Map by Ray Lundgren

For Christine K. Tomasino,
agent and good friend

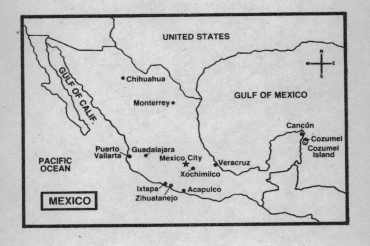

Chapter One

*I*t might have been the occasional light-headedness she felt in Mexico City's high altitude, or it might have been the pollution of the city. Then again, it might have been the overwhelming number of people jamming the streets, the subways, the buses, the sidewalks— everywhere. Of course, it might also have been the Mexican men who felt obliged to undress each woman they passed with their eyes. And for a shapely American blonde like Pat Jessup, with her distinctly Scandinavian looks, it actually became a challenge to navigate the city alone. It could have been any of these factors, or none, that made Pat feel melancholy today.

"I never should have left Cozumel," she muttered to herself as she stepped outside the front door of her hotel on the Avenida Hidalgo. "At least in resort towns you can walk around in a bathing suit and be inconspicuous. Here you practically need to be swathed in veils!"

She found a break in the swell of people rushing to

work and surged ahead, letting herself be carried along. It was sometimes hard to remember that she was in the middle of the third week of her "break out" vacation.

"Some vacation," she told herself under her breath as she joined the queue at the newspaper kiosk.

"Buenos días, linda señorita," smiled the ancient paper seller as Pat approached him.

"Gracias, por nada," Pat said rather curtly, tired of being told she was pretty by every man who spoke to her. Personally she had always thought her nose was too short and her chin too pointed, but these faults were undoubtedly overlooked because of her blond hair and extraordinary blue eyes, the shade of cornflowers.

"Los tres?" the vendor asked curiously as she picked up three Mexican newspapers and gave him a handful of change.

"Sí. Muchas gracias," she added gracefully, moving away.

"Gracias. Buenos días," he called after her.

Pat could at least congratulate herself on having majored in Spanish at college. Having only been to Mexico once at that point, on a vacation after her junior year, she still somehow knew that she had an affinity for anything connected with Spanish culture or language. And oddly enough, her desire to escape from all that had been bothering her at home was bound up with Mexico. Leaving her job, breaking off her engagement with Steve—none of it would have been possible if she hadn't had this one goal, this perfect destination, in mind.

Glancing at the headlines, she strolled past lovely Alameda Park. The world was in a mess, as usual, but all Pat was interested in these days was the want ads. She'd been kicking herself for days about not coming directly to Mexico City. Instead of wandering from Acapulco to Cozumel knocking on doors, as she had done, she should simply have gone to the source and answered ads in the paper. For an intelligent twenty-six-year-old with a degree from Boston University and a master's from Cornell in hotel management, she didn't seem to be too bright these days.

Well, your emotions are acting up, she told herself, picking up her pace as well-dressed businessmen jostled her. It's not easy to say good-bye to everything you know. Especially not when everybody tells you you're crazy to leave home.

Her father, dear Dennis, had been the only one to give her his blessing. But then, he had always understood. Her mother had fretted and worried and told Pat flat out that she was insane to break up with Steve.

"A doctor!" her mother had yelled at her tearfully even as Pat was packing for the airport. "In a year, his residency will be over. Do you know how much a cardiologist makes? Oh, it's not only the money, Pat. I never resented your father for not rising above himself. I never minded being the wife of an independent fisherman. But Steve is so right for you! You're so right for each other. Don't do this."

Of course, Pat knew she was running away. Steve had as much as told her he'd be waiting for her after she'd sowed her wild oats. He'd puffed on his pipe and mentioned quietly in his soft Western twang that he still loved her and wanted to marry her. If she had to take time out to think about it, that was fine with him. But he had to remind her that there was no question about his accepting the practice in Colorado that an old retiring doctor was leaving to him. He was going whether she came along as his wife or not.

His little woman! His wife! Pat marched stolidly

ahead, crossing with the traffic. Dr. Steve Elman didn't know the first thing about her needs, her passions, the way she intended to live her life. But then, she admitted rather sheepishly to herself, she didn't know either. All she was sure of was the fact that she didn't want any man—Steve or anyone else—putting pressure on her, telling her that after they were married she wouldn't have to work but could spend all her time raising their family. "A Denver housewife!" she'd yelled at him. "Don't you know anything about me?" But Steve had only smiled and assured her that things would work out.

The big question was, did she love him? Had she ever loved him? They'd been going together for two years now and she still wasn't sure. Steve was kind, terribly patient; he was attractive and responsible and very good with children, as her mother often pointed out, but Pat knew there was something missing. When he kissed her, there were no sparks, no real excitement between them. He regarded romance as a job to be done, and done well.

Pat suddenly realized that she'd been walking for half an hour. The warm November day was really getting to her, and she'd intended to stop for her breakfast long before this. She spotted an orange-juice wagon on the corner and gratefully went toward it, an oasis in this Mexican desert. Her mother had warned her repeatedly about eating anything sold on the streets, but orange juice was just squeezed oranges, right? How could she get sick from that? Dr. Steve certainly wouldn't approve, but he wasn't here, thank heavens.

"*Buenos días. Un jugo de naranja grande, por favor,*" she asked. The young man gave her an interested look, as if to ask how a blond American could speak with such an excellent accent, and poured her a tall glass. She paid him and began gulping down the sweet juice. It was wonderful, and it revived her spirits at once. Maybe today would be the day she found what she'd come to Mexico for.

"Por favor? Señorita?"

She felt a tug at her sleeve and looked down to see a little Indian boy. He couldn't have been more than ten, but his face looked old, and he'd evidently lived a very hard life in his brief time on earth.

"You want tour, huh? You want see Mexico City? I show you!" He began pulling at her arm, and she stopped him with a stream of very emphatic Spanish. *"No, gracias,"* she finished.

"Okay, no tour." The child's dark eyes appraised her. "I give you something better. I tell your fortune." His English was heavily accented, but she could tell he'd worked hard on his vocabulary.

"No fortune," she smiled. *"Gracias."*

"Lady, you gotta know the future!" he exclaimed. "Is *very* important. *Muy importante.*"

The juice vendor was roughly shooing the boy away, and Pat suddenly felt a pang of compassion for him. "Well, just a quick fortune, then. Not my whole life, okay? How much? *Cuánto?*"

"Is cheap! I tell you about next year only, okay? For a glass of *jugo.*" He licked his lips and put out his hand for her glass. She thought a minute, then shrugged in resignation and gave it to him. He drained the whole thing in one gulp and wiped his mouth on his grimy arm.

"Okay, kid, now the fortune." She stuck out her hand and he grabbed it, his brow furrowing in concentration as he examined her palm.

"You got *great* future!" He nodded after a few seconds. "All good things."

"Hmm." She tried not to smile. "Like what?"

"I see . . . I see a beach—beautiful white sand, right. You a tourist, right?"

She shook her head. "Not really."

"Sure, okay. So you on the sand and here comes the man. He's gorgeous like Burt Reynolds! But . . . but . . ." The child stopped and traced a couple of lines on her hand. "No, is *muy* handsome, very dark, he swims good! He like you a lot, lady."

"Does he now?" She couldn't prevent a small laugh, thinking of how the child had arrived at her fortune. Naturally, what would a blond American be doing in Mexico City but stopping over before going on to some resort? Presto, white sand and a dark, handsome stranger.

"Well, that's pretty good," she told him. "But you promised me a whole year. What happens after I meet this man who looks like Burt Reynolds?"

"You be very much in love and get married!" said the child incredulously, implying that only a very stupid person wouldn't be able to figure that out for herself.

"Oh, well, that's wonderful," Pat said, tucking her newspapers firmly under her arm. "Bye now!"

"Lady, what about *jugo?*" He came running after her.

"You drank mine."

"But that was before I told you such good fortune," he pouted.

Pat shook her head and reached into her purse for some five-peso pieces. "You win," she shrugged, giving them to him and walking away quickly before he could ask for more.

She hurried along the avenue, working her way toward the Zona Rosa, Mexico City's most fashionable district. She'd passed a nice little patisserie there the other day and since she'd been deprived of her orange juice she decided she'd treat herself to a nice breakfast. It was just nine o'clock, at least an hour before the traditional Mexican breakfast. She enjoyed the custom of grabbing a sweet roll in the morning, having a long leisurely lunch from two to five, and then a light dinner after nine. It seemed so civilized to eat this way, so much more relaxed than back home. Steve never could take more than twenty minutes for lunch, and by the time he got to her apartment in Marblehead for dinner, it was usually seven-thirty and he was famished. When they ate at her parents' house in Gloucester, he made an attempt not to wolf down his meal, but alone with her, he didn't much care. Pat remembered her father's whispered comment one night, "Doesn't the boy know his food has to get chewed before it starts on the trip to his stomach? He eats like he'll never eat again."

The more Pat thought about that, the more it occurred to her that it wasn't only food he wolfed down, it was everything. Steve Elman raced through life, never savoring or enjoying it. When he'd found a suitable mate, he had to hurry up and court her and secure her for his wife. They'd met at a party in Boston, and maybe it was their differences that had drawn them together that night. Steve had listened while Pat talked about her career goals, her search for the perfect little hotel to manage, her reasons for going into hotel management in the first place.

"You know," she'd said that night, "I haven't given up hope. I'm going to find it. My small romantic resort in paradise with an international clientele and the opportunity to really make a name for the place. It's got to be," she mused, "just the sort of place I'd want to go on my own honeymoon."

Steve had smiled warmly and urged her to keep

looking. But as the months went on and her current job at the Breakers in Magnolia got duller and duller, Steve stopped encouraging her. "Just think about a nice Colorado ranch house," he'd say. "Think about entertaining me, your husband, instead of those pokey old vacationers in Magnolia." He actually had a theory that Pat had gone into hotel management because of a repressed need to please people and make them like her.

"Psychological claptrap!" she said aloud, and several people on the street turned to give her a look. Blushing, she hurried down Hamburgo Street and turned onto Liverpool.

The odd thing was that the minute she'd made her decision to quit her job and her relationship, everything had fallen into place. Gone was the hesitating Pat who wasn't really sure she wouldn't be making a terrible mistake by not opting for security. In her place was a more assured young woman who only knew that there was more to life than taking care of the festering Breakers Inn or marrying dull old Steve Elman. There had to be more! Someplace in the world, Pat knew, she would find her heart's desire. Whether it involved work or a man or both, it was going to be full of romance, passion and heady excitement.

She saw the hanging signboard up ahead. *Dulces & Café*. She went inside, nodding a quick hello to the old man behind the counter. The smell of cookies baking and the warm odor of hot chocolate assailed her, and she sighed deeply, breathing it all in. This was more like it—the Mexico she had dreamed about and read about was different from the reality of Mexico City. The city felt very foreign to her, although she was fluent in the language. Now, sitting here in this café, she wondered if she shouldn't call it quits and start home at once. Her two weeks in the sun had relaxed her, and Mexico City was just too much of a hassle. Maybe she should go back—not to Steve, of course, but just back to Boston to look for another job in the States. There were dozens of fine hotels that might need an assistant manager, and she'd saved enough from her last two jobs to take some time off and write dozens of letters for dozens of interviews. Her notion about working in Mexico was probably just a romantic dream, not very practical at all.

She went to the counter, selected a flaky pastry and a large mug of dark Mexican coffee, and went back to her table near the window. The place was deserted, and she relished the quiet and the sweet smells after the pollution of her long walk. She opened her first newspaper and flipped to the want ads.

"Hotels, let's see," she muttered, running her finger down the column. There was a job for a waiter in Mexico City, one for a chambermaid, and a position for a pastry chef in Cancún.

"Zilch," she grumbled, flipping her shining blond hair over one shoulder. She picked up the second paper and thumbed through it. Not one position open under the hotel heading. It was just the same as her fruitless two-week personal search. The chain hotels had all accepted her resumé cordially and told her they'd be in touch if anything opened up in the future. Pat knew without asking that they were required by law to reserve their positions and job referrals for native Mexicans.

Of course, there was one lead she hadn't tried yet. One of her teachers at Cornell, James Travis, had mentioned the name of a man at FONATUR, the Mexican government agency responsible for the incredible boom in resort development. What was his name?

Cotrillo? Costasico? Something like that. She had her sheaf of notes back at the hotel. It certainly couldn't hurt to make an appointment with the man, and maybe her professor's reference could sway him, convince him to overlook the fact that she was an American. How stupid of her not to have gotten in touch with him already.

Filled with new enthusiasm, Pat opened the third paper before her on the table. FONATUR was the answer, of course! In the past eight years, they had financed the creation of such tropical vacation spots as Cozumel, Cancún, Veracruz and Puerto Vallarta. If anyone knew anything about Mexican hotels, it had to be the head of the agency.

The elderly gentleman behind the counter waved the coffeepot at her, but she shook her head. She would take the subway back to her hotel and try to arrange an appointment with the man before he went out to lunch. Señor Costilla! That was his name. Pat was no longer concentrating on the newspaper as her brain began whizzing around, mapping out new strategies. If she could convince the man that she had something to offer the Mexican tourist industry that no national could match, he'd surely give her a name or two, just a few new contacts to call. The newspaper slipped from her lap to the floor, and as she bent to retrieve it, she did a double take.

"Wow!" She grasped the paper and smoothed it in front of her. There was a three-inch box ad at the top of the Help Wanted page.

Assistant Manager Wanted
for Mexico's newest posh resort.
The Paradiso. Ixtapa/Zihuatanejo.
Must be fluent in both English & Spanish.

16

Salary commensurate with experience.
Contact Mr. T. Beckman (4-2807)

Pat's hands shook. It was as if Fate had floated down inside this café and kissed her lovingly on the head. Why, the job was tailor-made for her. Ixtapa, the newest, most exclusive resort on the Pacific coast. It was another FONATUR baby, if she remembered correctly.

She ripped the ad from the paper, threw a ten-peso note on the table and rushed from the empty patisserie, her heart fairly singing with joy. As she raced toward a nearby hotel to find a public phone, she had a premonition of the future.

Things are going to work out, she told herself happily. I just know it.

Chapter Two

$\mathcal{T}$hree days later, Pat was on a plane bound for the Zihuatanejo airport, a forty-five-minute ride from Mexico City. Her brief phone conversation with Mr. Beckman had gone so astoundingly well, she couldn't help but be slightly suspicious as she gazed down at the mountains below her. He had barely asked anything about her training or her experience, but rather, seemed in a great hurry to get things settled between them. His deep voice on the phone could have belonged to a man of any age, but Pat suspected he was in his late fifties or early sixties.

"Do you speak Spanish?" Beckman had asked right off.

"Yes, I was a Spanish major in—"

"Any experience?" he'd interrupted.

"I was the manager at the Breakers in Magnolia, Massachusetts, and before that, my first job was at the Holiday House in Niagara Falls."

"Hmm, I see. . . ." He'd sounded totally unimpressed.

"And I have a master's degree in hotel management from Cornell," Pat offered.

"Really?" That bit of information definitely piqued his interest. "I tell you what, Miss Jessup. I'll wire a plane ticket to your hotel so we can get together and talk about the job. Let's see, today is Tuesday, so you should be able to get here by Friday, in that case. I'll see you Friday morning, okay?"

"Ah, yes, fine, Mr. Beckman."

"Good. See you then."

That was it. He'd hung up abruptly, and Pat was left thinking that thirty seconds on the phone is no kind of preliminary to a job interview. She had hundreds of questions to ask him about the hotel, the area, the responsibilities of the job, but he'd given her no chance at all to say anything, even about her own background and capabilities.

Wonder if he's desperate, she thought to herself as the plane took a dip toward the ocean and leveled off at a lower altitude. Wonder if he's younger than I suspected from his voice. Wonder if he's married.

She gave herself a mental slap on the wrist, ashamed to be thinking just like her husband-hunting college roommate. Obviously, the only important thing was the job, and even if Ted Beckman was young and devastatingly handsome, she would have to keep her distance if he was to be her employer. The worst thing in the world was to get romantically involved with your boss.

Pat, he's probably as old as the hills! she cautioned herself as the plane took a turn and the fishing village of Zihuatanejo came into view. Then she forgot all about her prospective employer as she gasped with pleasure at the sight below her. It was breathtakingly beautiful. Tropical green mountains clustered together, each crowned with a halo of wispy clouds. They sheltered the incredibly green-blue waters of the Pacific, and it was hard to tell where the sky and sea divided. The azure color of the sea below promised wonderful swimming and even better daydreaming. Pat suddenly had a vision of herself ensconced at a lovely hotel, gazing out her office window, wearing her perfect, permanent tan, enjoying the quiet lapping of the waves against the sand.

As soon as they had landed, and Pat stepped off the plane, the balmy, fragrant air filled her lungs, washing away all the pollution of Mexico City, clearing her mind of the anxieties of the past few weeks. There was something healing about the clean scent, like an omen of good things to come. With a new spring in her step, she followed her fellow passengers into the terminal to collect her bags.

The conveyor belt had just started to snake around the baggage claim area and Pat filed over behind a group of Americans, eager to get their luggage and get on with their vacations. As she stood next to the far wall, watching the fretful expressions on the various pale faces around her, she noticed a short, middle-aged Mexican man wearing an embroidered white shirt, kelly green pants and white shoes. He seemed to be working the crowd, approaching one young woman after another with a gleeful smile and a mischievous twinkle in his eye. Pat amused herself by watching him being rebuffed by each successive American. But he never gave up—as soon as one had turned him down, he scampered off, undaunted. He shrugged apologetically to a statuesque redhead and then started to move toward Pat. She grinned good-naturedly as he approached, preparing her answer in Spanish. Evidently, her blond hair and beige cotton pantsuit made her a likely target for his attentions.

Maybe just a cabbie looking for a rich tourist, she surmised as she watched him walk toward her. But possibly an escort for hire. "You want lovely evening, señorita? I take you to romantic spot."

Oh boy, thought Pat, steeling herself for his assault.

"Buenas tardes," he began with a slight bow. "Ms. Jessup?"

"What? Oh, yes, I'm Pat Jessup." All of Pat's romantic fantasies flew out the window when he called her by name.

"Ah, finally!" exclaimed the little man with delight. "I think I look in vain for you all over Mexico! But permit me, I am Orlando Ruiz, Mr. Beckman's assistant. I am here to take you to the Paradiso."

"Thank you. It was very nice of him to send you to pick me up," Pat smiled, impressed at the savoir faire of Ted Beckman. Perhaps she had underestimated him on the telephone.

Orlando fluttered his hands at her gratefulness, as if to say it was nothing, merely a conventional courtesy.

"Your bags? Do you see them, Ms. Jessup?"

They were just coming along the conveyor belt as he spoke, and when Pat pointed them out, Orlando lunged to retrieve them.

"Oh, that's okay. Here, give me at least the wardrobe," she protested. The little man looked totally overwhelmed by the weight of her large suitcase.

"No, Ms. Jessup. I am to show you all the service of the Paradiso, so that you will see what to expect. Come now, the car is right outside." He hurried ahead of her to a white Mercedes sedan parked amid a profusion of compact cars and minibuses. Pat felt slightly conspicuous climbing into it while Orlando put her bags in the trunk.

"You don't mind, Ms. Jessup?" Orlando asked as he scooted in behind the driver's seat. "I must do a small errand in Zihuatanejo before we go to the hotel."

"No, no problem, Orlando. That way I get to see the neighborhood. And please call me Pat," she smiled.

"*Okay,* Pat," he nodded, stressing the colloquialism. He gunned the engine and jockeyed his way through the cabbies and parking lot attendants to the main road. At frequent intervals, Pat noted, there were huge, splashy billboards advertising the big Ixtapa hotels. "Come to Camino Real, Jewel of the Pacific," "The Aristos is Your Home Away from Home." There were even larger signs for the El Presidente and the Holiday House. What a shame to spoil the landscape like that, Pat thought as they whizzed along the narrow road. She was again struck by the perfection of the area—each tree and bush had just the right shadings of green to complement the abundant roadside wildflowers. She had never seen such lush, wild beauty. The perfect spot for my dream honeymoon resort, she thought happily as she leaned her head back against the cool burgundy leather. Now if the hotel lives up to my expectations . . . and if I live up to Ted Beckman's. . . .

The wind rushing by the open car windows prevented any further conversation between her and Orlando, and once the two-lane road became a real highway, Orlando put on the speed (driving like all the other madmen around them); all Pat could think about was her stomach dropping out. Driving, she had learned in her travels, was yet another manifestation of Mexican machismo. One man could never let another pass him, nor could he ever let his passenger relax and enjoy the

22

view. Not to drive fast in Mexico was evidently considered sissyish.

Orlando slowed the car slightly as they approached a traffic circle clearly marked with arrows toward Ixtapa, Zona Hotelería, Aeropuerto, and Centro. He whipped around the circle in the direction of the center of Zihuatanejo.

"You know, we are now in the sister city of Ixtapa," he yelled as he drove along the boulevard. "For years this little village of Zihuatanejo has been known as a hideaway for rich Germans, rich Italians, rich English people, some Americans too. But for a long time there was no way to get here. People would fly to Acapulco, then rent a van and travel days along muddy back roads and through swamps to get here. Were they surprised to find the lovely La Ropa beach after so much hard travel!"

"When was the airport built here, then?" Pat asked, suddenly very excited by the idea of this little-known gem that people would fight the elements to get to.

"Eight years ago," Orlando told her. "This was when the government took the undeveloped stretch of coconut groves three miles away and started to build Ixtapa. They asked a computer, you see. They fed in material on what guests are liking, what the geographical details about every undeveloped area on the Mexico coasts are. This is how they pick Ixtapa, Pat. You will see, how beautiful it is. Zihuatanejo is still for the people, you know, no big hotels. But Ixtapa, ah!" He fluttered the fingers of one hand in the air.

Pat grinned and turned to look out the window again to examine the business area of Zihuatanejo. The architecture was a curious mix of crowded stucco shanties, each with its open porch, and a considerable number of modern glass and concrete banks and small office complexes, many of them still under construction. The mix of rich and poor struck home. But the older buildings had a simple elegance all their own that stood out above the new.

Orlando turned down a narrow cobblestone street, bisected by huge square planters holding trees and flowers. Vendors sat outside on their porches in rocking chairs, hawking their wares noisily—everything from fruit, liquor and shoes to auto parts, light bulbs and gallons of paint were displayed in colorful disarray. One tiny street led into another and then into another with more stylish shops. Several had embroidered dresses hanging right in front, like banners in the breeze; others showed off the brilliantly crafted silver and abalone jewelry so famous in this part of Mexico. Pat found herself itching to get out of the car and explore on foot. My first day off, I'm going shopping, she vowed silently. Then, once again, she had to tell herself that nothing was definite. She was nowhere near being hired at the Paradiso.

It was curious how she'd just stepped off the airplane and felt at home here, as if there were no question in her mind about whether or not she would be hired or would accept the job. She realized suddenly that she had never felt as strongly about a place. It was as if the magic of Ixtapa had already cast its spell on her and held her in its power. Anything could happen here, Pat thought, from a job where I'm needed and appreciated to a romance that fulfills me. Even, she dared to think, a love affair that would grow deeper and blossom into a lasting commitment. Was she in love with the place, or merely with the idea of being in love? Pat didn't know, but she didn't really care. She had a wild, silly sensation, a lush new feeling about herself that was running out of control. And for the first time in her life, she didn't have to take charge and control it. She would allow it to take her wherever it would.

"Excuse me for just a moment, Pat." Orlando's soft voice suddenly brought her back to reality. He turned a corner and pulled up to the curb across the street from a small adobe church. "I must run into the *farmacia* to pick up a prescription for Mrs. Beckman."

"Oh, of course, Orlando. Take your time."

So there was a Mrs. Beckman. Well, of course, Pat, what did you expect? she grumbled to herself. Naturally a successful American running a big resort would be a married man. Pat was instantly brought up short in her own fantasies and took a breath to bring herself back down to earth.

Annoyed with herself for being so ridiculous, she got out of the car to look around. The doors of the church across the street were open and she could see the sunlight shimmering through the stained-glass windows along one side. It was a simple building, but elegant in its clean, square lines. It reminded her of a church back in Gloucester, a place her father had discovered long ago and had introduced her to when she was twelve. "I'm not a religious man, as you know, Patricia, but I need a place to be quiet in and the Fisherman's Chapel is where I can talk to myself." It was special there for him, he had told her, like the sea on a calm day. Whenever the catch was bad or life became too complicated, he'd go to that chapel to sort things out and put them back into perspective. Partly believing in its good qualities, and partly because she had nowhere else to turn, Pat had gone there herself the day she broke up with Steve, and had spent more than a few late afternoons there pondering her future before leaving for Mexico. Somehow, this little white church in Zihuatanejo had the same feeling about it, and she liked it immediately.

From the street, Pat could see candles burning on the simple wooden altar at the foot of the huge crucifix. The decorations were stark and bare, devoid of any excess ornamentation that might detract from the pure experience of being at peace with oneself.

Pat stared in from the vestibule, admiring the beauty of the chapel. She was so captivated by the place, she didn't even notice the group of workmen who had gathered outside, although they had certainly noticed her.

Four of the men wore dusty jeans and were gawking at the attractive young woman with her shining blond hair. The fifth, evidently the supervisor, was wearing pressed khaki pants, a beige shirt open at the collar and a bandana around his neck. His clothes were as dusty and grimy as the other men's, however, since he had been working along with them. Just at this moment, a small, fat priest wearing a brown cassock appeared from a side door of the church, scowling, and told the men to get back to work. One of them protested loudly, attracting Pat's attention, and she whirled around to see what the source of the commotion was.

"But, Father," the man pleaded mockingly in Spanish. "God has sent us a reward for our labors. Do you not see the miracle he has bestowed on our humble church?"

Pat couldn't help but smile at the man's audacity, but the priest was not amused by his comment and ordered the men to go finish their work.

Pat was determined to make herself as inconspicuous as possible. She'd really had it in Mexico City with prying eyes and lewd remarks, but she figured that as long as the priest was around, the men wouldn't get too rowdy. She left the chapel, with her head bent down, and started back toward the car. The priest smiled apologetically and hurried to her side.

"Señorita," he began, and then, shaking his head, he started again in heavily accented English. "Miss, I am sorry, so sorry. I apologize for their bad behavior. They mean no harm, you understand. It is only their way to give compliments."

"Certainly, *padre,*" Pat smiled. "I've been in Mexico for a few weeks, so I've been complimented before."

"Ah, these habits, regrettably crude." The priest fussed with his rope sash. "But such is the way here." Then his eyes brightened, and he asked, "May I ask, you are from America?"

"Yes, from Massachusetts. Actually, I grew up in a small fishing village called Gloucester, very much like Zihuatanejo."

"This is so? But how wonderful. My brother has moved to Texas and his letters are full of the excellence of America. Sometimes even I am envious of his new life in America."

"I see," Pat grinned, glancing over at the lingering workmen, who were only half-heartedly devoting themselves to their manual labor. "Tell me, Father, what is the name of your lovely church?"

"This is the Church of Santa Bárbara," he responded proudly.

"It's so beautiful. You know, I was just thinking that it reminds me of a chapel for the fishermen back in my hometown."

"Yes, certainly. And we have many fishermen, as you surely know, here in Zihuatanejo."

"And some good catches, too!" the workmen's supervisor called out in Spanish. He was perched up on a scaffold against the side of the church instructing one of his workers, but he stopped to gaze down at Pat. "Perhaps the *señorita* has come to our church to pray for a big handsome fish," the man laughed. "Like me."

"*Santos!*" The priest squinted up at him and shook his fist. "You of all people! For shame."

Pat turned and glared up at the man. She was about to call out something extremely sharp, but found that she could not. She was speechless as she locked eyes with this attractive man. He had a broad chest, piercing dark eyes, a trim mustache and thick, wavy dark hair that flopped over on one side of his forehead. His gaze held hers and she felt weak, as though all the blood had been drained from her. She was powerless to turn away, and way back, somewhere muffled in her memory, a bell rang. There was something about this man. . . . She couldn't put her finger on it. All she knew was that his presence did something to her insides she had never felt before.

There was a large stone gargoyle on the scaffold beside him, and the grotesque monkey's head seemed to join him in mocking her. The workmen, who were busy reinforcing the ledges where the gargoyles sat, chortled at his remark as their supervisor grinned innocently down at Pat. It was obvious that they all assumed she didn't understand Spanish.

Pat braced her hands against her sides, willing herself out of the hypnotic trance under which this handsome stranger had placed her. "*Señor,*" she began in his language, with her best Mexican inflection, "if you were the best catch in Zihuatanejo, I'm afraid I would have to throw you back. *Muy pequeño*—much too small."

The workmen howled with laughter, one of the older men nearly slipping off the ledge as he repeatedly slapped his thigh in enjoyment of her put-down. The rotund priest's jaw dropped in shock. The object of Pat's derision nodded slowly, as if acknowledging that he had just met his match. He almost seemed to enjoy her pointed comeback, and his dark eyes took on a different expression as they traveled the length of her slim form. Pat tried, but could not break eye contact with him. She was forced to watch as he examined her closely, and she felt the touch of his gaze as keenly as if it were his large, muscular hand. Now his eyes rested on her shoulder, before traveling languorously down over her breasts, and then reaching her waist. His scrutiny continued down the side of her thigh and the whole length of her long legs. It was not so much embarrassing as it was thrilling, a new adventure for her. This man's gaze was nothing like the leers she had encountered in Mexico. Instead, it was a challenge laced with admiration.

Pat, come off it, she told herself sternly. He's no different from any one of the hundred other guys you've seen during the past three weeks. But oddly enough, she told herself in the same breath that he was different.

"Señorita." The priest's voice brought her back to reality, and finally she was able to rip her gaze away from the man on the scaffold. "You speak excellent Spanish. It is not often that an American tourist has such a fine capability in foreign language."

"Oh, well thank you. I'm not exactly a tourist, though; I'm . . ." She could still feel him staring at her, and she did not dare to look up. She was enormously grateful when she spotted Orlando coming out of the *farmacia* with his package.

"Padre, I must go now. But I hope . . . would it be all right if I came to see you again?" She gave one last

glance inside the lovely chapel and knew that it might bring her comfort in the days ahead.

"I would be delighted. You must come for coffee some afternoon soon."

"I'd love to. Goodbye, now." She waved over her shoulder as she made her way back to the car where Orlando was waiting. He opened the door on the passenger side for her and gave her a deep, gallant bow after he helped her in.

"Just looking around," she explained as he started the engine.

"Ah, yes, is much to see in Zihuatanejo," Orlando smiled. "But now we go directly to the Paradiso. You must be tired after your journey. And a new place, well . . ." He set the plastic bag with the logo of the drugstore on it beside him on the seat. "Poor Mrs. Beckman," he clucked, indicating the bag. "I have gone to get her the drops for her eyes. She sees very little now, and it is getting worse each day, although sometimes it is surprising, the things she is able to make out. It is so sad, though, even the drops no longer help much." He shook his head in sympathy as he stepped hard on the accelerator. "Perhaps some day you will be kind enough to bring her here, to the Church of Santa Bárbara."

"Oh, I'd be delighted." Mr. Beckman's wife is going blind! Pat thought with a sudden pang of remorse. It must be so hard on them both. She was forced to reconsider her mental portrait of the man who might become her employer. Not a young, dashing jetsetter at all. Probably her first impression of his voice had been the correct one—he was an older man with many grave concerns and responsibilities. He and his wife had undoubtedly been in the hotel business in America, but had moved to Mexico because life was slower and easier on a woman with a handicap.

Yes, the picture was different from the way she had first assumed it to be. As the car sped along the road toward Ixtapa, Pat attempted to correct the images in her mind. But all she could see was the tall Mexican up on the scaffold at the church, smiling down at her.

Chapter Three

It was growing dark by the time they rounded the bend that led into Ixtapa, some three miles north of Zihuatanejo, but even in the dusky gray light, Pat could feel the vast difference between the two towns. As soon as they were in view of the ocean again, gigantic billboards reappeared on the highway with offers of eternal sunshine, azure water and nirvana on earth. Each Ixtapa hotel promised more than the next, and Pat couldn't help grimacing at all this hype. After the picturesque charm of the little fishing village she had just left, this seemed positively gaudy. But as Orlando took the last turn and the road sloped downward toward Ixtapa, a breathtaking panorama appeared. High-rises were usually not Pat's style, but there was an energetic feel to the row of hotels here. Against the ocean and flanked by high craggy cliffs were the posh resorts of Ixtapa, some still under construction, their bare beams reaching to the sky. Most were glass and concrete boxes, but the architecture varied with each one. Across the highway from the hotels lay a sprawling golf course, its perfectly green grass setting off the deeper hue of the palm trees. Pat had hoped for something less flashy, but she was excited by the incredible amount of growth and development. Which one was the Paradiso? she wondered.

"So, how do you like it?" Orlando demanded with a proud grin. His expression clearly told her how he felt about the place. It was as if he were taking full credit for Ixtapa all by himself. "Fabulous, no?"

"Yes, it certainly is," Pat agreed diplomatically.

"The hotels down on the strip are the older ones— the Aristos, the El Presidente, the Holiday House. All very nice, but nothing like our hotel."

Pat realized she had to take everything this loyal employee said with a grain of salt, but she couldn't help catching some of his enthusiasm. And if Ted Beckman's staff felt so good about the Paradiso, how did the guests feel?

"Look, up there," Orlando continued, pointing to his left. "The Camino Real, our biggest competitor."

Built into the side of the hill overlooking the ocean was a towering orange stucco structure that reminded Pat of a glitsy concrete bunker. It was awesome in its size, but too high-tech for Pat's taste. The most interesting thing about it was that it was built on levels, like a huge staircase mounting up from the sea. There must have been five hundred steps down to the ocean. How do the guests go swimming? she wondered. The place had its merits, but it certainly wasn't charming.

"Magnificent hotel. Even I must admit," Orlando sighed. "Three pools, many, many golf carts, nice restaurant, disco . . . but it's not the Paradiso," he finished with a satisfied laugh.

"Three pools!" Pat shook her head. "I suppose that's because it's too far a walk down to the ocean, eh?" She indicated the hundreds of steps.

"Yes, but you see, this was a necessity. It is too dangerous to swim in the ocean here. Tides are too strong. The bay in Zihuatanejo is good for swimming if you want the ocean. But our guests," he continued, "they don't like the salt water, or the pebbles underfoot. In the pools," he snapped his fingers, "no problem."

How odd, Pat thought. Why build a resort where the tides are too strong for swimming?

"Ah, there she is," Orlando pointed excitedly. "The Paradiso!"

Pat followed his gaze toward the structure in the distance. The hotel was built on another hill, set apart from the older resorts. It seemed to glare across at its rival, the Camino Real, on the other end of the beach like an enemy behemoth. The Paradiso was a modernistic structure of stacked yellow stucco boxes and rectangles, some angled oddly, almost defying gravity. Several of the windows were long thin frames, several were three-sided. The whole thing was a wild geometric aberration, made even stranger looking because of the floodlights highlighting random walls. It certainly attracted attention; no one could ever miss it from the highway. Well, Pat thought, I suppose I could make it my home if I tried hard. But her heart was pounding too hard to worry about the architecture of the Paradiso. This could be it, her chance for the best job of her life—and maybe something more besides.

"Beautiful, no?" Orlando asked, pulling over and stopping the car at the end of the long, straight stretch leading to the hotel.

"It's very impressive," Pat nodded.

"There is nothing like it in Mexico. It is designed so that each room is a duplex suite with a parlor and a bedroom above it. The restaurant on the roof, the Crystal Garden, is—how do you say?—a hexagon? Wherever you look, the view is tremendous. Then there is the more intimate dining room below, and also the ballroom where the big acts are booked. The Camino Real cannot say that they have entertained Cher, eh?" Orlando bragged.

"It really is something," Pat murmured, getting more excited as he talked. Yes, the architecture was disappointing, but for a big hotel with class entertainment, that was only par for the course. Pat's dream of her small honeymoon hideaway would have to take a backseat for a while. This high-tech fortress before her would surely give her room to stretch and grow, unlike the quaint and charming Breakers in Magnolia, where the liveliest activity was a rousing game of bridge in the evenings. To be the assistant manager of a place like the Paradiso was an enormous challenge. And who knows who she'd meet here? An Arab oil sheik, a wealthy American politician, maybe even an English lord or a French wine magnate.

Orlando pulled the Mercedes into the long, winding red brick drive that led up to the Paradiso, and Pat's stomach came alive with bounding butterflies. She felt tired and grimy, and prayed that she'd at least be able to wash up and change before meeting Mr. Beckman and his wife. But try as she might, she could not slow the progress of the car just by thinking, and Orlando drove up into the large open-air courtyard. Tall palm trees offset the bleak lines of the high, squared-off walls, and there were banks of plants and flowers everywhere, as if somebody, perhaps the architect, perhaps Mr. Beckman himself, had decided at the last moment to soften the initial impression.

As soon as Orlando brought the car to a halt, a porter rushed up to open Pat's door. "Take Ms. Jessup's luggage to twenty-two," Orlando instructed him, handing him the car keys. "Pat, if you will come with me, I'll show you to your suite. Beautiful, no?" he repeated as he watched her glance inside to the well-appointed lobby.

She nodded as she walked behind him, taking it all in—the legion of dusty-rose sofas and armchairs, all casually arranged into conversation groups; the plush mocha rugs; the interesting Mexican pottery holding fresh-cut flowers of every color and variety. The efficient hotel personnel stood at the ready in their immaculate white shirts and pants. The lobby was alive with activity, Pat noted with satisfaction. Somebody was doing something right. And yet, her brain began to spin with possibilities. She could see so many places for creative improvements, just a touch here and there, but significant enough to promise return visits from the clientele. Oh, if Mr. Beckman gave her the chance, what wonders she could do! There was no reason why this giant, modernistic monolith couldn't be imbued with a little of the charm of a cozy *posada*. The Paradiso was a gold mine of untapped treasure, and it would be a long overdue challenge for her professional skills.

Orlando stopped at the front desk to pick up the key to Pat's room, and then led her down the long, cavernous corridor to a short flight of stairs. They climbed to another corridor lined with doors, each one a different shade of blue.

"This is the senior staff wing," Orlando explained as

he fumbled with the key in the lock. "You are staying in the suite vacated by our last assistant manager. It will remain yours, naturally, if it pleases you . . . if you join us," he smiled encouragingly. "And I do hope that you will, Pat."

"I hope so, too, Orlando." What happened to the last assistant manager, Pat wondered. Fired? Quit? She was dying to ask Orlando but felt it might be an indiscreet question. She didn't want him reporting too much back to his employer. Well, I'll just have to ask Mr. Beckman myself, she decided.

"Now!" Orlando threw open the door and flipped on the light switch. Pat gave a small gasp of delight—the place was wonderful! A sunken living room, tastefully furnished in Danish modern, was accented with brass Aztec ornaments. A spiral staircase led up to the bedroom loft over the living room; the far wall was a thick glass pane, affording a splendid view of the ocean. And there were fresh flowers everywhere.

"Mr. and Mrs. Beckman asked me to extend their invitation to you for dinner tonight. But only if you feel up to it, of course."

"Oh yes, I'd love to meet them," Pat replied eagerly, the butterflies once again returning to her stomach and beginning their little dance.

"Excellent. They will be awaiting you then in the Ventana del Mar, the downstairs restaurant, at nine. You do know that in Mexico the dining hour is quite late?"

"I'm used to it by now, Orlando. Actually, I prefer it. I never start getting hungry till then, anyway."

"Ah!" he exclaimed, clapping his hands in delight. "Then you must have a Mexican soul."

"More likely a Mexican stomach," Pat joked, and Orlando laughed appreciatively.

"Then I will inform Mr. Beckman that you will be dining with him, if you will excuse me now. Please, make yourself at home. I am at your service," he assured her. "You know, we say here, *mi casa es su casa*."

"My home is yours," Pat translated. "That's lovely."

"You are so fluent," Orlando complimented her. "I know you will love it here, and we will all love you. Now, I am taking up much of your precious time, so I will vanish. If you need anything, you only have to call the front desk and they will beep for me."

"Thanks, Orlando, you've been wonderful," Pat smiled. "But I think all I need now is a shower and a nap."

The small, cheerful man grinned and nodded before showing himself out.

Pat looked at her watch and exhaled with relief. Only seven-fifteen. Plenty of time to relax. And then . . . the moment of truth.

At ten to nine, Pat was just putting the finishing touches on her makeup. Initially, she'd thought about wearing a very simple dress and barely any makeup, but then she reconsidered. Plenty of time to be a plain-Jane business-type in the morning. Tonight, she would show the Beckmans that she possessed the style and pizzazz necessary to the image of a fabulous resort. She chose a ruffled peach georgette dress, with a full flowing skirt over its own dark apricot slip. She bound her abundant hair in a sleek upswept style, letting a few tendrils curl around her face.

Fortunately, Orlando had sent Rosa, one of the chambermaids, to see if Pat needed anything, and Pat asked if she could possibly have her dress pressed. Miraculously, Rosa was able—with a radiant smile—to get it back to her in only half an hour. Pat couldn't help thinking that Ted Beckman had a way with his staff. The service at the Paradiso was unobtrusive and very efficient, and also gracious.

When Pat was ready to go, she gave herself a final glance in the mirror. Not bad, girl, she thought appraisingly as she examined the slim, well-turned-out reflection before her. If only her turbulent emotions could match the calm exterior. Something had been churning inside her ever since she'd arrived that afternoon, some new magical element that had turned her from an anxious girl running from a burnt-out affair to a competent, attractive young woman eagerly dashing toward life with open arms. What had caused this transformation? she wondered. Well, whatever it was, Pat was grateful for it.

She followed the signs toward the Ventana del Mar, passing through the lobby and down a series of steps toward the larger of the two swimming pools, which was suffused with multi-colored spotlights. Pat had to stop and admire the extraordinary waterfall at one end of the pool, its cascading sheets of water falling behind beautifully arranged rocks. The effect was magnificent.

The restaurant, with its side wall made entirely of glass, gave the diners a terrific view of the water and any evening swimmers still paddling around in it. Pat went around to enter through the front door and she blinked a couple of times to accustom her eyes to the dark. Each small table had a candle in a glass lamp for illumination, and the overhead recessed lights were turned down to a dim glimmer. The tables were on several levels, those closest to the glass wall on the highest tier. A long bar, with every bar stool now occupied, stood along the side, making a cozy alcove for couples somewhat removed from the rest of the dining room. The other walls were wood-paneled, and the place was designed so that the tables were well removed from one another, affording a sense of intimacy. A gigantic vase of fresh flowers graced the maître d's table, and there was another on top of the baby grand piano at one end of the room. An attractive young man in black tie was playing a soft Cole Porter melody when Pat walked in.

"Yes, *señorita,* may I help you?" The maître d' came to her side at once.

"Oh, yes. My name is Pat Jessup. Mr. Beckman is expecting me for dinner."

"Of course. Please follow me," he responded with a knowing smile. She surmised that word had gotten around that she was in the running for the job.

Pat followed him across the restaurant and up three levels to the choicest table in the house. Her stomach was tied tightly in a knot of fear and excitement when the maître d' led her to a couple at the far end of the dining room.

Mr. Beckman, she was surprised to see, was not a paunchy, balding man in his sixties, nor was Mrs. Beckman an elegantly aging, tragic figure. They weren't a married couple at all, but mother and son. Ted Beckman rose to take Pat's hand as she approached the table. He was very tall, well over six feet, and his sandy hair, cut fashionably short, was brushed over his forehead like a little boy's. He was about forty, Pat guessed, and in terrific physical shape. The golden hair on his hand tickled her own, and his dazzling smile, showing gleaming white teeth, was totally disarming. His mother, a small woman with a neat cap of pure white hair, was probably in her seventies. She wore a navy dress and very thick eyeglasses.

Pat was indeed flummoxed, but she kept her wits

about her and had the good sense not to act as if she'd expected anything different. Trying to compose herself, she smiled weakly.

"Ms. Jessup, I'm Ted Beckman." His clear hazel eyes and roguish expression really knocked Pat for a loop.

"Pleased to meet you, Mr. Beckman."

"No, you have to call me Ted."

"And I'm Pat."

"This is my mother, Ruth Beckman."

"Hello, Mrs. Beckman." Pat reached over to take the woman's hand as she settled herself in the third chair at the table.

"You don't mind if I squint at you, I hope." Mrs. Beckman kept a firm grasp on Pat's hand and drew her closer, toward the candlelight. "I just want to get a good look at you, and this place is pitch black."

"I know what you mean," Pat smiled as the elderly woman put her face just inches away from hers.

"My, you are stunning, dear," Mrs. Beckman announced after a few seconds.

Pat blushed, somewhat put off by the woman's frank assessment.

"Now, don't mind my mother, she's trying to get on your good side," Ted laughed, easing the mood. "How was your trip here, Pat?"

"Oh, just fine. The connection from Mexico City was excellent."

"I've ordered a local Mexican wine," Ted said, changing the subject abruptly and signaling for the waiter, who was standing directly opposite. "Hope that's okay."

"Yes, certainly." Pat couldn't help but admire the man's flair and assertiveness. It stuck out all over him. Even in this brief period of time, she fathomed a great deal about him. The man was clearly a go-getter, a person who knew what he wanted and took it without asking permission.

"I tell you, I'm working on making flight connections from the States easier, and it's a real headache. There's no problem getting to Ixtapa if you happen to be in Mexico already, but I want more direct connections."

"My son thinks the air traffic starts and stops in Ixtapa," Ruth Beckman interjected, reaching for the basket of rolls. "It just isn't true."

"Well, there are resorts that command more attention, but we're young, just starting out. You'd heard about us before you answered the ad, Pat?"

She chose her words carefully. "I did hear a lot about Ixtapa from my professional friends, travel agents, and ah, my former teacher at Cornell. But aside from one ad campaign in a major magazine several months ago, I hadn't really seen a lot of publicity."

"Yes, well, that's going to change."

The waiter came back bearing a bottle of wine in a standing ice bucket. Quickly, he uncorked it and poured a bit into Ted's glass so that he could taste it. When Ted was satisfied, the waiter filled the three glasses and disappeared.

"To Ixtapa, long may it flourish," Ted toasted.

"And to many profitable business relationships—and other kinds, too," Ruth added pointedly.

Pat smiled down into her glass, wondering how much matchmaking Ruth did on her son's behalf—although he didn't seem like the sort of man who'd take anyone's advice on a woman. Or on much of anything else, for that matter.

"We'll get down to specifics tomorrow, Pat, but maybe you'd like to know something about how we came into existence, eh?" Ted was studying her face as he spoke.

"A computer, I believe," she said, taking a sip of the dry wine. It was cool and refreshing; it also took the edge off her anxiety.

"Ah, you've done your homework. Excellent!" Ted nodded. "Yes, after the success of Cozumel and Cancún, FONATUR—I suppose you know who they are— decided to do a little statistical research. How often did guests swim in the ocean? Did they prefer a swimming pool? How many return clients were couples? Young or old? How many families? Did the kids want an activities program? What about entertainment for the adults? So they fed the results into a computer and came up with the plan for Ixtapa. Building over the past eight years has been truly astounding, and its pace is picking up daily. If you want a job that's going to lead somewhere, Pat, you're on the fast track here. Now, tell me about yourself."

You would shift the focus onto me, she thought, glancing down at her menu and clearing her throat. "I'll, ah, give you a resumé with my professional background at our meeting tomorrow, but maybe it would be helpful right now to know what my interests and goals are?"

"Please, you two!" Ruth interrupted. "I'm getting ravenous! I'm going to eat the table and the piano over there if we don't order soon. And remember, Ted, I thought we decided no business after nine."

"My mother's right," he laughed, giving a warm, hearty chuckle which made Pat feel less threatened at once. "No more serious talk. Just some *guacamole* and perhaps a fresh fish caught only hours ago. One last question, though, Pat. How does the Paradiso strike you so far? Watch it," he joked, "anything you say will be held against you."

"Let's see," Pat smiled diplomatically, ticking the

items off on her fingers, "the staff I've met is enthusiastic and well-trained, the rooms are tastefully done, the
guests seem active and pleased, although I haven't
talked to any of them yet. I can go into my other
impressions tomorrow."

"Thank God!" Ruth sighed, waving her menu at her
son.

"I like your answers," Ted said thoughtfully. "I like
them a lot. And now, how about some dinner?"

Pat settled back into her chair with a feeling of relief.
She'd passed the first test, at least. But she couldn't get
over the sensation, as she chatted with the Beckmans
over dinner, that her answers were not the only thing
Ted Beckman liked about her.

Chapter Four

Pat awakened to the sound of birds right outside her window. The clock on the bedside table read eight. Fine, that was plenty of time to get ready for her ten o'clock meeting. Slipping on her robe, she went over to draw the drapes, and yawning widely, she gave a good yank. The sight that greeted her was magnificent, and it made her forget her anxiety, if only temporarily. The staff quarters were on the lowest level of the building, so that the windows afforded a clear view of the small beach. Today, the morning sun gave the sand a honey-gold luster and hit the water with heart-stopping brilliance.

A flock of terns, ridiculous little birds with long legs and an impatient manner, ran along the beach near the waves. As soon as a wave broke, they would scamper away in a perfect imitation of Groucho Marx. Pat couldn't help but laugh as she watched them. She flipped the catch on the glass door and walked out onto her patio for a breath of air. It was growing warm already, but the fresh breeze kept it from being uncomfortable.

Pat leaned out over the balcony, resting her head in her hands, propped up on her elbows. It did smell like home, like Gloucester. She had never imagined being able to recreate that feeling she'd had as a little girl when her father took her out on his fishing boat, but here it was, palpable and undeniable. First, the lovely chapel for the fishermen in Zihuatanejo, then that unmistakable smell in the air. Maybe I will find a home here, Pat thought with a rush of excitement. Maybe this won't be just a job, but something more.

But the first problem was getting the job. This was no time to be daydreaming. Pat left the door open and went over to her closet. She'd given Rosa most of her crumpled dresses and skirts the night before, and they had all been back, pressed and hanging neatly, when she'd returned from dinner.

"Now, what shall it be?" she mused, scanning the rack. "Ted Beckman saw the social me last night; now he'll get the business me."

By nine-thirty she was ready, dressed in a crisp white linen shirt and matching jacket and a navy pleated skirt. She grabbed her portfolio and, glancing at her watch, hoped she'd have time for a cup of coffee before the interview.

The desk clerk in the lobby directed her to the courtyard where breakfast was being served. When she'd settled down at a table with her coffee, she was startled to see her prospective employer coming toward her with his breakfast in hand. It was certainly odd that he wasn't dressed for their meeting. She wondered if this was some new kind of employer scare tactic. Her stomach knotted. It was going to be awfully awkward to talk with him when he was dressed for tennis and she was dressed for business.

"Good morning," he grinned, pulling out the seat next to her. "Beautiful day, isn't it?" He squinted up at the lemon-yellow sun.

"Good morning. Yes, it's lovely."

"Say," he frowned, noting the empty coffee cup in her hand. "That's not all you're having for breakfast, I hope. There must be something in my spread that appeals to you."

"It looks terrific, honest," she shook her head apologetically. "It's just . . . I don't get hungry this early." She willed herself not to mention her jitters, although he seemed like the kind of person who might have been sympathetic. Still, his choice of attire made her stay on her guard.

"Well, don't worry, the chefs stay out here until noon. We start serving early because we found that the golfers crave their ham and eggs before starting out. Frankly, as long as I've lived in Mexico—let's see, it's twelve years now—I've never been able to wean myself away from my native California eating habits."

"Oh?" Was this the beginning of the interview? Why should Ted start telling her about himself?

"Actually, I'm happy I ran into you. Listen, as long as you don't mind, why don't we have our meeting out here instead of in my office. It's too nice a day to be cooped up indoors."

"Fine," Pat responded, understanding that he must have planned it this way. The only thing she couldn't fathom was why.

"So, let's begin at the top. How do you like the Paradiso? Is it everything you ever dreamed of in a resort?" he grinned mischievously.

"It's that and more," she said tersely, thinking that the interview would go nowhere if he was going to fish for compliments instead of ask her legitimate questions.

"I don't think we really got a chance to go over my background on the phone, Ted," she said before he could interrupt. "So I've brought a copy of my resumé and several references—from my former employers and my professors at Cornell." She briskly unzipped her portfolio and slid the top sheet across the table toward him.

He barely glanced at it, scanning the page as though he were speed-reading, while he drummed his fingers on the table. "I'm glad to see you've got experience," he said after a few seconds, "but I'll tell you, Pat, what counts in my book is not a person's record of achievements, but rather what their abilities are. What I want to know is, what can you do for me now, today?"

"Well, I . . . it seems to me that would depend on how much freedom I'm given in the job."

He seemed pleased at her answer. "Listen to me," he said earnestly. "If you're good, if you want to get ahead here, all you have to do is come up with an idea and I'll help you implement it. Okay, let's get down to basics. The Paradiso is far from perfect, I'm aware of that. What would you change here if I let you?"

Pat looked away, out to the ocean, considering her words carefully. This was the first job interview anyone had ever let *her* conduct, and she was beginning to enjoy that. "Let's see, I'd start with the beach problem. Your fancy computer put you several long staircases away from it. That's too much for older people—no, let me change that—it's too much for anyone on vacation to walk. I remember seeing an elevator-cable car in Quebec City that runs between the lower and upper parts of the city. I think they have one like that in Capri, too, called a funicular. Well, it's a big job, but I suppose with the proper funding, you could manage something like it for the Paradiso."

"You know, it's uncanny." Ted's green eyes held hers in an intense gaze. "I've been in touch with the Quebec city planner about that very idea. Even if the ocean around Ixtapa isn't the best for swimming, we do want to take advantage of that beach. Okay, good. Next?"

She laughed. "Wait a second. Do you think I should solve all your problems for you in just one meeting? That's a lot of free advice."

He looked a little embarrassed, but in a minute, he was laughing along with her. There was a camaraderie growing between them—Pat could feel it in their conversation and in the interest they both had in the business. "Well, let's go on to the personal stuff, in that case. Says here on this resumé you majored in Spanish at B.U. Still pretty fluent, are you?"

"Yes, oddly enough. Since I've been in Mexico, about three weeks now, a lot of idioms and vocabulary have come back to me."

"Good. Why'd you come to Mexico to look for a job?" he asked flatly.

"Well, I figured I had nothing to lose. I had no opportunity to be creative at the two places I worked in the States, so I figured I'd follow my dream. Ever since I got out of Cornell, you see, I've had this goal. I wanted to be part of the finest tropical resort known to man." This was stretching her dream a bit, but Pat figured it couldn't hurt.

"I guess you've stumbled on it, then. All right, now to the nitty-gritty. How are you with difficult guests? What about supervising staff? Are you organized? God, do I need someone who's organized!"

"I think I can answer pretty positively on those," she nodded modestly. "At my last job, the place in Magnolia, the clientele was elderly and needed a lot of handholding. I only supervised two people there, but at the Holiday House I had a staff of twelve. And I'm extremely organized. I think my strongest suit is creativity, though. I had all kinds of ideas for improving the Breakers—you know, advertising, special off-season weekend rates, better deals for travel agents who steered business our way, special ethnic menus one or two nights a week. But my boss believed that the old ways are the only ways. I don't want to find myself in that situation again."

"You won't," Ted said firmly. "I'll give you all the free rein you need, how's that? To be honest, I've seen four applicants since our last assistant manager left us a month ago. None of them had the guts you seem to have, although they were all older and more experienced. I think you'll work out beautifully."

"Um. Do you mind if I ask—"

"Anything. I believe in complete openness with my staff. What is it?"

"Why did your last assistant manager leave?"

"Oh, well, she was ready to move on, I suppose. She'd been with us a year, and well, let's just say, we had our personal differences." He stood up abruptly from the table, and Pat could see she had touched a sore spot. Maybe he fell in love with her, she thought. But she had no time to ruminate about Ted Beckman's past, because he was talking briskly and was evidently eager to end their meeting.

"I tell you what, Pat," he said. "I'm willing to take you on for a two-week trial period. During that time, I'd like you to make a list of changes and improvements you want to implement at the Paradiso. Your regular duties will count as well, and at the end of that time we'll see how we like one another, and how much we see eye to eye." He gave her an appraising look that for some reason seemed less than professional. Then, in the blink of an eye, he was business-like again. "What do you say? If you work out, and you're happy here, the job is yours."

"Sounds fair to me," Pat nodded.

"Good, great. Oh, by the way, I haven't mentioned your salary yet." Ted named an astronomical figure and Pat's eyes widened in shock.

"What!"

"That's pesos, Pat."

"Sure, it's fine." She blushed as she computed the figure into dollars. Actually, it was more than fine. Mrs. McIver at the Breakers had only been paying her a little over half that.

"I'm really happy about this. Shall we shake on it?" He extended his large, tanned hand, and it nearly encompassed her small one when he took it. "Your two weeks start tomorrow, which means today is yours to get oriented and to enjoy yourself. If you need anything, just ask Orlando."

"That's awfully nice, thanks." She was too overwhelmed to say much else. Here she'd conducted her own interview and she had the job! Excitement bubbled up in her like champagne. There was so much to plan and think up and put into motion.

"By the way," he continued. "I'm throwing a formal dinner party tomorrow night for a potential investor. Some of the local gentry will be there, and I'd like you to come and get acquainted."

"I'll look forward to it," she nodded, wondering

what on earth she was going to wear to a formal affair. She'd have to find something in town this afternoon.

"Wonderful. I've got to run now. See you in my office tomorrow morning at eight-thirty sharp. Have a nice day—bye!"

"So long, Ted." She watched him march off toward the tennis courts, amazed at herself and the ease of the thing. Maybe she was growing up. It was odd, but ever since she'd broken up with Steve, she'd become more aware of her own potential. And now, this beautiful, lush place was hers! Well, for two weeks at least.

Her first impulse was to call home and share the good news with her parents, but still feeling slightly insecure about the whole thing, she decided that celebration was a bit premature. Besides, she might not get the enthusiastic reaction she wanted. Her mother hadn't exactly been thrilled at the notion of her daughter leaving home, fiancé and possibilities for a "normal" life. Her father was always happy about her successes, but even he might balk at the notion of a permanent job in a place he'd never heard of.

Well then, the first thing to do was get some money wired to her from her bank in Marblehead and go shopping for this upcoming dinner party. That meant a trip to town, with specific instructions from Orlando about where to send a telegram and where to find some frothy, gorgeous concoction that would knock everyone's socks off. Except Ted Beckman's, Pat decided as she went to find her guide and mentor. It would be better for both of them to keep everything perfectly professional and business-like.

Then, with a small whoop of delight that caused the three chefs and several pool loungers to turn around, Pat was off to start her errands.

* * *

"Maybe I should have taken Orlando up on his offer to let me borrow a car," Pat muttered to herself as she walked the rickety old bicycle up the hill leading out of Ixtapa. She was in such an adventurous mood, and after one of the gardeners had kindly offered to lend the new assistant manager his bike, how could she refuse? But dressed as she was, in her tight jeans and crew-neck red cotton sweater, she was a prime target. Cars slowed down when they passed her and an entire road crew stopped work to take a gander at the pretty blonde pedaling along. Somehow the attention was easier to take today. She had a new home and a new job, and nothing was going to spoil her good mood.

Pat saw the top of the hill in sight and started riding again, tooling along the red brick road until it hit the highway. She stopped to glance back at the hotel strip where Orlando had described a small shopping mall, as he put it, but she decided against Ixtapa. That lovely fishing village was only three miles distant, and she was in good physical shape. So she persevered, ignoring the hot sun and the cars until she reached the sign pointing the way to the Zihuatanejo *centro*.

She reached the top of the hill and started to pedal harder, breathing deeply of the fragrant heavy breeze that caressed her face and limbs. She would need a good sunscreen, too, until she was safely tanned. She burned easily and couldn't afford to be walking around the Paradiso looking like a lobster.

Wherever she looked now, everything was green and lush. Even the shacks and stray dogs that proliferated along the highway seemed to blend harmoniously with the landscape. Things seemed less foreign to her today, and she knew they would become part of her, a new part she was seeking to explore. It all seemed to fit, to belong just like this.

The *centro* came into view, and Pat started looking around to get her bearings. Orlando had mentioned several nice boutiques right near the Playa del Popolo, the large public beach near the middle of Zihuatanejo, not far from the church and the *farmacia* where they had stopped the night before. If she could find the church again, she could work from there.

Somehow, without realizing it, she wanted to find the church for another reason. That man, the supervisor who'd been working with his men, had not left her mind. Throughout her dinner with Ted and Ruth Beckman, even at the interview this morning, she had wondered whether she would ever see him again if she stayed in the vicinity. It was just not like her to think this way, and she tried to put him out of her mind, but found it impossible to fight the feelings.

Now she could see the church steeple over the low buildings of the town. The round Spanish bell tower, its gentle arches displaying the bells, called to her. Pedaling down the narrow cobblestone streets, she took in everything around her—the skimpily-clad children playing, the shop owners, just now opening their metal grates to start the day's work, the young men betting with each other for an extra cigarette. And then Pat saw something she could not believe. There was an old Indian woman, carrying a basket of fish on her head! The fresh fish had been stuck into a bucket of ice head downward, so that their tails fanned up like the points of a crown on the woman's head. She was just stopping at the door of a nice-looking restaurant, attempting to sell her wares. Pat was so fascinated watching the unusual sight that she didn't see the large pothole right in front of her. The bicycle bucked like a horse and threw her unceremoniously into the street.

"Ow!" She'd braced her fall with her hands, and they stung terribly.

"Señorita! Pobrecita!"

Strong arms were lifting her from the rough pavement, and even before she looked up, she knew whose they were. He smiled down at her, never releasing his grip on her arms. His dark eyes held a look of concern tinged with amusement—he had not forgotten their barbed interchange of the previous day. The identical reaction she'd had to his hypnotizing look overcame her again, and as she stammered her thanks for his assistance, she had to force herself to pull away. His fingers on her slim arms were like vines wrapping themselves around a tree—they belonged there.

"Gracias," she managed.

"De nada. Hay daño?" He seemed very worried that she might be hurt.

"No, no." She tore herself away from the shadow of his imposing body. He was wearing a worker's uniform today—a khaki shirt, work pants and a red bandana around his neck. But all she could see was the strength of his black eyes, set far apart over his high cheekbones. He was truly the handsomest man she'd ever seen.

Hopping back onto the bicycle seat, she started off, enormously embarrassed.

"Hasta la vista!" he called merrily after her. *"Adiós!"*

Blushing furiously, she pedaled faster, around one corner, down a long avenue, then into another section of the town. All she knew was that she had to get as far away from the man as she could. What was this effect he had on her? Here she'd been complimenting herself on how well she'd handled Ted Beckman, how she'd learned to control a situation with a man. And yet this guy had her totally flummoxed; she couldn't even walk straight or think straight around him. Vowing to keep out of his path, and therefore out of Zihuatanejo, as much as she could, she stopped at the first bank on the street and sent her telegram.

Chapter Five

There was scarcely time to get ready. The guests were due to arrive any minute, and as much as Rosa had helped, Pat was still dissatisfied. Tonight she had to look perfect.

She had found the most wonderful dress she had ever seen in her life hanging in a tiny shop near the beach. After a long and fruitless search, she had finally spotted some interesting dresses in the window of a boutique. When she had explained to the proprietress that she needed something for a very special occasion, the woman had ushered her into a back room filled with handmade Mexican wedding dresses. Pat selected the first one the woman had showed her, a snow-white creation of tucked voile, with off-the-shoulder lace sleeves. The lace was repeated at each of the three tiers of this amazing floor-length concoction. A white satin ribbon at the waist completed the look.

The only real problem was the price. Pat knew that

she was no good at all at haggling, so she didn't even try. Instead, she wandered around the room, looking at poor substitutes and sadly shaking her head. Eventually, the owner of the shop threw up her hands.

"This is your heart's desire, is it not?" she asked Pat in Spanish.

"Well, yes," Pat admitted. "But it's considerably more than I wanted to spend."

"No, you must have this one," the woman said decisively, nearly throwing the gown back into Pat's arms. "A bride must always have her heart's desire."

When Pat tried to correct the woman's mistaken impression, she refused to listen and promptly lowered the price of the dress, explaining with a shrug that she was a terrible businesswoman. When intuition told her to sell a certain garment to a certain customer, there was no arguing.

Now, as Pat sat in front of her dressing table mirror, putting the finishing touches on her makeup, she thought fondly of the woman. People really are different here, she mused. They use their hearts more than their heads. I like that.

There was a soft knock at the door, and Rosa came in to help Pat put on her gown.

"Are they all here yet?" Pat asked anxiously, reveling in the feel of the lace on her bare arms.

"So many people! And you should see the rich German banker, I think he is called Herr Dorfmann," Rosa giggled, doing the hooks at the top of Pat's gown.

"Yes, he's a big investor in the Paradiso. Mr. Beckman particularly wanted me to meet him."

"But you will laugh!" Rosa went on. "All the gentlemen, they are in black ties, and he, he is dressed like a mariachi player!" She doubled over with amusement.

"You don't mean that," Pat smiled.

"Yes, for he must always be different. Very wealthy man," she added.

"Um, who else is there?" Pat asked as she wound up her hair and Rosa pinned a cluster of delicate white flowers in it.

"I do not know the names, but Orlando has told me there are others here from the government agency in Mexico."

"From FONATUR?"

"Yes, that is it. And all the hotel owners and their wives. Some of the town council. And naturally, the mayors of Ixtapa and Zihuatanejo. It is a fine group."

"What are the mayors' names, Rosa?" Pat thought it would be polite to know somebody's name when she walked into the room.

"Mayor Sánchez, he is the mayor here in Ixtapa. And Mayor Ribera is from Zihuatanejo."

"Thanks, that's a help. Well." She got up from the dressing table and did a little pirouette in front of Rosa. "How do I look?"

"Oh, *señorita, linda, linda!* You are truly beautiful."

"If you say so, then I suppose I'm ready. Lead the way."

She eased the lace sleeves back up over her shoulders, thinking that it would be more proper for formal introductions, and followed Rosa out into the corridor. At the glass elevator, leading up to the Crystal Garden, the two women parted, and Pat took a deep breath, steadying herself for the evening. The specially designed elevator was made of glass, and it afforded a breathtaking view of the Pacific and Ixtapa Island.

Pat pressed the restaurant button and the elevator slowly began to ascend. She took in the wondrous sight of the full moon and stars hanging majestically over the

59

tumultuous waves. Tonight was going to be wonderful; she could feel it.

The elevator came to a stop on the top floor and opened onto the shimmering Crystal Garden. In keeping with its name, the entire restaurant was glass and crystal. Everything in sight, from the glass-topped tables and Plexiglas high-backed chairs to the plates and flatware, was see-through. Even the floor was made of frosted glass tiles, lit softly from below. The huge hexagonal room was divided at intervals by giant crystal formations, as though somehow in the middle of Mexico, icicles had formed. Some of them rose over twelve feet to the skylight ceiling. No matter where you looked in the room, the landscape outside was visible, nothing detracting from the natural beauty of sea and sky and mountains. Truly, Pat thought as she looked around, Ted Beckman was a genius, and she was privileged to be working for him.

"Sweetheart, for heaven's sake, I've been looking for you." As if called up by her thoughts, Ted appeared at her side, looking elegant in his well-cut tuxedo and ruffled shirt. "I must say," he breathed in her ear as he drew her toward the crowd in the middle of the floor, "I hired you for your professional capabilities, but your beauty may do just as much to attract business."

Pat was glad that the room was dark, so he couldn't see her blushing. "Well, thank you. Now, who do I meet first? Herr Dorfmann, Mayor Sánchez, or Mayor Ribera?"

Ted laughed appreciatively at her savvy preparation for the evening. "No, wait a second. I see my mother with Señor Costilla, he's the head of FONATUR in Mexico City. Good man, very smart. Ah, here we are!"

Ruth Beckman was peering up at a dapper-looking man of about sixty with a nearly bald head that shone in the overhead lights, dim as they were. Ruth had chosen a long burgundy crepe de chine gown with seed pearls at the neck, and she looked wonderful.

"Pat, darling, you're a picture!" Ruth exclaimed as they came near.

"Señor Costilla, our new assistant manager, Pat Jessup," Ted cut in.

"How do you do?" she asked with a dazzling smile. "I believe we have a mutual friend. I was a student of James Travis at Cornell."

"Jimmy!" exclaimed Señor Costilla. *"Mi amigo* Jimmy! How is he?"

"Very well, thank you. I spoke to him only about four weeks ago, actually."

"Please send him my warmest regards when next you see him." The man swooped a couple of glasses of champagne off a passing waiter's tray and handed them to Pat and Ruth. Pat couldn't help but notice the pleased expression on Ted's face. He was looking at her like he'd just hit a vein of gold.

"Pat, I'd like you to meet Herr Hans Dorfmann. Will you excuse us please, Señor Costilla?" Ted asked.

"But naturally. Pat, may I call you Pat? We must talk later and exchange news of my dear old friend."

"I'd love to," Pat grinned as she allowed Ted to whisk her away.

"That's great!" Ted enthused, sotto voce. "There's nothing like contacts, eh, Pat? I didn't know you were a pal of his."

"Oh," she smiled mysteriously. "I have all sorts of assets."

"Which I will enjoy discovering," he murmured. "There's our investor now. Okay, Pat, don't laugh. He's dressed for a costume ball."

"I've already been warned," she told him as they

walked past the bandstand. A group of Mexican musicians dressed in red and black uniforms was just warming up, but they all stopped to stare at Pat. Tonight, she didn't find the attention annoying at all. She knew she was collecting points.

"Herr Dorfmann, I'd like to introduce our new assistant manager, Pat Jessup. She's from Massachusetts."

Pat choked back a guffaw and took the man's proffered hand. But instead of shaking hers, the rotund German, in his ridiculous sombrero and gold brocade jacket and pants, swept it up and kissed it.

"I am enchanted," he said with a thick German accent.

"Thank you," Pat nodded.

"I've been telling Pat about all our plans for improvement, Herr Dorfmann," Ted said hastily. He was suddenly terribly obsequious, which made Pat wonder if it was hard to get on Herr Dorfmann's good side when it came to doling out money. His peculiar mode of dress indicated that he was awfully eccentric.

"We shall see, eh, Ted? Improvements are tricky things, is this not so, Miss Jessup? Sometimes you can go too far, ruin a good thing."

"Well, I think—" Pat began, but she was interrupted by an impatient tugging on her arm.

"I must take Pat away from you gentlemen," Ruth Beckman interrupted. "Nobody else around to guide me to the powder room. I'll bring her right back," Ruth promised without waiting for a response. When she had dragged Pat forcefully past a tight knot of people standing behind one of the crystal stalactites, Ruth raised her voice over the music and asked, "Having fun?"

"Sort of," Pat shrugged. "But I feel like my smile's stuck on my face. All part of the job, I guess."

"Yes, you're a terrific choice when it comes to that," Ruth smiled. "But I don't envy you."

"Oh, why?" Pat stopped and turned to look at the little woman beside her.

"Working for my son," Ruth chuckled.

"A taskmaster?" Pat asked nervously. Suddenly she wondered what she'd gotten herself into.

"You'll find out," Ruth told her, taking her arm again. "I don't want to spoil it by spilling the beans. Oh, there he is. The very person I wanted you to meet. No, I can't see his face," she said when Pat looked extremely surprised. "It's the way he holds himself. Like he's the only man in the room. See?"

She pointed a few brief yards away to a tall dark man standing with his back to them. Ruth was right, he did have a particular stance, different from the other men around him. His back was straight as a ship's mast, and he had a kind of still grace, like a cat in the jungle, holding still just before pouncing on his prey.

"Oh, Santos!" Ruth called. "I want you to meet my friend."

The man turned around, smiling, and Pat gasped. No, it was impossible. How could he be here? It was the workmen's supervisor from the church, the man who'd helped her up when she'd fallen from her bicycle, the man who had her dreaming the wildest thoughts imaginable day and night.

"Santos, this is Pat Jessup. Pat, Santos Ribera, mayor of Zihuatanejo."

"What!" Pat blurted out. Her jaw dropped in astonishment. She realized she was being terribly rude, but she couldn't help it.

"Good evening, Miss Jessup," he smiled. His eyes were teasing, reminding her of their two earlier meetings.

But how could this be the same man? He was dressed to the teeth in a tuxedo that covered his muscular form, but permitted any eye to see the outline of the body beneath. He wore the elegant outfit the way he did his khaki work clothes—making it seem comfortable, like an old friend he had casually wrapped around him. Pat couldn't take her eyes off his hands, the hands that had lifted her gently off the ground. Not white and soft, but calloused and work-scarred, they were as dark as his handsome face. Pat was totally dumbfounded, and all her diplomatic tactfulness had fled.

"Pat, dear, do say something," Ruth prompted her. "Or the mayor will think you're an Ixtapa snob who never strays into his province."

"Oh, ah, I'm so sorry. It's just that—"

Santos took her by the arm and took Ruth by the other. "The music, I find it a bit loud. Shall we go out into the roof garden, ladies?"

"You two go ahead," Ruth smiled, extricating herself. "I said I'd spend most of the evening with Frau Dorfmann. She hates these affairs, and I promised Ted I'd keep her amused. Just between you and me and the wall, though," Ruth snickered, "I think she's hiding so no one will associate her with her husband. Some getup he's got on!" With that, she vanished into the depths of the Crystal Garden.

"Shall we?" Santos asked Pat, not waiting for an answer, but guiding her firmly away from the people taking their seats for dinner at the various tables.

She kept her head down as they walked toward the Plexiglas doors to avoid facing him. She was enormously embarrassed. Thinking that the mayor was just a guy making a pass at her, and answering him back as she had! She surely wouldn't stay in Ted's good graces by offending the mayor of Zihuatanejo.

But when he'd whisked her onto the flower-laden patio and there was silence all around them except for the relentless sound of the sea, Pat had to look up at him. There it was, that plainly challenging look on his face. He'd enjoyed making a fool of her! As she tried to glance away, he grabbed her by both elbows, laughing, his mischievous grin growing wider at her discomfort.

"I am pleased to be formally introduced at last, Miss Jessup. I was beginning to fear our relationship would consist of one accidental meeting after another. You see, humble workmen seldom get the proper recognition."

"Those who deserve it always do," she replied quietly, meeting his gaze.

"A point well taken. I think I *do* deserve it. Now, you must admit that a fellow who donates his time to the church after he has put in a full day's work in the mayor's office can't be all bad."

"I never said you were—" Pat began, but he cut her off.

"Truly, after yesterday, when you ran away from me, I was hurt to the core. I was certain you were not even interested in getting to know me."

"But you spoke in Spanish; you were dressed—"

"My native language and my choice of dress. Tell me, Miss Jessup, tell me you weren't interested. I dare you."

The twinkle in his dark eyes was naughty and suggestive, and it called up all the forbidden thoughts that had, in fact, been running through Pat's mind since the moment she first saw him. Her hands were damp and sweaty, and she knew her heartbeat was a great deal faster than normal. This man's presence caused a shower of sparks to start, like a faulty electrical connection, raining from her head down to the core of her being. But when she didn't answer his challenge, he whispered softly, "You seem like an intelligent woman, Miss Jessup. And I am, modesty aside for the moment, an intelligent man. I'm sure I will find a way to pique your interest."

"Mayor Ribera, there is nothing in this world that does not interest me," she said cheerily to break the mood. "Shall we walk?"

They moved closely together around the perimeter of the Crystal Garden's roof. Every star in the sky was out now, forming a brilliant kaleidoscopic background for the heavy moon. The night was so well lit, Pat could see Ixtapa Island clearly, each tree near the shore silhouetted against the deeper forest behind it. She wanted to speak, to carry on a perfectly sane and ordinary conversation with this man, but it seemed impossible. She was too full of the night and the tropical Mexican haze that fogged her mind and blinded her senses. A half hour passed in complete silence, as they walked and occasionally stopped to admire the view.

"You can feel its beauty, can you not?" Santos spoke at last. "Long before the Ted Beckmans of the world came and built high-rise hotels and gave extravagant parties, there was this." He stretched out his arm to encompass the view. "This belongs to everyone, to the meanest peasant who toils the earth. It is my heritage, and I love it deeply."

"I can see that," she breathed softly, understanding a little more about this mysterious man. She was curious as to what he meant by his comment about Ted, but she decided to let it alone. It wouldn't be wise to discuss her employer with the mayor of Zihuatanejo. Her loyalty, no matter what turmoil her emotions might be in, belonged to her new job.

"Not this town, if you wish to call it a town—this strip of prison bunkers for the rich. Even the mayor here is a puppet, for who should he govern? The waiters? All of their families live in Zihuatanejo." He turned to her, one eyebrow raised. "You can see I am an outspoken man, but when I saw you that day at the Church of Santa Bárbara, I knew you were not an ordinary tourist, impressed by great numbers of swimming pools and designer-fabric drapes. You were touched by antiquity, and by things that have meaning."

"Now just a second," Pat interrupted, trying not to be overcome by the moonlight that suffused his handsome face with a new kind of warm attractiveness. "There are all kinds of beauty, you know. And modern architecture, in its own way, has majesty and power."

"But not lasting," Santos said firmly. "I wish to know what you were doing at the church." He turned to lean against the balustrade and folded his arms across his chest.

"Just admiring it. It reminded me a lot of a church back home."

"And home is . . . ?"

"Massachusetts. On the east coast."

"I know it well. I went to Harvard Business School in Boston." He smiled smugly at the uncomprehending look on Pat's face. "Yes, it is so. Even the mayor of a small Mexican town can be educated abroad. It was most interesting, especially on weekends when I could escape to the ocean. *That* reminded me of home."

Pat laughed in embarrassment for her naiveté. She was the provincial—not he. Not this keen-eyed, perceptive man, who never failed to go right to the heart of the matter. And then he began to talk about America, and she felt a pang of homesickness. For the next hour or so, she forgot where she was, so vivid were the pictures he painted for her of her own home.

"Tell me," she asked curiously when there was a brief lull in the conversation, "what were you doing at the church yesterday?"

"Restorations, Miss Jessup. We are trying to maintain the Church of Santa Bárbara as a historical landmark, and there is much to do to compensate for centuries of neglect."

"How old is it?" she asked.

"Seventeenth century. Built by a Spanish priest named Hector Madero, who took his vows late in life, after he had amassed a fortune. He was a rich nobleman in Seville, you see. His dream was to build a cathedral of his own in the New World and he traveled widely before selecting Zihuatanejo. He was as struck by its beauty as you were, Miss Jessup. Now, do not ask me how he had managed to hold onto his fortune after he became a priest, but somehow he commissioned twelve marble gargoyles to be carved by the finest Spanish craftsmen while he set about building a temporary chapel, to serve until he could build his cathedral."

"And he never did it?" Pat interjected.

"No, the materials, the time, the workmen were all lacking. And so, the little stucco chapel became the focus of all his attentions. When the gargoyles were shipped to him six years later, again Fate intervened. Only seven of the twelve survived the voyage intact. But he persevered and set about reconstructing the facade and had ledges made for the gargoyles, which happen to be the only ones in all Mexico. We are doing our utmost to restore the ledges, and eventually, the whole church. It might please *Padre* Madero, wherever he is."

"That's fascinating." Pat could see the dedication and love for this church shining in his eyes. This man had more sides to him than anyone Pat had ever met. He had a true love for his people and his heritage, but he didn't scorn the advantages of an American education. He was evidently a prestigious figure in the area, and yet he could toil and sweat next to his men for the sheer pleasure of making something more beautiful. And unlike most people Pat knew, he had great respect for the past, something she, too, admired deeply.

"I think that's an admirable project. And you're doing a great job—even if you do harass women from your scaffold."

He looked at her sharply for a moment, and then he threw back his head and began to laugh. The deep, warm chuckle was infectious, and pretty soon, Pat couldn't stop herself and laughed along with him. He grabbed both her hands and held them in his large ones, close to his chest. "You are a person whose good will I will try hard to earn," he promised in a soft voice. "I sense that you are a strong woman, and a caring one, Patricia. How I will enjoy getting to know you."

For a brief second, he released her hand, and touched her right shoulder, stroking the lace sleeve of her gown gently with his fingers. His hand seemed unnaturally warm, as though he were running a fever.

Pat had never in her life been so affected by a man's touch. It traveled to each part of her body and made her dizzy with pleasure and excitement. But before she could even respond or pull away, as she knew she ought to, there was a noise on the other side of the patio. Santos and Pat whirled around to face a flushed and annoyed Ted Beckman.

"Pat! I've been looking everywhere for you. The dinner's almost over, and a few people are going to make speeches. Naturally, I'd like to introduce you formally to the community. If you're not too busy," he spat out with an angry glance at Santos. Pat noticed that he hadn't even acknowledged the mayor's presence.

"I'll be with you in a second, Ted," she said softly. "I must have lost track of the time."

"Evidently." He stood his ground, and it seemed obvious that he wasn't going to move until they did.

"I have somehow managed to rob Miss Jessup of her appetite," Santos shrugged, taking her by the arm and leading her briskly past Ted. But as soon as they were through the doors of the Crystal Garden, and the noise of the crowd covered his words, Santos whispered in Pat's ear, "What I meant to say was, I have robbed her of her appetite for food."

She laughed nervously and drew her arm quickly from his. And yet she could still feel the imprint of his hand on her shoulder. The sensation refused to go away. "I beg to differ, Mayor Ribera. Actually, I could eat an entire chicken *mole.*"

"Good!" he laughed. "Then we'll continue our conversation later, shall we?"

"By all means," she nodded, already moving back toward Ted, who was motioning her toward his table. As she walked away, she could feel Santos's eyes on her, as palpable as his hands.

"I'd like to remind you," Ted said evenly when he had seated her beside him, "that being seen and available to the guests and my personal clients is part of your job."

Pat frowned and swallowed hard. He seemed unreasonably upset about the time she had spent with Santos, and as she examined the controlled set of his face, she was reminded of the mayor's harsh words against Ted and his designs on Ixtapa. There was clearly no love lost between the two men, and she decided to make it her business to find out why. Right now, though, her only object was to placate her boss and do her job.

"The night is young, isn't it?" she smiled at him cordially. "Now, what's the order of business? Herr Dorfmann or Señor Costilla? Or should I say hello to Mayor Sánchez? I'm ready for work now, Ted," she assured him.

"Well good, that's fine." The anger vanished from his face, and suddenly he was the hale and hearty Ted she had seen before. At least he didn't hold a grudge, Pat thought as Ted tapped on his glass to call for everyone's attention. She would keep that in mind for the future.

But she wondered, as he made his presentation and introduced the first speaker, if his upset had anything to do with jealousy. Even if it did, Pat decided, she wasn't going to let it get to her. She felt slightly light-headed and unaccountably happy, as though she'd just been given a surprise birthday party. Could it be the intoxicating presence of Zihuatanejo's mayor?

Watch it, girl, she warned herself. He may be more than you can handle.

Chapter Six

"*A*re you sure this is okay with Ted?" Pat asked Ruth nervously as she steered the luxurious white Mercedes down the Paradiso's long drive. After his marked disapproval last night, Pat didn't want to do anything else that might incur his wrath.

"I told you, sweetie, it's fine with him." Ruth fluttered her hands impatiently. "Orlando's busy with a truckload of new gardeners, you did your work this morning and I want to go into Zihuatanejo. So it's logical—you can take me!"

"Your logic, Ruth, leaves something to be desired," Pat laughed, steering carefully into the traffic on the main road. She had awakened that morning to the cry of the pelicans, swooping down for their breakfast beneath the waves, and the first thought in her head was that she had to be logical about the previous night. What could the young mayor's flirtation actually mean? He was a politician, wasn't he, and the most diplomatic tack would naturally be to get on the good side of the Paradiso's new assistant manager—particularly if his relations with Ted were strained.

"I think you should go past the Playa del Popolo first. It's always so lively there," Ruth interrupted Pat's reverie. "You know, sometimes I get sick and tired of the stuffy crowd over at our hotel, so when Orlando has errands to run, I always beg him to take me down here. I have this retinal disease, you know, and I can't drive. It just keeps getting worse, and so far no brilliant doctor has discovered a thing he can do about it. Sometimes I surprise myself, though, I can even make out the small print on menus; other times it's like looking through a pane of smashed glass." She sighed. "When Al was alive—that was my husband—we went everywhere, did everything. My eyes were fine then. But one day he had a stroke, and poof, my whole life changed. So naturally when Ted and Arlene invited me down, I agreed."

"Arlene?" Pat half turned to her, but managed to keep an eye on the road.

"Ted's ex. She was a sweet girl. I liked her. But I knew Ted was making a stupid mistake when he made her vice-president of Paradiso Enterprises. But he insisted."

"Why?"

"Because, sweetie, Ted is turned on by ambitious, capable women. They just move his motor, you know. He's not too interested in the sweet, stay-at-home type, or the quiet Mexican wife and mother—which reminds me that I was telling you about Santos Ribera's mother. He's been promising me for months to take me over to her house for an afternoon, so when I saw him last night, I cornered him."

"Do you know where she lives?" Pat asked. Actual-

73

ly, she was far more interested in what Ruth had just told her about her failing eyesight and about Ted's failed marriage, but she was aware that this was neither the time nor the place to talk about those things. It also occurred to her that her guilt in taking off from work on her first day had more to do with going to find Santos than it did with shirking her duties.

"Some place up in the hills. Oh, you'd never find it, dear. We're going to the town hall to get Santos first, and he'll take it from there."

"Okay. But I shouldn't be gone too long, Ruth. You know I'm only working on a two-week trial basis," she fretted.

"You silly! You've already got the job. Ted *loves* you! Believe me, I'm his mother. I can tell when he's smitten, and I don't need my eyesight to do it."

"Ruth," Pat protested, very embarrassed. "It's not a question of love. It's creativity, organization, supervisory skills and dealing with people. It's—"

"The only one you have to deal with is my son Ted. And don't talk back. Now, when you get to the end of the road leading to the beach and you can't go any further, take a left. I think the town hall is near there."

Pat wondered how Santos would act toward her when they met today. Would it be the same as last night, that electric current passing back and forth between them? Or would she see the professional mayor, busy with paperwork and telephone calls? Either way she was looking forward to it.

The *centro* was small, so despite Ruth's shaky directions, she found the town hall in minutes and parked in the lot behind it. The hall was in an open field plaza with municipal offices flanking three sides and the fourth opening onto the bay. The mayor's office was a starkly simple one-room affair in the corner of the plaza with a gilt-letter sign over the door, announcing his title. Inside, Pat could see Santos sitting by himself in a straight-backed wooden chair. Aside from the plain metal desk, strewn with papers, there was a phone, a rickety chair for one visitor, a wall calendar, and one standing goose-necked lamp. The ultimate in simplicity. The only luxury the mayor had allowed himself was setting his desk so that it faced the beach rather than the wall. He must love that view, Pat thought, looking out at the white-capped waves under the azure sky.

"Is this it?" Ruth squinted at the sign. "I think it says mayor or something—that's what he told me. Thank God you have your eyesight, and you know Spanish, Pat."

Without waiting for Pat to help her up the steps, Ruth charged bravely ahead, pulling her companion by the hand. It was odd—whenever Ruth really wanted to see something, she seemed to be able to will herself to do it. Either that, or she had substituted instinct and pluck for clear vision.

"Oh, Mr. Mayor, we're here!" Ruth sang out as they approached his door.

Santos jerked around, an annoyed expression on his face, but when he saw who was interrupting him, a relaxed smile softened his features. Pat stood behind Ruth, telling herself not to stare. And yet, he was staring right back.

"Ruth, Miss Jessup, I am glad you have come early."

"You haven't forgotten your promise, now?" Ruth eased herself into the other chair as she spoke.

"My mother is expecting you," he countered. "I think she has ransacked the stores for banquet preparations. Even from here, I can smell her tortillas baking over the hot fire."

"Well, that'll be welcome after the awful meal we

suffered through last night. But you two were lucky—
you missed most of it."

Pat gaped at her in astonishment, and Santos burst
out laughing.

"Well, what are we waiting for?" Ruth asked. "The
work will keep till this afternoon. Or tomorrow, for
that matter. Let's go."

"Ah, Ruth." Santos came over to her and waggled a
finger in her face. "You are just like your son, always in
a hurry, always impatient." Then he turned to Pat.
"You must be careful, Miss Jessup. These Beckmans
will make you *loco*."

"Oh, I don't know about that," Pat grinned, taking
in yet another incarnation of Santos Ribera. From
brash workman to elegant gentleman to mayor of
Zihuatanejo. In his cream-colored suit and open collar,
he was definitely as devastating as he had been the
previous night.

"Come on, Santos," Ruth muttered, tapping her
foot. "Are we going or aren't we?"

"Of course, Ruth. Immediately." Shaking his head,
he picked up his phone, dialed three numbers and
informed someone in rapid-fire Spanish that he'd be
out for a few hours. Then he set down the receiver and
smiled at the two women. *"Vámonos!"* When he came
over to usher them out the door and put his hand lightly
on Pat's elbow, she felt weak all over again—but she
was beginning to like the feeling.

He led them out the door and across the plaza to the
parking lot, where he pointed to a dusty black VW
Rabbit.

"We can take the Mercedes," Pat offered, indicating
the Beckmans' car several yards away. "There are three
of us, and it'll be more comfortable."

"Miss Jessup." Santos wheeled around, his black

eyes glinting with sharp criticism. "I am the servant of the people. How would it look for me to ride in Mr. Beckman's luxury automobile?"

Pat pursed her lips, thinking privately that his comment and the way he'd said it were totally unnecessary. She wasn't some fat-cat capitalist; she was only thinking of Ruth's comfort. And she did not like being lectured. It reminded her of the way Steve used to talk to her when she said she didn't want to go to Denver. But Ruth had already settled herself in the back seat of the VW and was ready to go.

"Get in, Pat," she called when she noticed the two of them glaring at each other. "We'll be perfectly fine in here."

Pat had no choice but to get into the passenger seat. He was the mayor, after all, and part of her new job was to make nice with the local politicians.

Santos got behind the wheel with a grunt of annoyance, and without a glance at Pat, he gunned the car out of the lot and down the narrow street, through the *centro* and down to the traffic circle just outside the village.

He drives worse than a Mexico City cabbie, Pat thought sullenly, gripping the sides of her seat. Another one who thinks it's macho to drive like a maniac.

At the traffic circle, Santos followed the sign marked Zona Hotelería, but when it split off, he took the left fork onto a narrow, winding uphill road that looked down on the bay. As they climbed higher, Pat could see the landscape unfold beneath her, and her bad mood dissolved as she took in the breathtaking sights. Flowering bushes framed the rocky cliffs leading down to the deep blue water, and there, sitting out in the middle of the exquisite bay, was a three-masted schooner that might have been transplanted from the early nineteenth

77

century. The little fishing boats gathered around it like moths attracted to a flame.

"What *is* that?" Pat asked.

"A training ship for our navy," Santos answered proudly. "All Mexican sailors must learn how to sail in the old tradition before they board a modern ship. The old ways, you see, Miss Jessup, are important to others besides myself."

She shot him an annoyed glance, but he just smiled smugly to himself, as though he knew perfectly well that it was only a matter of time before she came around to his way of thinking. Well, she decided, if that's the way he is, he's got a lot to learn about me.

But before she could work herself into a state, Ruth piped up from the back seat, "Where does your mother live, Santos?"

"Near Las Gatas Beach. I don't know why I did not think of this myself, Ruth. The two of you have a great deal in common, I believe, except that you do not speak the same language. But people always find ways to get around that," he added, stealing a look at Pat out of the corner of his eye. She couldn't help feeling that he was saying and meaning two different things.

"Ah, there it is. Over there." He pointed to the edge of the bay directly opposite the Playa del Popolo in the middle of town.

"Las Gatas? The Cat Beach? That's a funny name," Pat commented, looking over at the lovely houses set up high in the hills. Each one was terraced, affording a perfect view out to the water from any level.

"It is, and especially because there are no cats around here. The dogs take care of that. Only my cat, El Presidente, as I call him. But he came with me from Massachusetts and survives very nicely with me on La Ropa Beach, where I live. Down there." He pointed to the right, to a stretch of beach sandwiched between craggy rock formations. It was perfectly gorgeous.

"Las Gatas," Santos went on, "was named by the conquistadors when they took it from the Tarascan kings. They had trouble pronouncing 'Tarascas,' and so, for their convenience, they settled on 'Las Gatas' because it was easier. You see, at one time, Zihuatanejo was the exclusive royal Indian resort—many centuries ago. Just as Ixtapa is now becoming the royal resort of the international jet set."

"I don't see why you—" Pat cut in sharply, but he reached over and patted her hand in a placating manner.

"Now, now, I was not being critical—only telling you a bit of history. Where was I? Oh, yes, La Ropa, which means 'clothes,' was so called because whenever there was a shipwreck, the tides would wash the debris up on this beach. Often, the sailors' clothes came first, and the sailors—poor devils—afterward."

"Santos, you're gruesome," Ruth grumbled. "I hope you don't entertain your mother with such stories."

"But she told them to me!" he exclaimed, laughing. "You will see, you will like her."

He sped down the road for another mile or so, following the curve of the bay. Finally, he came to a stop at the side of the road where a cluster of small stucco dwellings were enclosed by a low stone wall. Tied to a palm tree on the lush green lawn was a small black-and-white goat, straining to graze on the tall grass just beyond his reach. As Santos led them across the lawn to his mother's home, Pat was struck by the unspoiled beauty of the place. The care that was lavished on the sprawling garden and the trellis of roses was mirrored in the simple elegance with which the house had been maintained. There were three outbuildings clustered around the main one, but nothing about the little complex suggested ostentation or great wealth. Pat couldn't help comparing the quiet simplicity of Zihuatanejo with the overbuilt hotel strip in Ixtapa. This place called out to her soul and soothed her spirit.

Santos went up onto the front porch and called out to his mother, who emerged almost at once, a wide smile on her face. She was much smaller than her son, a petite, round woman whose dark hair was streaked with gray. She drew her tall son down to her level and gave him an affectionate kiss on each cheek, then she examined him closely, asking in Spanish how he was and if he was taking care of himself. Pat was struck by the contrast between her mature, lined face and her long, straight hair, worn loose like a schoolgirl's. She could have been anywhere from forty-five to sixty.

"Qué linda!" exclaimed Señora Ribera, taking Pat's hand. Then she bowed almost formally to Ruth and said, *"Buenos días, señora."*

Ruth greeted the woman as though she were a long-lost friend, and although the two knew scarcely a word of each other's language, they began an animated conversation with words and hands, one overlapping the other. In less than a minute, Santos's mother threw up her hands, laughing, and led Ruth into her house. The smell of spicy Mexican food wafted out as she opened the door.

Pat smiled as she watched them together and heard the simple phrases they repeated back and forth to each other. She had seen the Gloucester fishermen and their French-Canadian colleagues communicate this way when they came in at the end of a long day. As Santos had said in the car, they had some common bond that allowed perfect understanding. Because of the genuine desire to get through to one another, they found a basic level of communication. If only it were that easy between men and women, Pat thought ruefully.

"Shall we join them?" Santos asked, but before Pat could answer, he grinned mischievously and went on, "No, they need some time to get acquainted. Let's go down to the beach."

Calling in to his mother that they would return within the hour and that he was hungry enough to eat the goat whole, Santos grabbed Pat's hand and dragged her over to the long flight of stone steps that led down to the beach.

"Mayor, I really don't have a lot of time," Pat protested. "Actually, it's my first real day on the job, and I—"

"I think we now know each other well enough to cease the formality. If you will allow me to call you Pat, I would like very much for you to call me Santos."

"Yes, sure, but you see, I—"

"Pat, my dear Pat, you have not been in Mexico long enough to accustom yourself to Mexican time. Now is lunch and then, the siesta. For centuries, we have done things this way. Even Mr. Beckman's schedule board cannot change it. You will be a far better employee at his establishment when you have learned the luxury of long Mexican afternoons. This is when people get to know each other, when they indulge in the most special of hours." He stopped on the step and turned to her, his face only inches from hers. "We must do the same as the older women and allow the sun to pass across the sky while we share the most perfect time of day. Come!" he urged her.

What could she do? He was so appealing, so boyish and compelling, that she found herself walking willingly behind him, her palm warmed by the embrace of his large hand. His fingers held hers tightly, so that he could guide her down the steps. But when she looked up and took in the view of Las Gatas Beach directly below them, she knew she could never have passed up this opportunity. Flowering trees dipped their branches into the water all along the tiny cove, which was studded with pieces of pastel-colored coral, ranging from off-white to deep rose. The gentle waves washed the coral over and over so that it shone in the sunlight like bits of a star that had fallen to earth. The beach was deserted except for one man who was working on the engine of his "water taxi" and an old Indian woman stringing coral to sell to the tourists.

"It's beautiful here," Pat murmured as they took the last few steps down to the beach. "I love it, Santos."

"Then you have very fine taste," he said approvingly. "But you have yet to see the beach where I live, so you must reserve judgment on which is your favorite."

She blushed and looked away, wondering if he intended to take her to "his" beach.

Santos bent down and quickly eased off his shoes, then ripped off his socks. "You cannot walk the beach in shoes," he told her, reaching over to undo the straps on her sandals. "Your toes must feel the warm sand."

Again the touch of his hand sent an odd but wonderful sensation coursing through her. To do something as intimate as remove her shoes would have been unthinkable in Ixtapa, but here, it seemed normal and correct.

"Now, we shall walk. That's all right, just leave them here," Santos assured her as she stooped to pick up the sandals. "No one will take them." He linked an arm through hers and drew her forward, toward the line parallel to the waves. "I used to come here late at night when I was a young boy. To see the moon, the stars.

But," he turned to her, grinning, "it is even better with a beautiful companion."

She did not look at him, but kept walking, wondering suddenly how many beautiful companions he had brought to this lovely beach, and to La Ropa, near his house. He was a very attractive man and a fascinating person. Pat simply assumed that many women must have been interested in marrying him. And had he ever considered one of them?

"Tell me, Pat, what brings you to Mexico?" he asked her earnestly. "Are you searching for a good love or running from a bad one?"

Pat flushed and gave a nervous little laugh. How could he ask such a thing? Could he read her thoughts? It was almost as if he could tell there had been a Dr. Steve Elman in her past.

"What makes you think it was love?" she shrugged, holding back her mane of blond hair from the breeze that had sprung up suddenly. "Why wouldn't you assume it was just a search for a good job? Hotel management is my business, and a resort like Ixtapa is a challenge for me."

"A challenge, yes. American women are always on the lookout for a good challenge." He shook his head. "When I was at Harvard, I don't believe I ever met a woman who did not use that word more often than any other."

Pat felt her hackles rise at his scoffing tone. What had started so nicely as an afternoon interlude had turned into something quite different. "Tell me about Harvard," she asked, hoping to change the subject. She was curious to hear him talk about himself, and particularly about what had made him travel to the United States.

"I'll tell you about Harvard," he nodded, "if afterward we can return to the topic of love." With a funny, mocking smile, he continued, "All right. When I was in business school I wanted to be a shipping magnate," he laughed.

"And what happened to that dream?"

"Well, my father already controlled all the shipping for the banana trade along the Pacific. He was priming me, you see, to take over the business. But after he died, I had time alone to think about what I really wanted out of life. My mother and I already had more money than we could possibly want. So, after just three years on my father's banana throne, I sold the business and ran for public office."

Pat nodded, newly intrigued by this unique individual who would give up a successful business empire to follow his heart's desire. The way he explained it, it seemed so logical, so right. "And what made you choose public office over anything else?" she asked.

"My father, although I loved him dearly, was an exploiter of men, I am sorry to say. He lived like a rich American, sapping Mexico for his personal pleasures. His attitudes were wrong," Santos announced, slamming a fist into his palm for emphasis. "Tradition and the past meant nothing to him, and people were only interesting so long as they fit his purposes. And do you know, eventually I saw that his business was making me the same way. I sold it just in time, before I was totally corrupted."

Pat examined his handsome, tanned face, filled now with serious intent. "You really believe in preserving traditions, don't you?"

"I believe there is nothing in the world as important to a poor people like ours. When you have nothing material to call your own, you need something intangible, but still very precious, that no one can take from you. I want my people to take pride in themselves—and I want to give them back everything my father and his associates robbed from them."

Pat shook her head. "That's a tall order for one man to fill."

Santos saw the disbelief in her face and laughed gently. "Do not worry, my dear Patricia. I do not feel that I must save all of Mexico all by myself."

She smiled with him, glad to see that he didn't take himself seriously *all* the time.

"Now, I have satisfied your curiosity; you must do the same for me."

"Oh?" She turned to pick up a beautiful shell that had been washed up by the waves. Actually, she couldn't face him, because she knew what he was going to ask.

"I am an acute observer of human nature, Pat, and I can tell easily that you did not only come to Mexico for a job. Something else drew you from your home—am I correct?"

"Well," she admitted, still examining her shell, "I guess. In a way."

"And what was that?" he asked her patiently.

"I needed . . . I wanted to find out something about myself. I suppose I'd been doing the same old thing in the same old way long enough." She looked up at him and shrugged. "That's about it."

His eyes narrowed and he took her hand, leading her closer to the lapping waves. Then his arm slipped around her, but only in a casual way, as if he were simply steadying her stance on the wet sand. "When I was younger," he began, "my father selected a woman for me to marry. I was a dutiful son, and she was very beautiful—also from a wealthy Mexican family—and so naturally, I accepted. I even let myself believe that I loved her, for a while."

Pat stared at him, astonished. Why was he confiding this to her?

"Then, when I went to America to school, something changed within me. I knew it, although I could not define it. The world was no longer so black and white, but it had many beautiful colors."

Pat couldn't help herself. "And when you came home," she broke in, "you told her you couldn't marry her."

"No," Santos shook his head, his arm still resting loosely over her slim shoulders, "she told me. After one evening together, she knew that we were not destined one for the other. Our souls did not call out to each other. My father was furious, of course. But we had made the right choice. And," he said, his dark eyes meeting hers, "my soul still searches."

Pat let her breath out and realized that she was trembling slightly, although the afternoon sun was warm. "Sort of the same thing that happened to me," she murmured.

"I knew that," he said softly. "I was only waiting to hear it from you. Even the day when I saw you at the church, I felt we shared a common bond, a similar language. Does your heart not tell you the same?"

His hand gripped her shoulder and pressed her closer. Somehow, she found herself turning toward him, drawn by a force she could not control. His eyes burned down into hers, and spoke to her in an eternal language, asking her a question to which there was only one answer. They stood drinking in the sight and smell of one another, held for a moment in time by a thin web of hesitation.

At last he broke through, his mouth coming inexorably closer to hers. His lips hovered tantalizingly near, but he did nothing, letting her find her own inclination. Then she moved toward him and the moment was complete. Their lips met and they kissed, longingly but gently. Pat closed her eyes to the sensation, but still she was aware of his strong hands, now on her back, now on her waist, at last in her hair, as he let the kiss grow and blossom like a tropical flower. Her breasts arched to meet him, and as he pressed her tightly against him, she sensed that her thighs were trembling, her legs scarcely able to hold her upright. His mouth opened on hers and she met his intensity with a passion she had never dreamed existed inside her. For that moment, the world was lost to them both.

When at last they were able to draw apart, they stood still, the waves lapping at their toes, both panting for breath. Pat could still feel the impression of his lips on hers—her body was alive and pulsating with a million different sensations. But above it all was her blank astonishment at her own capacity for desire. Throughout her life, she had longed to feel this impulsive, marvelous, blinding passion that would close her eyes to everything but the man she adored. And yet, here she was, alone on a beach with a man she hardly knew. And why had *he* moved her this way?

Suddenly embarrassed, she looked away, and he gently reached to cup her chin in his hand. "Pat?" He looked at her questioningly. She wanted to believe that he was sincere, but her own doubts about the way she reacted to men were too ingrained.

"Let's start back," she said hastily. "Your mother and Ruth must think we've drowned or something." She couldn't cover her nervousness, and as much as she wanted to talk about it, she couldn't.

"If you wish," he nodded politely. Without another

glance at her, as though he respected her right to explore her own feelings in her own time, he began walking, and she followed quietly by his side. The tide was ebbing now, and Pat concentrated hard on watching the waves wash away the footprints they had made. Was this what their relationship would be like? One brief moment of bliss obliterated before it could grow?

Pat was so absorbed in her thoughts, she almost missed Santos's words when he began speaking again, after several long silent minutes.

"But I did not quite finish what I was telling you about why I decided to make such changes in my life." His words came tumbling out briskly now, as though he were addressing an audience at a political rally, as though they had never kissed at all or held each other suspended in time and space. "Despite what I had learned at my father's knee, I wanted more—just as you do, Pat."

"Yes," she said, looking up at last. "I can understand that."

"I felt I could give more, and by doing so, I would receive back many times over what I had put out. Now, take the Church of Santa Bárbara, for example. It is unique in our country for its history, its wonderful Spanish gargoyles. Once it is restored, it will be there forever, and the people of Zihuatanejo can rejoice that it is their special landmark. Do you see, Pat?" He stopped walking and turned, taking her hands in his and grasping them tightly together. "Once the people can take pride in their town, they may not feel that it is useless to develop it. My hope is that eventually they will care enough to grow more cash crops for themselves, to start their own businesses so that they can prosper for themselves, rather than wait for rich investors." He looked out at the sea, then back into her clear blue eyes. "More travesties like the hotels in Ixtapa will not help Mexico. But tradition will."

Pat frowned at him and drew away. On the one hand, she was extremely grateful to him for not mentioning their spontaneous interlude together. She *did* need time to think about it. But on the other hand, she found it extremely disconcerting the way he could just bounce back and start talking about "the people" and their problems as though nothing at all had happened. Unless that was exactly how he felt about it. But the other thing that bothered her was Santos's grim determination. He was so set on his one course, he could see no other alternatives.

"There's nothing wrong with encouraging the tourist trade here, Santos. That produces money as well—money that will go, in part, to your people. Listen," she smiled, as a fantastic idea hit her. "What if I could convince Ted Beckman to work with you? Maybe start a hotel management trainee program at the Para-diso—"

Santos shook his head sadly as he cut her off. "I thought you understood me," he frowned. "But you have heard nothing I said to you today. If you intend to stay here in Mexico, Pat, you will have to learn that you cannot interfere in the way things have been done before. New ideas are not necessarily good ideas, nor can a woman hope to settle what exists between two men. For that matter, it would be well for you to learn your job before you begin to preach to others."

"Now just a second," Pat exploded, suddenly seeing red. How could this man have been so tender with her only moments before? Now he was treating her like a recalcitrant child. "Talk about preaching! You give me the big lecture on tradition and tell *me* not to preach! You tell me about how to fix Mexico and accuse me of interfering! Let me tell you, Mayor, you've got a hell of an attitude problem!" She was so angry she could scarcely get the words out. "And as for a woman not butting into a man's business, well, that notion went out with the Middle Ages!"

He stared at her with a steely gaze. "I believe you mentioned that my mother and Ruth should not be kept waiting. In that, at least, we agree. Come, if we do not hurry, the banquet will have ended." He marched ahead of her, planting his long legs one after the other in the wet sand. Pat didn't even try to catch up to him. Her head was pounding with rage, and with some other emotion she could not define. Whatever Santos Ribera was, he was not a man to be trifled with.

But I'm no pushover either, Pat thought decisively. And pretty soon, maybe not tomorrow or the next day, but eventually, he is going to learn that he has met his match. The battle isn't over yet.

Chapter Seven

The next three weeks flew by so fast Pat scarcely had time to recall what her fight with Santos had been about. What with her dizzying work schedule at the Paradiso and getting to know the area, she was too busy to worry about the mayor's chauvinistic attitudes. The job was turning out to be much more than she had ever expected, and that excited her. She was free from the mundane matters of hotel management, such as monitoring the staff, keeping peace in the kitchen when the high-strung chefs started in on one another and soothing the ruffled feathers of hotheaded guests, because her two assistants took care of those matters brilliantly. It was very clear, after the first week, that Ted had other plans for his new assistant manager. In their daily meetings, every morning promptly at eight-thirty, he made it clear that he trusted her and valued her opinions.

"I have a feeling you'll be better than me at finding

out how the guests feel about us, Pat," he told her one morning in his spacious glass-enclosed office on the top floor of the Paradiso. "FONATUR'S been dragging its feet on advertising, and it concerns me that the only intrepid voyagers to Ixtapa are people who heard about it firsthand from friends or associates. And God knows what it's going to take to turn them into repeaters!" He ran a hand through his short, well-trimmed hair, and Pat could see how concerned he was. Laid back Californian though he might be, he didn't hide his feelings very well, at least not from her or his mother.

"Building a clientele through word of mouth is just going to take too damn long," he continued. "We could be wiped out by then."

"Where do you think the real problem lies?"

"The problem is that we're losing out to the Yucatán," Ted sighed, walking over to his gigantic three-dimensional model of Mexico's Pacific coast. "Cozumel and Cancún are hot right now, plus they've exploited the eastern U.S. market very well. It's a convenient hop from New York or Washington. But us, I don't know. It seems like Texans and Californians are the only ones who know about us. But look—" He motioned to the model. "We're right in line with Acapulco and Puerto Vallarta, so why not steal some of their business? They're old hat now, anyway, as far as I'm concerned. If we had the right kind of advertising, we could get forty percent of their crowd easily, don't you think?"

"Maybe," Pat ventured, not exactly sure about all this. Way back, tucked somewhere in her mind, Santos's words kept playing over and over, like a broken record. He thought the tourist industry was big enough right now for his town. But then, she asked herself, what did he know about hotel management anyway?

"See, FONATUR is afraid we'll kill the trade in the other resorts if we pour on the steam. They want it both ways, natch. And we're not tried and true, so they balk whenever I ask for more money."

"You know, Ted, you're right about this word of mouth problem," Pat nodded. "I mean, Acapulco's practically a household word, and who's ever heard of Ixtapa? For that matter, who can even pronounce Zihuatanejo? They call it 'that Z place,' do you know that? Say, I've just put my finger on it!"

"What?" He whirled around, immediately interested.

"Well, I'm sure people must be confused by the few ads they *do* see. We need to convince people that Ixtapa and Zihuatanejo are only a couple of miles apart, and that this is a whole resort area, not just a golf course with some palm trees in the background."

"Pat, you're a genius!" Ted got up and grabbed her by the shoulders enthusiastically.

"No," she smiled, extricating herself from his grasp. "Just observant."

"Okay, all right, whatever you say," he blustered. He seemed rather embarrassed to have touched her—or was she imagining things again? "So, how do you propose that we go about clarifying ourselves, getting the word out simply and clearly that we're the chic-est, best new spot in Mexico?"

"How about free vacations for the biggest travel agents in New York, Boston and Chicago for starters? Most people choose a vacation spot through an agent, so I think we should go to the source. Convince the professionals, and they'll take care of the word-of-mouth ads. We could even offer them a more generous commission or some kind of bonus for every tourist they send our way. Then," she went on, getting more excited as the ideas began coming fast and furious, "we should start lobbying with the airlines. Every flight, except the few direct ones a week from L.A. and Houston, is two stops, so all the Easterners have to go through Mexico City and worry about changing planes. A direct hop from New York would convince lots of doubtful tourists that Ixtapa is worth a visit."

"Now you've got it!" Ted gave a whoop of delight as he came to her side and shook her hand vigorously—man-to-man, or partner-to-partner. "I'm sure I could get one of the airlines to go for it on a six-month trial period. Pat, this is great. *You're* great."

She grinned at him, enjoying the boyish glee with which he greeted anything that meant more business and, therefore, more profit. "By the way, Ted, speaking of trial periods, mine was up over a week ago. You haven't told me yet whether I have the job."

"Well, you must be out of your mind, or else ridiculously modest. Of course you've got the job, you nut! There's no way I'd let a gem like you get away."

"Uh-huh." Pat snapped her small notebook closed and grinned at him. "I thought I had it, but I just wanted to make sure before I did anything else ingenious for the Paradiso."

"Well, don't keep me in suspense. You're my employee now, you know—can't hold anything back."

"Okay." She went over to the plush suede couch and settled herself back in the pillows, feeling justifiably pleased with herself. "We agree that one of our major problems is the popular misconception about who's what down here. I'd like to call a big meeting of the local hotel owners, merchants, restaurant owners, public officials, etc., of both Ixtapa and Zihuatanejo. If we all get together on this, maybe we don't have to wait for FONATUR. We could run ads ourselves in the States that would clarify the business of who we are and where we're located. If everyone will chip in for a sizeable campaign—contribution according to yearly revenues —we'll all benefit. And as organizers of this cooperative venture, the Paradiso wins great public relations as well."

"I love it, Pat! Do it!" Ted went to his desk and began writing furiously in his own notebook. "It's a brilliant scheme. Oh, listen, would you do me one favor? Invite Hans Dorfmann, okay? He's still sitting on the fence about the deal I'm trying to nail down with him, and maybe your meeting will convince him that Ixtapa is no minor league operation. I keep having this feeling he's on his way back to the Yucatán with his deutsche marks."

"What's this deal all about?" Pat asked curiously.

Ted shot her one of his charming smiles and shook his head. "I hate to discuss things before they take shape, Pat, even with you. I promise you, though, if things go right, you'll be part of it—a big part." When she made a face and seemed to be about to ask another question, he continued, "Investors have to have a sense that a project is special, and for that reason, confidentiality is essential, Pat. You'll be the first to know when I break the news."

She shrugged and got up to leave, no longer quite as smug as she'd been a few minutes before. Sure Ted trusted her, he loved her ideas and he gave off definite signals that his interest was not only professional. But when it came to something big, she was just another employee. And he was just like every other man she knew, reluctant to share the "affairs of men" with a mere woman. God, they were annoying!

"Take time off from your other duties to get this started, would you, Pat? The sooner you get everyone involved in this ad campaign, the sooner Dorfmann will agree to be my partner, and the sooner I can include you in this project."

"Well, that's about as much incentive as any employer has ever offered me," she responded truthfully, still miffed that he was playing cat-and-mouse with her. "I'll see what I can do."

"Catch you later, Pat," he nodded, picking up his phone to make a call. She knew that she'd been dismissed.

Sighing as she left Ted's office, Pat's head was whirling with a variety of unrelated items. Starting to get the word out about the conference, making up an agenda, getting Herr Dorfmann to cooperate—the difficulties were evident. And the largest one, she was certain, would be getting the mayor of Zihuatanejo to attend. Naturally, Santos would have to be there, and this would give her ample opportunity to demonstrate just how capable a woman could be. As she hurried down to the mail room, she realized she was actually relishing the idea of showing him what she could do. It could not be denied that the man had gotten under her skin. There was no escape from his subtle power over her. He both infuriated and stimulated her, and he raised her emotions to fever pitch.

She tried to clear her head of the image she kept having of that kiss on the beach, that wonderful moment when the differences dissolved and their hearts spoke more loudly than their heads. But it was difficult to reconcile all the elements that separated them.

Suddenly deciding that it was about time she got down to work, she made up her mind about the rest of the morning. Since Ted was giving her free rein on this conference, and since Mexicans always did business in a personal manner, she could go into town and start chatting up everyone she intended to snare. As she walked down to the parking lot to borrow one of the hotel cars, she debated with herself whether it would be wise to go to Santos's office for a casual visit so that she could start getting him used to the idea of this meeting.

Oh, admit it, girl, you just want to go see him, Pat told herself angrily as she selected a yellow VW bug and went to the attendant to get the keys. It really ate at her that he hadn't called or come by or sent a note in three weeks. Well, if the mountain won't go to Mohammed, she decided, starting off down the drive, she would have to go to the mountain.

She prolonged the moment, teasing herself with the thought that maybe she wouldn't go after all. But she was feeling so good after her brief chats with several of the local merchants and hotel owners that she took a deep breath and turned down the road that led to the Playa del Popolo, right across from the town hall. She sat in the car for a couple of minutes, watching a group of tiny youngsters set up their fruit stand on the low wall across the way. How was Santos going to react when she just waltzed in to see him? Well, why did she care so much, anyway?

Because you're infatuated with him, you big ninny, she suddenly realized. And with what in particular? Not his family's wealth or his Harvard degree—she'd known Ivy Leaguers before and was not impressed. But Santos was something else, a man of unpredictable contradictions and off moments of tenderness amid his macho bluster. He was a rich man who scorned the trappings of class, a person who genuinely cared about those not as well off as he. But what intrigued her the most about him was that he was still searching for love—as Pat herself was.

She bravely walked to the door of his office and knocked, half hoping he would be out, helping the workers at the church or seeing to the affairs of his town. But as luck had it, he was sitting calmly by himself, jotting notes on a yellow legal pad, and he seemed startled to see her. A range of emotions crossed his face, at last settling into the polite, cordial Santos she had seen several times before. But there was still a hint of something else behind his smile.

"Pat, how good to see you!" he exclaimed, rising from his chair and walking to her. She had forgotten how tall he was, how the shock of dark hair framed his strong features. She had forgotten, too, her interior reaction when she was near this man. The sensation was embarrassing, but pleasurable at the same time.

"I hope I'm not disturbing you," she began.

"Not at all; I was just about to leave for lunch. Will you join me?"

She said yes immediately, wondering if he really did want to see her. His manner was slightly distant, and she could not read his expression at all.

He spoke briefly to his secretary on the phone, then took Pat by the hand and led her out to the plaza. "No dispute over cars today," he teased, reading her mind. "Let's walk—the restaurant is quite near."

The various shops were just beginning to close up for the long siesta, and Santos had a word for every vendor and storekeeper. He stopped to chat briefly with the foreman of a construction site that looked like another bank to Pat. She couldn't take her eyes off two of the workmen, boys scarcely out of their childhood. When Santos had said *adiós* and they walked on, she said, "Those kids were just helping out, right? They were only about ten or eleven."

"True. But they are employed just as the older men

are. And they are fortunate to be employed, Pat, because it puts food on their mothers' tables."

When she sighed and looked downcast, Santos chucked her under the chin and laughed heartily, "They do not mind! They would rather be toiling with the men than locked up with the babies in school. When I was their age, I envied such boys. I was only carrying a book bag when they were carrying bricks."

She shook her head, uncomprehending. "I guess there are some things we'll never agree on. I think kids should be allowed to be kids."

"And *I* think," Santos growled, "that you enjoy a good argument. Here, this is the best fish place in town."

He led her through the doorway of the Mesa del Capitán, a charming but touristy seafood restaurant owned, he said, by a British expatriate. Pat was surprised—she would have expected him to select a humbler and cheaper place patronized by the locals, particularly after the conversation they had just had. But as soon as they walked in and the waiters greeted their mayor with smiles and calls of *"Buenos días!"* she understood. Santos reveled in the prompt, specialized service he got here. The owner rushed in to shake the mayor's hand and greeted Pat with a deep bow, and as soon as he had disappeared again, Santos confided, "He is English by birth, but in his soul, he is Mexican."

Interesting, Pat thought as she studied the menu. He was usually against foreign entrepreneurs like Ted and Hans Dorfmann. Again, it struck her how Santos Ribera thrived on contradictions.

"What's good here?" she asked when he yanked her menu away.

"Everything. I will order." He began to signal for the waiter, and Pat felt herself getting mad all over again. It didn't matter what her opinions were, as long as Santos decided he was running things.

"But I—" she began.

"No, no, I insist." He began rattling off a variety of dishes to the waiter in Spanish, interspersing his order with some hearty jokes. Even though he knew she understood what he was saying, he persisted in this buddy-buddy routine with the waiter.

Why is he like this? Pat thought despairingly. I thought he was deeper, more sensitive.

"Is your job going well?" he asked her casually, without a trace of interest, when the waiter had left for the kitchen.

"Excellently. My employer seems pleased, and now that my two-week trial period is up, I'm not on probation any more. I'm here to stay," she added pointedly.

"A fact which gladdens my heart," he smiled, reaching across the table to take her hands. But she pulled away.

"Oh, really?" Where was the man who had kissed her so passionately, who had stirred her soul? His words sounded hollow to her today, and naturally, she blamed herself. She'd mistaken her first impression of the man for the real thing.

"Yes. I am very happy you are remaining in Ixtapa. It gives me the opportunity to see you often. And to teach you many things," he added in a different, lower voice. He took one of her hands and brought it to his lips, kissing it softly. Their table was in a secluded alcove, so that no one could see them, but Pat felt uncomfortable and she squirmed in her seat.

"Do you know why I did not call you or come to see you?" he asked, his lips trailing delightfully up her hand to her wrist.

"No." She could scarcely get the word out.

"I wanted to see just how much you cared—how much the moment we shared on Las Gatas meant to you. A man and a woman must never force what exists between them." His other hand reached up to stroke her face and she had to control her breathing, which was coming in short, desperate gasps.

"How do you know that anything really happened that day?" she asked, really wanting a straight answer.

"Oh, my Patricia. I know, and so do you."

Pat looked away, embarrassed, just as the waiter returned with a huge platter of oysters for their appetizer. She grinned at it, snapping out of her spellbound mood, and started laughing.

"And what amuses you?" Santos asked, squeezing lime liberally over the plate.

"It's just . . ." She had to stop laughing as he popped an oyster in her mouth. "Well," she went on, after she had swallowed. "This is a little obvious, don't you think?"

"What is?" he frowned.

"The oysters, Santos. *Ostras,* isn't that what they're called? Oysters are supposedly aphrodisiacs."

"Which neither you nor I are in need of," he countered with a suggestive glance.

Pat took a deep breath and swallowed. "Sorry to disappoint you, but I find these rather tasteless. I guess the warm water of the Pacific does something to the quality."

"What are you saying?" Santos was instantly on the defensive. "These are the finest *ostras* in Mexico."

"Maybe," she shrugged, spearing another with her fork. She was sort of enjoying his discomfiture. "But they're not as good as back home."

"Spoken like an American," he sneered, suddenly

hostile. "You are nurtured on frozen food, yet you have the nerve to criticize something you are incapable of appreciating." He quickly moved the platter away from her.

"Now *you're* wrong," Pat said calmly. "My father always made sure I ate the freshest fish in the Atlantic. He caught it himself. He's an independent fisherman in Gloucester, did I tell you that?" Pat gave him an innocent smile, watching his face change. She could see him readjusting his ideas about her. Naturally, he'd assumed she was a spoiled American from a well-to-do family.

"What's wrong?" she smiled. "You look like you don't believe me."

"No, I . . ." he began.

"Santos, not all Americans are rich businessmen, bent on exploiting the poor. My father only exploits fish, just like your friends here in Zihuatanejo."

"I see." His eyes were no longer distant, nor did he joke about her ideas throughout the rest of the meal. Suddenly he seemed to have a different appreciation of her, because of her background. Unlike other men she knew, including Steve, Santos was impressed by a family who struggled and won, as opposed to one who had succeeded financially. Pat could see traces of envy in his face. Just as he had wanted to carry bricks instead of books as a child, now he seemed to long for a past that would place him squarely among his people. And he admired Pat because she came equipped with such a past.

This revelation had opened the door for them. Without anything being said directly, it was understood that they had changed toward one another. It seemed odd, even though she was fiercely attracted to this man, that she had to wave a red cape in his face to get him to move. Like a bull in the ring, he was forever in need of a challenge. And Pat firmly resolved that she would provide just that.

Pat was never exactly sure how she'd managed it, but she got the meeting organized in less than a week. Time was of the essence, because Herr Dorfmann was leaving for Germany in just a few days, and Ted had expressly asked that he be included.

"I'm not going to make it myself, sorry," Ted told her the morning before.

"You're not coming to the meeting?" Pat asked incredulously. "But the point of the whole thing was to show the Paradiso as leader of the pack."

"I know, sweetheart. And you're perfectly capable of doing that yourself. I have complete confidence in you. Look, I forgot I had a prior appointment with Señor Costilla at the FONATUR office in Mexico City. You can handle it, Pat."

Pat pursed her lips nervously. "Ted, you've told me yourself, Mexicans do business because of their personal contacts. I've been here only a month—less—and you want me to head up the whole shebang?"

"Yes, I do. Have a ball," he said airily as he left to pack for his trip.

Pat thought about this all day and all that night. Ted had done it on purpose, of course, and he was testing her. It wasn't that she was uncertain about her skills, but it had been like pulling teeth to get Santos to agree to attend, and who knew what some of the others would think of her big push for an ad campaign.

Pat woke up on the morning of the big day feeling determined and competent. She dressed as she had for her interview with Ted, in the white and navy linen outfit, and wound her blond mane up in a severe chignon. She wanted to look as businesslike as possible.

The huge conference room of the Paradiso began filling up at nine o'clock. The hotel and restaurant owners mingled with the local politicians, bankers and small businessmen at the long table where coffee and pastries had been provided. Pat stood at one end of the table, surveying the room. One of her main fears was already beginning to materialize. The big Ixtapa hotel owners had gathered in a tight bloc and were only talking with one another. The less well-dressed group from Zihuatanejo stood apart, eyeing their neighbors suspiciously. Santos had told her that the Ixtapans considered the Zihuatanejans backward and stubborn, and on the other hand, the Ixtapans were looked on as capitalist conquistadors by his people.

If I could only start with a rousing game of musical chairs, Pat mused as she called the meeting to order. Above all, she wanted to keep the mood friendly. A pitched battle here would be doubly disastrous. Not only would the two factions inhibit their own progress by working against each other, but a display of chaos and bitterness would convince Herr Dorfmann that Ixtapa was the wrong place to invest his money. And if he wasn't pleased, Pat was going to have a lot of explaining to do when Ted got back.

"Buenos días, señores. Por favor, tan pronto como posible. Es tarde." She hoped she didn't sound too schoolmarmish, calling them to order this way. She glanced over at Herr Dorfmann, seated by himself in a corner, sipping his coffee and quietly taking in the scene. He was conventionally dressed today in a dark blue suit and red tie, but he looked as cunning as ever. Ted had raved about the man's legendary investment

instincts, how he'd been known to pull out of deals at the last moment because he had a hunch that things weren't right. Pat just hoped the vibes he was getting from the two camps wouldn't drive him out of the room.

She checked her list as the men took their places to make sure everyone she'd invited had arrived. The only one missing was Mayor Santos Ribera.

That contrary troublemaker! she fumed. He'd disapproved of the very idea of this meeting, and undoubtedly, the fact that a woman was running it drove him wild. Well, too bad for him.

"*Señores,* gentlemen, may I have your attention please?" she asked once in Spanish and once in English, and in a moment, the room was silent.

"Now as you know," she continued, "we're here today to discuss the feasibility of—"

The door opened and was slammed shut. She looked up, annoyed, to see Santos standing there, immaculate in a pair of white duck pants and a navy blazer.

"Pardon me, Miss Jessup," he murmured rather sarcastically, grinning broadly at her. "Please, continue."

"I will," she said evenly, "as soon as you find yourself a seat, Mr. Mayor."

Santos sauntered to the far end of the table and took his place among the contingent of small hotel owners from Zihuatanejo's La Ropa Beach.

"Now, as I was saying," she went on, trying hard not to look at him, "we're here to discuss the feasibility of a mutually financed ad campaign aimed at the American tourist market. We want to promote the Ixtapa-Zihuatanejo area as one resort."

"Why should we pay to spread lies?" Santos interrupted.

There were shocked murmurs all around the table. Over the hubbub, Pat said icily, "Pardon me, Mayor Ribera?"

"Why should tourists be fooled into believing that the two cities are one? They are not. Your ads would be a fraud." His tone was smug and defiant. It was almost as if he was daring her to answer back.

"Perhaps you don't understand the benefits of advertising," she said stolidly, determined not to let him undermine her position. "We want everyone to be aware of the fact that Ixtapa is only a few miles from the Zihuatanejo airport—it's easy to get to."

"Am I to understand that you want to create the impression that Zihuatanejo is only an airport? It is far more beautiful than Ixtapa, and therefore, is a more desirable resort."

Pat glared down the table at Santos as a hot debate broke out. Mayor Sánchez of Ixtapa was turning red, and the Zihuatanejo hotel owners were busy congratulating their mayor. Santos just kept looking at her, unperturbed by what he had started.

"Señor Ribera, you're misconstruing our intention here. The ad campaign is going to benefit everyone in both communities. The ads are going to reflect the separate characters of the two cities." Why are you being a stubborn, pig-headed idiot! her eyes asked him.

"But why should this vulgar Mexican Las Vegas benefit from Zihuatanejo's beauty? We have nothing to gain by associating with you because we are a paradise in our own right—and have been for centuries."

He would throw in tradition, Pat groaned inwardly. "Señor Ribera," she said aloud, trying to make herself heard over the arguing, "we are not here to make value judgments on the two towns."

"*I* am here, Miss Jessup, for the sole purpose of

protecting the city I govern. Ixtapa's interests are certainly not those of Zihuatanejo."

"No matter what you personally feel about big hotels," she protested, "the fact remains that they are necessary if this area is to survive as a competitive resort."

"The big hotels are for the foreigners, not for the Mexicans," interjected a small jewelry-store owner from the Zihuatanejo *centro*. "They rob us of business. And I must add that they are financed in large part by foreigners who invest in Mexico only to take profits from this country."

"Sí! es verdad." Santos clapped the man on the back. "The Americans and Germans are particularly guilty of this."

Herr Dorfmann did not flinch at this obvious slur. He said nothing, but fixed his pale blue eyes on Santos, sizing him up.

Pat was beside herself, almost unable to keep her outward cool. If Santos had planned to sabotage her meeting, he had succeeded beyond his wildest dreams. If he was only here to mock her, then that made it worse. It seemed likely that Ted would fire her if she lost Herr Dorfmann, but oddly enough, that possibility did not seem as awful as having Santos Ribera as an enemy. "Señor Ribera, if you would—"

"Excuse me, Miss Jessup. My intention is not to be rude. I only wish to point out that this meeting has no value for myself and my fellow Zihuatanejans. I am leaving, and I urge them to do the same." With that, he pushed his chair back and drew himself up, his back straight as he marched proudly from the room. One by one, his contingent of followers left after him.

Pat read nothing but disapproval on the faces of the

Ixtapa hotel owners. They shook their heads in disgust and slowly, they too began to leave. Pat didn't even try to stop them. Santos had just declared war, and she really didn't want to be caught in the crossfire. She sighed and looked over to see how Herr Dorfmann was taking all this, but his chair was empty. Naturally, she should have expected that. She closed her eyes and tried to wish herself far away. What would her father say to her if he were here, she asked herself. *Don't let 'em get to ya, girl.* Yes, that was good advice. But it was awfully hard to act on. Santos had already gotten to her—and now he was doing everything in his power to destroy her.

At seven o'clock that evening, Pat was sitting on the sofa in her suite, gazing out the window at the dark ocean. Ted was due back any time now, and it would be astounding if he didn't call her up to his office for a full report. How could she tell him that Santos had insulted Herr Dorfmann in front of all those people? Ted couldn't seem to stand the sight of Santos anyway. Did he know she'd been seeing the mayor on something other than a professional basis?

God, it was so confusing! As furious as she was with Santos for his awful behavior, part of her was completely prepared to defend him if Ted started in with wild accusations. Boy, you really are hooked, she told herself in disgust. The man doesn't give a damn about your work or your position in the community, and you're treating him like he was your lover or something.

She was startled by a knock on the door, and as she whirled to answer it, her heart pounding, she prayed it wouldn't be Ted. She wasn't ready for that yet.

"Oh, Orlando," she smiled when she opened the door and saw his face beaming at her. "Am I glad it's you. Come on in."

"I am so sorry, Pat. Mr. Beckman, he is back. I thought of making up a story, telling him you have gone fishing. But it is too late in the day for fishing."

Pat had to laugh. "I take it he knows about the meeting. Or should I say, the disaster?"

Orlando nodded solemnly. "He ran into Herr Dorfmann at the airport."

"Oh, no," Pat moaned, dropping into the nearest chair.

"I am not sure what they spoke of." After a minute he said, "Yes, I am sure. I have worked for Mr. Beckman now six years, and I can tell when he is not happy."

Pat said nothing, but rested her head in her hands. Well, the jig was up. At least getting fired would solve one problem. She'd never have to see Santos Ribera again.

"He said to tell you he'd be in his office in half an hour."

"Okay. Thanks, Orlando."

"Also," he went on, "this just came for you." He handed her a telegram. "I debated with myself, tell her first about Mr. Beckman or give her the message. I don't know," he shrugged. "Maybe now you have good news."

"It better be," she smiled. "Tell your boss I'll be in his office at seven-thirty. And thanks, Orlando."

She waited until she heard the latch click behind him before glancing down at the yellow envelope in her hand.

Maybe I won the lottery, she thought glumly. Or

109

maybe some cousin just got married and my mother couldn't wait to tell me.

She ripped open the envelope and read,

Dear Pat,

Your father is at Mass. General recuperating from a mild heart attack. Don't be alarmed; he's all right now. Steve says he may have to give up fishing, but not to worry now. Please call soon.

Love,
Mom

Pat felt the tears well up and start to spill down her cheeks. All thoughts of Mexico, of the meeting, of Ted and of Santos vanished, and in their place was a mental picture of her father's boat, tied to the dock in Gloucester, floating by itself on the dark waves.

"I know what you want to talk about, Ted," she said when she burst into his office. "But I can't now. Look, my dad's just had a heart attack. I don't know how serious it is, but I've got to be there with him. I'll send you a cable from Massachusetts about when I'll be back."

He looked puzzled at first, then slightly annoyed and finally slightly embarrassed. If he had intended to fire her, this obviously was not an opportune time. And although it never occurred to Pat until she was finally on the plane, she—and her father—had bought herself a little time.

"Well, I'm . . . naturally, I'm sorry to hear this, Pat," he muttered. "How long do you think you'll be gone?"

She gave a sigh of exasperation. "I really have no idea. I'll let you know. I've got to go pack, Ted."

Without waiting for an answer, she turned and fled, mostly because his attitude was driving her back toward self-pity. The one person she couldn't cry in front of was Ted Beckman. She raced back to her room, threw a few things in her suitcase and didn't bother to think. If she caught an evening flight, she'd be at the hospital sometime in the morning. The only thing in her head was the urgency about seeing her father. As soon as she'd looked into his eyes, she'd know how serious it really was.

The night was pleasantly cool, and Pat took several deep breaths as she hurried out the front entrance of the Paradiso. A line of taxis, bringing diners who weren't staying at the hotel, was inching its way past the door. The Paradiso was the most active place in Ixtapa at night, thanks to its elegant restaurants and exclusive nightclub performances.

As soon as the first cab had emptied out, Pat jumped in and slammed the door. *"Buenas noches,"* she said. *"Por favor, al aeropuerto."* But suddenly, she realized she had somewhere else to go first. *"No. Al centro. Quiero ir a iglesia de Santa Bárbara."*

She wasn't exactly sure why she wanted to visit the church, but it had something to do with that Fisherman's Chapel back in Gloucester where her father had taken her when she was little. It was a connection to home, and she felt that it would soothe her and prepare her for the journey.

She let the cab go and tried the side door of the lovely stucco chapel. The flickering altar candles were dim, but gave her enough light to see by. She eased herself into a rear pew and set her bag down beside her.

She wanted to cry, but found she could not. All she could do was clench her fists and curse herself for not being at home when it had happened. She loved her father so much—why had she gone so far from him? Of course, he had never said anything against it, and had written her a wonderful congratulatory letter when she informed him that she had the job. But now she felt guilty, and she didn't like the sensation.

"I better go home," she muttered under her breath. Slowly, she walked from the chapel, shutting the door and starting down the dark street toward the *centro*, where she knew she could find another taxi. Signs of life began springing up about a block away from the church. It was eight-thirty or so, still too early for Mexican dinner, but the shops of Zihuatanejo were crowded and strains of music filled the air.

She walked for about three blocks in a kind of trance, as mental images of her father crowded out all the guilt. After all, Dennis Jessup was the one who had taught her that the heart was just as important as the head when you made your decisions; as long as one didn't overbalance the other, and you kept them on an even keel, "one port and one starboard," as he would say, then you were all right. Pat smiled as she remembered her father, back from a long day of fishing when the catch had been mediocre. "Well," he'd always say, "those fish are just like stubborn women. When they don't want to, they don't!"

Her father had passed on to her his wonderful sense of humor, his deep concern for others. Her father had given her the freedom to live her own life. Yes, she thought, I wouldn't be in Mexico now if it weren't for

Dennis Jessup. The real question, though, was if she wanted to remain.

Her dream of the perfect job and the perfect man— both of which she was going to find in Ixtapa—had fizzled. She'd been completely incapable of controlling the conference and utterly unable to fathom the man. Maybe when she was back in Massachusetts, the whole thing would take on a new perspective. At least she hoped it would.

She reached the main street of Zihuatanejo and turned the corner toward the *mercado,* where she saw a line of taxis. As she crossed the wide avenue, she happened to look into the window of a small café. Several men were laughing and drinking beer at the front table.

"Oh no!" When she saw Santos's laughing face, all her good intentions fled. He was the last person in the world she wanted to see right now. But it was too late, because he had already spotted her.

Clutching her bag to her side, she half walked, half ran across to the first taxi. Santos caught up to her easily and wrenched the suitcase from her.

"I have to talk to you," he said earnestly. "Please, Pat."

"I don't have time now—I'm afraid it'll have to wait."

"It can't wait!" Taking her by the other hand, he yanked her down the street toward his car.

"Santos, I've had enough of your high-handed manners for one day. I frankly don't give a damn what you want me to do anymore."

He dropped her bag and turned her around to face him, his black eyes piercing her very soul. "What has happened to you?" he breathed.

"I have to go home. My father's ill—I just got a telegram. I'm on my way to the airport." Saying the words aloud pressed the button inside her, and she started to cry. At first the tears fell softly, but in a moment she was sobbing and couldn't stop. Santos held her quietly, letting all the emotion pour out. People passing on the street looked at them curiously, but they were oblivious to everything around them.

When Pat was still at last, he reached up and gently wiped her wet face, stroking each tear away with his work-hardened fingers. "There are no flights out of Zihuatanejo to Mexico City at this hour," he said quietly. "You will have to wait till morning, Pat. But I'll see to it that you are there in plenty of time." He opened the door of his Rabbit and put her bag in the back seat before ushering her around to the passenger side.

"Why don't you just drive me back to the Paradiso?" she asked, cursing herself again for being so stupid. In a small town like this one, you didn't just rush off to the airport at all hours and expect your plane to be waiting. "I'll get a cab as soon as I wake up."

"No," he said. "I feel you shouldn't be alone tonight." He put his key in the ignition as though this were an established fact.

"Then where are we going?" she sniffed.

"To my home."

She was too exhausted to protest. Her fury at Santos hadn't diminished one bit since this morning, and yet she was grateful for his solicitousness. He's not horrible all of the time, I guess, she thought as he put the car in gear and screeched out of his parking space.

"Do you have to drive like that?" she pleaded, wondering if she should call her mother or the hospital or somebody.

"Tonight, I do," Santos answered firmly.

They drove in silence toward La Ropa Beach, and in a few minutes, he jerked the car to a halt and got out. The road was deserted, and Pat strained in the darkness to see the outline of a house somewhere.

"Up here," he gestured, pointing to a path by the side of the road covered with flowering trees. Their lush perfume spread out into the cool night. Behind Santos, Pat scrambled up the short flight of stone steps leading to a neat, one-story stucco dwelling. It was very much like his mother's house, only smaller.

He threw open the door and Pat heard an odd sound, like a baby's cry or a dog's bark, she couldn't decide which it was. As Santos flipped on the lamp on the large desk near the entrance, Pat was startled by the sight of a large, muscular calico cat with a white face and paws. He gave another wail and jumped down to rub himself forcefully against his master's legs.

"El Presidente," Santos said by way of introduction. "When I brought him here, his name was Pussywillow —he was an old alley cat I met at Harvard. But when he arrived in Mexico, he was so brave and chased away so many dogs on the beach, I renamed him El Presidente. Here, you can sleep in my room." He threw open the bedroom door and brought her suitcase inside. The room was small but cozy, with a large bed close to the door and an overhead ceiling fan. There was a variety of gaily-colored rugs hanging on the walls and a big window that looked out over the beach. The sound of the waves was so loud, Pat could almost believe they were right on top of the water, although the house was several yards above the beach.

"And if I take your room, where will you sleep?" Pat asked sarcastically.

"In the living room," Santos growled, walking past

her and nearly tripping over the huge cat, who followed him everywhere. "Are you hungry?" he called from the other room.

"No, just tired." Pat wandered around the bedroom, wondering why on earth she had let Santos drag her off to his house. How stupid of her not to have called for flight times! Now she was stuck with both her worry for her father and her anger with the man in the next room. Santos would pick this occasion to be nice, gentle and utterly devastating with his concern and his hospitality and his damn, unavoidable, sexy presence! She gritted her teeth, asking herself why she was so upset that he had decided to sleep in the other room.

"Are you coming out, or have you decided my company is unsuitable?" he called.

Pat sighed, looked around the comfortable room again and walked out into the living room. Santos was fixing something in the kitchen, a raised area on one side of the big room. A long serving bar connected the two sections. He produced a large carafe of white wine and a bowl of *guacamole* from the refrigerator.

"Please sit down. I won't bite," he said very seriously.

She skirted the large desk, strewn with papers, and wandered over to the long couch, covered in sturdy white cotton duck. The room was very simple, but the wonderful Mexican masks and bright fabric throws gave it an elegance all its own.

"Santos," she said as he sat on the couch a good distance from her and placed the food on the coffee table. "I don't really think I want to be here. I'm very angry at you, and I've got a lot on my mind."

"You're angry because of the conference." He shook his head ruefully. "Yes, I will admit I was hard on you.

That German investor will think twice before he helps your Mr. Beckman again."

"He is not *my* Mr. Beckman, and I'm glad you at least admit how badly you screwed things up."

Santos pressed a glass of wine into her hand. "I did what I had to do, Pat. Now, to you, it seemed that I alienated everybody, am I correct?"

"You are most assuredly correct."

"No. I did not. You don't know the Mexican temperament, Pat. Every Mexican loves to argue, and he loves a good loud fight. So, those Ixtapa hotel owners will not hold a grudge. It is our way. Besides, I totally disagreed with your ideas—and your employer's—for changing my city. I had to fight you."

Pat got up and walked away from him. He was so infuriating! "I suppose you and I don't have a lot in common," she shrugged. "And now, if you don't mind, I'd like to call the hospital and let them know I'm coming tomorrow."

Suddenly, she felt his hands on her shoulders. "I am truly sorry about your father, Pat. Come, the phone is in the bedroom."

Together they walked slowly into the other room, and Pat waited while Santos dialed directory assistance. After interminable delays, they got Massachusetts General, but it was impossible to get hold of anyone but a floor nurse in cardiology. Pat left a message for her mother and hung up with a sigh.

"You must try to sleep now," Santos said, taking her hand. They were sitting close to each other on the bed, their legs touching. Pat was feeling so many things, she was almost unaware of the new sensation starting deep within her when Santos turned to kiss her. It was a light kiss, so brief it might not have been there at all.

"We have a lot in common," Santos said as he got up to leave. "But sometimes those who are closest do not get along. The stakes are too great."

"Maybe," she began, but then he pulled her up beside him and enveloped her in a fierce embrace. His mouth was hungry and demanding, and she found herself giving as she never had before. She threw her arms around his neck to press him closer, but he was already there, his strong, hard body entwined with her small, delicate one. That kiss expressed what words could not, and when it ended, they stared at each other, awed.

He placed a fingertip on her lips and smiled. "I'm not sure I'll sleep tonight—but you must." He turned and went to the door, but before closing it behind him, he gave her a look so caring, so intense, that it shot through her heart like an arrow. Then he was gone, and she was staring at the spot where he had been.

Weakly, Pat eased herself back onto the bed. Her mind and body in total turmoil, she undressed and crawled under the covers. Santos was in that bed with her, although he was not in the room. He had invaded the most private place inside her and awakened a new set of emotions. Pat closed her eyes, trying to blot out the sight and touch and smell of him, but it was impossible. When the dawn broke, his presence was still as close as it had been the previous night, and she knew that she had fallen totally and irrevocably in love.

Chapter Eight

*H*e took her to the airport early, and there was an unspoken agreement between them. When Pat returned, she knew, they would either have to resolve their differences or their budding relationship would be crushed.

But in the meantime, there was her family to consider. During the long trip home, Pat asked herself what she would do if her father was seriously ill. She couldn't leave him again without being certain that everything was okay. Stop jumping the gun, she told herself as the pilot announced that they would be landing in Boston in a few minutes. Just take it easy, one thing at a time.

She gazed out her window at the wet runway and sighed. After eleven hours of travel and three planes, she only wanted a hot bath and a warm bed. She wasn't used to cold weather, and the pilot had informed them that it was twenty-six degrees outside. But a spark of excitement was growing in her now about seeing her parents again. Worried sick though she was about her father's illness and her mother's reaction, she still felt happy that she was on her way to see them. Shrugging off the chilliness, she claimed her baggage, got her passport stamped, and stepped out into the cold to hail a cab.

They whooshed along the wet roads, heading out of the airport toward the Callahan Tunnel and Massachusetts General Hospital. Pat kept blinking at the passing landscape—it looked so foreign to her after less than two months away. No palm trees, no flowers; only clumps of hardened, dirty snow and power lines strung over bare maples and oaks. After the beauty of Zihuatanejo, this was an additional shock.

She kept trying to picture her father's mischievous face and the way it must look now. She remembered all kinds of stories about how a heart attack could change everything. People's hair could turn white overnight; they could age twenty years; they could become old and feeble in the course of just a week.

No, she told herself fiercely, that won't happen to him. My father's different. He'll be out on that boat of his within the year. But as she paid the driver and walked up the circular drive to the main entrance of the hospital, she wondered if she was being unrealistic.

Please let him be all right, she prayed silently. He has to be.

The elevator door opened, and Pat stepped onto the antiseptic-smelling floor of the cardiology wing. Again, she imagined her father's face, and it gave her the courage to keep walking.

"Pat . . . Pat!"

A familiar voice drew Pat out of her stupor.

"Pat! Are you okay?"

Steve Elman, dressed in his white doctor's coat, with

a stethoscope hanging around his neck, came bounding down the corridor toward her.

Pat stopped where she was. Oh, God, she thought. Just what I need now. I should have known he'd be the first person I ran into.

"Pat!" He grabbed one arm, causing her shoulder bag to slip down and fall to the floor. They both dove for it at once. "My God, you look awful!" he said, retrieving it by its strap.

"I've just spent eleven hours on airplanes getting here. My father's just had a heart attack. How am I supposed to look, Steve?" Pat asked wearily.

"Sorry," he laughed nervously. "You're right, absolutely right. Well, it's nice to see you. How are you? You've got a great tan, I'll say that for you."

Pat stared at him incredulously. Could she ever have thought herself in love with this shallow, awkward person? It was impossible not to compare him with Santos. But she had changed a great deal in six weeks and that counted for a lot, as well. "I'd like to see my father. How is he?" she asked impatiently.

"Coming along nicely. It was a pretty mild cardiac, but he's going to have to settle down from now on," Steve responded, turning on his professional, concerned tone. Pat knew that he really did care, and it was therefore even more upsetting that he sounded so cheery, as if he had just put on his bedside manner because company was coming.

"He's had his warning," he went on, "and now he has to listen to it."

"He's got to go back to work," Pat said adamantly. "If he can't fish, that'll be the thing that kills him. He's not made to sit around and stare at the wall."

Steve shook his head. "Frankly, Pat, I don't think it was his work that caused the attack."

"Well, that's a relief. But what was it?"

"I think he was distraught over your moving to Mexico. It upset him, although he didn't want to let on, and that put a strain on him. His heart couldn't take it."

Pat glared at her former fiancé in fury. "And I suppose he'd be in the pink today if I'd moved to Denver with you! Is that what you're saying, Steve? Oh, what the hell do you know, anyway?" She rushed past him, starting toward the door of her father's room.

"No, Pat, you don't understand—"

She whirled on him. "Steve, it's *you* who doesn't understand, me or my father. I think I'd like to ask him for himself how he feels about my move. Now, if you'll excuse me—" She pushed open the door, turning her back on him abruptly.

"Did you come all the way from Mexico just to disturb all the poor, ailing souls in this hospital, girl?" Dennis Jessup asked in his lilting Nova Scotia brogue. "I could hear you all the way down the hall."

Pat went to him at once, dropping her bag on a chair. He was sitting up with his arms folded on his chest; a long IV tube ran from one arm to a tall pole by his bedside. His face was paler and more drawn than Pat had ever seen it, but other than that, he seemed okay. She grinned broadly and went to embrace him, being careful not to joggle the pole. When she leaned back and sat down on the white sheet, she noticed a brightly colored plastic puzzle cube lying in his lap.

"Dad, how do you feel?" she asked gently.

"Miserable!" he proclaimed emphatically.

"Are you in pain? Where is it?"

"In my lap."

"What!"

"Yes, girl. This toy is making me batty. My room-mate's grandson left it here yesterday, and I've been trying to figure the damn thing out ever since. Do you know that there are eight-year-old children who can get all these colors sorted out in less than thirty seconds? The devil's children, if you ask me!"

Pat chuckled at her father's tirade and leaned over to give him a peck on the cheek. He hasn't changed a bit, and thank God for that, she thought, enormously relieved. "You're terrific, you know," she smiled. "And it's great to see you."

"And you too, girl. Your mother said she got a message you were coming. She's down in the cafeteria now, getting some coffee. They won't let me have any, so she doesn't like to drink it in front of me," he confided, fiddling with his puzzle once again. "Damn thing! Well, I tell you, it must take a different kind of skill from going out in a boat and bringing in a good day's catch. Now that takes real talent!"

"Right . . . . Have the doctors talked to you about going back to work?"

"Oh Lord, yes!" He roared with laughter, and that started him coughing. Pat hastily poured him a cup of water from his bedside carafe and pressed it into his hands.

"Please take it easy, Dad. It'll take time, but you'll adjust."

"Adjust, my foot! I'm shocked to hear you say that, Patricia. I'm going back to work and no doubt about it. You know, these doctors—your friend Steve and the others—they don't know what fishin' is all about, no, indeed. And Steve's the worst of 'em. He's a bit of a chucklehead, if you ask me."

"Why do you say that?" she asked, stifling a grin.

"Oh, he comes in here every day with his big, sad face, whispering real low like he was at my wake, for God's sake. He's the kind of doctor who can talk you into your grave, you know what I mean? You were smart to give him the boot, Patricia."

She took her father's hand and gave it a squeeze, wondering what he'd think of Santos. Two down-to-earth men who say what's on their minds. I guess they'd like one another—in between arguments.

"Listen, I'm on your side, remember that," she said, "but you have to think about the consequences. What if you had another heart attack out at sea? You wouldn't be able to get help fast enough."

"Patricia, let me tell you something," he smiled. "The heart is a very clever organ. It's kind of like a bartender, if you'll forgive the comparison. Besides keepin' the liquids flowing, it gives free advice. Now, my heart tells me that I've got to go back to sea. If I don't, well, I'll just waste away playin' with this plastic cube here for the rest of my days. I'm no fool, Patricia, I know I won't be able to do as much as I used to, but I've got to do something. See, I trust my heart a lot more than I trust these doctors. And I don't want to hear any talking back." He pointed a finger at her when she seemed about to protest. "You followed your heart's advice when you went down to Mexico. Did your heart give you a bum steer?"

"Well . . ." She considered for a moment. "I don't know. I guess not, on the whole." Of course, it was this quality that she and her father shared in common that made her choose a life different from any she had ever imagined and fall in love with a difficult, wonderful man who occasionally infuriated her and brought her to the boiling point. But she wasn't about to go into that right now.

"Take my word for it," Dennis Jessup nodded, setting the cube on his night table with an annoyed grunt. "Listen to your heart and you'll never go wrong. I've done it now for fifty-nine years, and I'm not about to stop. I'd be disappointed in you, Patricia, if you didn't do the same."

She looked into her father's strong face and knew at once that he was right. Whatever it might cost her, she would have to listen to her heart.

"Now, daughter of mine, I think I need a bit more rest. I seem to get tired very quickly these days. You go search out your mother and have a cup of coffee for me."

She smiled and got up, reaching behind him to fluff up his pillows. As she started out of the room, she heard him ask, "You'll be around for a while, won't you?"

"Yes, of course," she answered, hesitant to say for just how long.

"Good, good." He slipped down under the covers, the news relaxing him immediately. "Give me an hour or so, then come back here with your mother."

"I will, Dad. It's so good to talk to you." Impulsively, she rushed back to the bed and kissed him once again.

Suddenly his arms tightened around her in a bear hug, and she could tell he'd only lost a little bit of his strength.

"Thanks for comin', Pat," he whispered tenderly.

"Go to sleep, you old salt," she said, holding back the tears that threatened to start up again. She loved this man so much, and she understood now that he was alive because he wanted to be, because of his will to survive. He had listened to his heart.

"I'll see you later," she said as she walked over to the door.

"So long, Pat." He winked just as she left the room.

Late that night, after visiting hours were over, Pat and her mother drove home to Gloucester. It seemed odd to sleep in her narrow single bed again, to see all the knickknacks and posters her mother had never thrown away. They didn't talk much that evening, since they were both exhausted, but Pat was painfully aware that her mother kept staring at her as if she were a stranger.

Well, it was true; she was different. Mexico had changed her, and Santos had also. Before she drifted off to sleep that night, she imagined him there with her, lying beside her and holding her tenderly. His hands were everywhere, caressing and stroking, and his kisses were alternately gentle and passionate. But what about the difficult side of him, the side that refused to acknowledge her as a competent woman, the pigheaded, arrogant side she hated? Well, she would simply have to resolve that when she got back home.

Home? But wasn't Gloucester home to her? She realized that even her perception of the word had changed. Now it encompassed a great deal more than the past and her parents. She fell asleep enormously confused, wondering how she would ever sort it all out.

The next morning, Pat sat at the breakfast table nursing her third cup of coffee, gazing out at the docks. Most of the fishing boats were out now, but the empty docks and the gulls flying low over the water made her think of Zihuatanejo. She was homesick! The view from her parents' kitchen was so similar to the one from Santos's office—she'd never noticed that before. Could that have been part of what made her fall in love with the place so quickly?

The screen door banged, and Mrs. Jessup came in, loaded with bags from the supermarket.

"Hey, you should have yelled," Pat said, taking the bags from her mother. "I would have carried those in."

Anya Jessup did not look well. She was taking her husband's illness very hard, and Pat was worried that her mother might come down with something. It seemed strange to Pat that she had always considered her blond, handsome mother as a very independent person. Now, overnight, she had turned worrisome and nervous, constantly harping on her fears for the future. There were tiny lines around her eyes and mouth that Pat had never seen before.

"That's all right." Mrs. Jessup was already unloading the various bags. "I didn't want to waste time. We should be getting to the hospital. This whole thing has just changed my whole routine, you know," she laughed nervously.

"I understand, Mom," Pat nodded. "You get used to one way of doing things, and then it's hard to change."

"Yes . . . the change will be hard on all of us." Her mother sighed forlornly.

Pat exhaled in exasperation. If only her mother would snap out of it! If she kept up this fretting when her father came back from the hospital, there would be nothing but friction between them. Maybe she should stay in Gloucester a while and ease the transition for them.

But it's their problem, she thought, watching her mother stack cans of vegetables in the cabinet. I can't solve it for them.

"Steve Elman has been really wonderful," Mrs. Jessup said as she started on the last bag. "He's a fine boy, a really excellent doctor."

"Um," Pat muttered absently.

"I was just thinking," her mother said, taking a seat at the kitchen table. "Pat, are you really going back to Mexico?"

"Yes, Mom, I told you—"

"But, do you honestly intend to spend the rest of your life there?"

Pat shrugged, feeling the pressure mounting in the room. "It's a little premature to say. I've only been down there a couple of months. But I have to give the job a chance. I've scarcely started getting things moving there."

"But . . ." Her mother fluttered her hands in the air as though she were searching for a concrete answer. "I simply thought, in the light of what's happened to your father, well, I assumed you'd want to give some thought to settling down, finding a man—"

Pat looked at her curiously. "And you think all the good men are around here, is that it?"

"Well, certainly one of them is! Pat, I worry about you. The thought of you being down in that godforsaken place is so terrifying to me. It's so far away from reality! Now, I don't think you realize what a sensitive and concerned person Steve is, and how much he still cares about you. He called at least once a week after you left, and he's been so good to your father in the hospital. Maybe if you gave it another chance . . ." She let the possibility hang in the air.

"Come on, Mom. It's finished. I just don't feel anything for him."

"Feel? Oh, I suppose you have some romantic notion that all love is deep passion every minute of the day!"

"Maybe every other minute," Pat joked, but her mother didn't even smile. "Mom, now he's using you to get me back. I don't like that one bit."

"It's just that he has no other way. Pat, he's a doctor, a wonderful man. And he's going to inherit a practice in Denver."

"We have to get to the hospital, Mom. Please, I don't want to discuss this!"

Her mother's eyes narrowed suspiciously. "Have you met someone down there? Is that it? Is it your boss, this Ted person?"

"No. Well, I have met an interesting man there, but that's not the reason I'm going back. And it certainly has nothing to do with my lack of interest in Steve Elman."

Her mother eased herself out of her chair and started for the door. "I don't understand you, Pat. You're so different from the girl we brought up. Particularly since you've been in Mexico—why, you even look different."

Pat smiled as she followed her mother out to the car. "I guess that's pretty accurate. I *feel* different about myself. Listen, Mom, yesterday Dad told me to listen to my heart. He's absolutely right. And my heart tells me that Mexico is where I belong right now. It doesn't mean I'm abandoning you two—you understand that?"

Her mother didn't answer, but climbed into the passenger seat, allowing Pat to drive. The two women were silent all the way to the hospital, and Pat couldn't help but feel sad. Growing up wasn't always the easiest thing to do.

Her father was discharged from the hospital exactly one week later, and he looked like a caged bird about to be set free. Anya Jessup led the procession to the car, carrying sheaves of menus, medical instructions and prescriptions. There was no denying that Dennis Jessup was going to have to make some concessions to his illness.

129

The attendant took him down to the elevator in a wheelchair while Pat finished packing up the few possessions he'd brought with him. She was on her way out the door with his suitcase and the flowers his friends had sent when the door swung open. Steve Elman stood before her with a rather sheepish expression on his face. His pipe was clamped firmly between his teeth.

"Pat! I'm so glad I caught you."

"We're just on our way home," she said hastily. "Thanks for everything, Steve. I really appreciate what you did for my father."

"All in a day's work," he shrugged, fixing his open stare on her. "I thought maybe tonight after I've gone off duty—I'm not sure what time that'll be—we might have dinner and talk."

Pat sighed. "I'm afraid not."

"But your parents will want some time to themselves, and you probably haven't had a good square American meal in months. I'd love to see you, Pat."

His expression was so earnest and enthusiastic, like a puppy trying his hardest to please.

"It's very nice of you," she said, wanting to be polite and casual, "but I only have so much time to spend with my folks. I'm going back next week."

"So soon!" He looked dismayed. "I'd hoped that you, that we—oh, Pat, listen, I'm still offering. The residency's over July first, and I'm due in Colorado on the fifteenth. You could meet me here, we could get married, then pack up the car and drive out west. How's that sound?"

"It sounds," she said thoughtfully, "like something you want to do, not like something I want to do. I'm very sure now, Steve. The answer is no."

Without waiting for his shocked response, she walked past him out the door and down to the elevator, which was just filling up with a crowd of visitors. Thankfully, she ducked into the car and when the door shut, it closed off a part of her life she was glad to let go of.

The next morning, she drove over to the Gloucester Western Union office. First she sent Ted a cable informing him that she would be back in five days, on the following Thursday. Then she sent one to Santos. It read:

"All's well. Coming home."

Chapter Nine

The plane landed at the Zihuatanejo airport at about five PM. She hadn't mentioned her time of arrival to either Ted or Santos, and she debated for a minute as to where to go first. It felt good to be back, and yet she had so many questions. What sort of mood would Santos be in? And Ted? Did she still have her job, or was she just returning to collect her things?

One of the eager minibus drivers grabbed her bag from her hand and asked her destination. She hesitated, then told him to take her to the Paradiso. She wanted to see the man she loved more than anything, but duty raised its compulsive head and informed her sternly that she had to deal with her job first. The repercussions of that disastrous meeting two weeks earlier were probably still being felt all over Ixtapa.

Nervous as she was, there was a kind of joy in the realization that at last she was really doing what she wanted. Even thinking about her mother's suggestion that she return to Gloucester, or about Steve's proposal, made her shake her head ruefully. Mexico was where she belonged, and somehow, she intended to stay.

"You know, Bobby, Mama would just love it down here."

Pat turned slightly to the woman seated beside her in the cream-colored minibus. She was a middle-aged redhead with a thick Texas drawl.

"Now, how do ya know that, Ella honey?" her burly husband guffawed. "We've only been here two minutes."

The couple laughed together and started to discuss the various retirement homes in the Southwest, where their parents lived. Suddenly, Pat thought of her father, and a pang of remorse shot through her. Dennis Jessup was too young to retire. But what if he didn't recover as quickly as he'd promised her he would last night? She bit her lip, staring out at the passing view along the highway. Something good was bound to happen to her father—and to her—it was only a matter of time. As for her mother, well, Pat just hoped she could adjust, and that her depression would lessen eventually. But it was hard to be awfully positive about Anya. She was far less able to cope with crisis than Pat's father. As Pat gazed at the stucco shacks that dotted the landscape, she was able to make out a variety of tired-looking women washing clothes in a tub or pounding cornmeal for tortillas. They all reminded her of her mother.

She was still immersed in thought when the minibus rolled up to the front entrance of the Paradiso. The Texans were gone, and she hadn't even been aware of it when they got out. Grabbing her bag and taking a deep breath, she marched inside and greeted the various doormen and desk clerks who said hello to her. But her cheery nods were a cover for her real feelings. She just wanted to run to Santos and let him wrap his arms around her, to soothe away all the anxiety and pain.

No, you've come to beard the lion in his den, and you can't back down now, she told herself, handing her bag to one of the bellboys and instructing him to take it to her room. She pressed the button for the elevator and seconds later, she was ascending in the glass cage, passing over the beautiful view on her way up to Ted's office. The sun was just beginning its descent, and the sky was filled with a soft, rosy glow.

The door opened on the top floor, and she tried not to think as she walked down the corridor to Ted's office. His door was open, and he was buried in his enormous ledger books, a frown creasing his brow.

"Hello," she said quietly at the door.

His head jerked up. "Pat! Oh say, I forgot you were coming back today. Well, thank God you're here. The place is a shambles. Come on in." He waved her to a chair, where she sat, somewhat puzzled by his attitude. And he hadn't yet asked about her father.

"Listen," he went on, swinging around in his chair and leaning toward her. "Two weeks can be a hell of a long time in the hotel business when you're short a valuable hand. I hope you're willing and able to work double time for a few days."

"Ah, certainly," she murmured. Then she still had her job! Well, that was one thing to be thankful for.

"Okay, now. I have just one request. You kind of bollixed things up for me with Hans Dorfmann at that meeting, but I have a feeling the dust is going to settle, and then we can make another foray. He did go back to Munich, but I called and explained everything. Believe it or not, he hasn't given up on me yet. Must be my charm and business know-how, huh?" he chuckled.

"And I've talked to the other Ixtapa hotel owners, too. They were very impressed with you despite what that idiot who happened to get himself elected mayor did to mess things up. They want to go ahead with the ad campaign without any input from Zihuatanejo, and that's fine with me—better, in fact. You can get on that right away. Oh say, how's your father? Sorry, I've had so much on my mind I clean forgot."

Pat cleared her throat, feeling her stomach muscles tighten. The man was a machine! He had nothing at all on his mind but business. "About as well as can be expected," she answered shortly.

"Well, glad to hear it. I know it's tough to see your parents get sick. When Ruth started going blind, it just about killed me. But there's nothing you can do about it, right? It's really in the doctors' hands."

"That all depends," she said, getting up to go to the window. "Every once in a while you *can* do something about it."

"Hey, now don't get yourself into a state," he said, coming over to her. "I need you in one piece right now. When you talk like that, you sound just like my ex-wife, Arlene, wanting to take care of the whole world. It's my firm belief that the best thing you can do is carry on as usual when things like this happen."

Pat stared at him in disbelief. She wanted to tell him what he could do with his glib, facile advice, but she realized it wasn't worth the effort. He was obviously incapable of understanding how she felt.

"Take my advice, Pat," he went on. "Get back to your work. Throw yourself into it totally, and you'll forget all your troubles. And speaking of work, I've got enough here to choke a horse. You get some rest tonight and start on that campaign tomorrow morning. And listen," he said as she walked to the door, a grim expression on her face, "stop worrying! It'll be all right, believe me."

She didn't turn to face him. She only wanted to get out of his office.

"Pat, would you do me a favor?" he added.

"Yes?"

"Stay away from Ribera. He's a real troublemaker. Ruth tells me he's, ah, personally interested in you, and I just want to warn you. He's a snake, not to be trusted."

Pat stood there with her back to him, breathing hard.

"You run along now—maybe Ruth and I will catch you at dinner."

"Maybe," she muttered as she hurried down the corridor to the elevator. But she knew perfectly well that she would not be in Ixtapa at dinnertime.

Santos told her on the phone to meet him at a small hotel restaurant on La Ropa Beach called the Pelicanos and she left for it as soon as she had showered and changed. She had decided on a red crepe dress with a splash of yellow flowers across its full skirt and tiny spaghetti straps holding it up. The dress made her feel cheerier than she actually was. As she drove through the darkening streets of Zihuatanejo in one of the Paradiso's staff cars, Pat felt a twinge of excitement that had nothing to do with the dress. She was going to meet the man she loved. Of course, she had no idea whether the feeling was reciprocated, but that did not matter to her right now. The only important thing was to satisfy this urgency churning within her, to talk things over with somebody kind and sympathetic. Afterward, she could get it all sorted out.

The Pelicanos was tucked away on a rutted dirt road, and she was forced to slow the car to a crawl as she maneuvered over the last pothole into the hotel's courtyard parking lot. A few well-placed floodlights illuminated the small two-story dwellings that surrounded a blue-tiled pool. The pool was split into two long sections that wound their way through an avenue of flowering bushes and tall palms. The foliage was so dense here, it almost camouflaged the stucco living units placed at irregular angles around the courtyard.

Pat smiled as she looked around and started to follow the sparkle of the pool toward the main hotel area. This was it! Just like her dream. The perfect honeymoon hideaway she had always imagined. A couple, chattering loudly in Italian, was just leaving their room, and Pat followed them to what she assumed was the restaurant. There at the end of the path, the pool opened up into a rough oval, and beside it was the dining area, a sunken pit covered by a tremendous *palapa,* a thatched umbrella made out of palm branches. At the near edge of the pit was a sleek fruitwood bar shaped like the hull of a ship, ending in a prow with a figurehead pointed proudly up at the sky. The sounds of a Mozart violin concerto stole softly through the air, mingling with the crash of waves from the beach, which was only twenty or thirty yards from the restaurant.

"Good evening." A lithe, dark man, casually dressed in a T-shirt and khaki pants, approached her. "You are, I believe, waiting for Señor Ribera?"

Pat smiled at him and nodded, puzzled by the man's German accent. She had seen him at the meeting, but hadn't heard him speak. He appeared to own this place, and he knew that Santos was expecting her. And *she* knew how Santos felt about foreigners.

"Please, be seated. He has just gone into the office to make a phone call. May I bring you a drink?"

Pat ordered a tequila sunrise and the owner vanished

to fill her order. She sat by the low wall of the dining area and gazed out at La Ropa. Now, this was beautiful —this was paradise.

"Have you yet realized that this is the real Paradiso?" Santos's voice startled her. Before she could respond, he bent and kissed the soft skin below her ear. A tingling sensation started where he had touched her and traveled like lightning over her entire body.

"Good evening," he said, going around to sit opposite her. "I hope I haven't kept you waiting. Did my friend Kurt take care of you?"

"I just arrived," she told him. "Is he the owner?"

"He is. And I know exactly what you are going to say. Why is he my friend if he is not a Mexican and he owns a hotel in Zihuatanejo? But before I answer, you must tell me, how is your father?"

A wave of relief coursed through her. She knew she could talk to this man, and that he would understand. But at the moment, she was still drained from her encounter with Ted.

"He's okay; I'll tell you all about it in a minute. Give me a chance to just sit here a second, would you? I feel like I've been flying around nonstop since I landed."

"Of course," he nodded, as a young waitress approached them with Pat's drink and a beer for Santos. "Whenever you're ready." Then he lifted his glass to Pat and said softly, "To happy endings."

"To happy endings," Pat repeated, taking a sip. "Now tell me what you meant. Why is your friend Kurt so different from, well, from Herr Dorfmann, for example?"

Santos's white teeth gleamed in the semidarkness as he smiled and leaned forward, evidently eager to explain. "My friend Kurt," he began, "is a protector of beauty. He understands the Mexican ways, and he has worked hard to get what he wants. About fourteen years ago, he discovered Zihuatanejo on a vacation from his job with an architectural firm in Baden. He fell in love with the place, naturally, and decided he would move here."

"In fourteen years," Pat pointed out, "anyone would learn the Mexican ways."

"But he has only been here four years! He found it impossible to purchase property, nor would FONATUR subsidize a foreigner. Eventually he got around it."

"How?"

"He found a partner who happens to be a Mexican, and he fell in love with her. But he didn't realize it at first. Only after they'd worked together for two years did they discover that they'd been in love all the time."

"What!" Pat looked at him in surprise.

"Yes, this is so. I know you feel that people must be hit by a lightning bolt all at once for it to be real and this is how I feel also." Pat looked into his dark eyes, hooded by their heavy lids. He had never confided his deeper feelings to her before, and she was proud and flattered that he would do so now. *My father would like him after all*, she decided suddenly.

"There is a law on the books which states that any business must be fifty-one percent owned by a Mexican national. Kurt could only control forty-nine percent but he trusted his Mexican partner implicitly; you see she already owned a hotel in the Yucatan so he figured she had the experience he lacked and he had the love for Zihuatanejo. She often travels to her other hotel and gives Kurt free rein here. And he does a fine job. His clientele comes from France, from Italy, from

South America, from Germany, of course. There's Margarita at his table." He pointed over to the owners' reserved table, and sure enough, there was a tall, elegantly dressed brunette smiling up at her husband.

"Well, good for him," Pat murmured. "Is there any other hotel that gets four stars from you around here?"

Santos thought for a moment. "None. The beachfront resorts in Zihuatanejo are pleasant, but none have the panache of the Pelicanos. The Ixtapa hotels, well, let's not go into my opinion about those."

"No," Pat laughed. "Let's not."

"I tell you, though, there is one location with enormous potential. It lies dormant because no one has been intelligent enough to complete the project. Come on, I'll show you." With a nod over his shoulder to the owner, he got up and drew back Pat's chair. He led her through the tables of diners to the stone steps leading onto the beach. The sound of the waves was closer now, and when Santos took her by the hand and helped her over the barrier, her heart began beating rapidly. The sound matched that of the water hitting the rocks.

They kicked off their shoes and started to walk, following the receding line of the surf. Everything was dark now, and most of the La Ropa restaurants were serving dinner. There was no one else around.

"Look, can you see out there?" Santos stretched his arm, and she followed the direction with her eyes. "Do you see the flags flapping in the wind?"

"Way out? Halfway toward Las Gatas?"

"That's it."

There was a huge unfinished structure terraced into the rock. Floodlights hit it at various angles, giving it an eerie, awesome majesty. It looked like a castle in progress.

"That's the Royale. There have been three builders

140

up to this point, but no one has touched the work in a year."

"Why not?" She peered into the darkness.

"The three were foreigners, and they went in independently, without the aid of FONATUR. Unlike my friend Kurt, they never thought to marry a Mexican national. So, you can see how difficult it is to build into the rock, and an entire waterfront would have to be constructed so that guests could arrive by water taxi. Consequently, each developer gave up when he ran out of funds. Truly, the Royale could have been a jewel." He shrugged and drew her onward. "Let's walk, Patricia."

For a few moments, they went on in silence, their toes gripping the wet sand. It was odd, but Pat felt as though the weight of the past two weeks with her parents was rolling off her, slowly leaving her more contented than she had ever been. Naturally, she was still concerned about her father, but being with Santos had eased the worry.

"I don't ever remember this kind of quiet at home," Pat murmured after they had been walking for a few minutes. "It kind of soothes you, takes all the stress away, doesn't it?"

"It's true," Santos agreed, walking along beside her. He had not taken her hand, but his presence was so strong, she practically felt his touch. "What I love about Mexico is most clear here. The pretense stripped away from everything, nothing but sea and sand, the mother and father of us all."

She stopped where she was and a pain gripped her, coursing through her. Santos sensed her hesitation.

"Do you want to talk about him now?" he asked softly.

"Yes, I . . . I guess so. I just don't know what to say.

I mean, he's out of the hospital, not in any immediate danger, but I can't stop worrying about him. He may never be able to work again, and that's what eats at him, worse than any physical symptom." She sighed and turned to him. "The doctors think it's too much stress for him to get back on his boat—but he knows that lying around idle would be the worst thing in the world."

"Then evidently, he must do what he has to." Santos put an arm around her waist, and they walked easily together, as he accommodated the size of his steps to hers.

"I only hope he's as okay as he tells everyone. I couldn't bear it if he had another attack and I wasn't there. If he died, I'd . . . I don't know what I'd do. Oh, I know they say heart attacks these days are as common as colds, and a good percentage of patients just bounce right back, but I don't know. Oh God, I feel so—" She hugged herself and looked out at the ocean. "I feel awful for leaving him. I wanted to sit with him, you know, and talk the way we used to. When I was little, we were so tight. He would take me out on the fishing boat sometimes in the summer on good days, and I remember when he got a really big haul, he'd tell everyone that I was the reason, that he couldn't have done it without me. Oh, maybe I should go back."

She bit her lip to keep back the tears, but they were inevitable. They came unbidden, overflowing and destroying all her resolve. Santos would think her just another weak female, she was certain. After months of trying to show him how strong she was, here she was dissolving in tears in front of him.

"I think you should stay here," he said quietly. "You'll know if he needs you."

"What . . . what do you mean?" She sniffed back another flood of tears.

"We know these things." Santos turned her to face him and held her chin in his hand. "Did I ever tell you about the night my father died?"

"No."

"I was away on a business trip for him in Brazil. I was in my hotel room when I felt it. Despite our differences, our bickering, our disagreements, we were one that night. When I called my mother, I learned that he had suffered a stroke at the very moment when I felt the pain. He died that night," Santos said simply. "And you, too, you have a soul that reaches out. You will know when something is wrong. That may not help your father, but it will help you to make your peace with death."

She shut her eyes, hearing his words and slowly accepting them. Then she opened them and let her gaze linger on his handsome features, illuminated only by starlight. "You're a very wise man, do you know that?"

He laughed gently and pulled her along. "Not so wise—only experienced. Come, let me show you my favorite place on La Ropa."

The hidden cove was tucked away behind some huge rocks. As he helped her over the top, she gasped with pleasure. A tiny beach lay before them, completely sheltered from the main beach, and washed by smaller waves. Without a word, Santos sprinted ahead toward the water, stripping off his blue dress shirt as he went. She watched the strong muscles of his back contract and straighten before he turned to her, and the sight of the thick mat of dark hair on his chest made her dizzy. He held out his arms to her and she walked into them in a trance.

"Me permite esta pieza, querida?" he whispered, and she nodded. They danced together on the sand, swaying to a music that moved both of them, a silent melody that stirred their souls. Pat was unable to control the sensations of her heart and body. Perhaps it was weakness because of her father, perhaps it was the end of a long chain of events that had led her to this realization: she wanted him. The tie growing between them was stronger each day, and it was too late to turn back.

Pat ran her hands up his spine to the soft hair on his neck, and he grasped her firmly, reaching down to flatten her hips against his. Slowly, he stroked her thighs and molded them to his own. Her breath came in short gasps, and she was lightheaded, aware that the moment for which she had waited was now at hand.

He kept up the pressure, and she felt the hardness of his masculine body become even more insistent. His body spoke to her and wooed her, and when they stopped moving in the dance, she was barely conscious of it.

"The first day I set eyes on you, I knew, and you did also. Do you recall? I asked if you were praying for a handsome fish. And now—look at me—I am caught in your snares. I want you, Pat," he sighed, lifting her and cradling her in his arms. She was powerless to speak or even breathe properly. His left hand slipped up under her mane of hair, and he brought his mouth down on hers, taking it fiercely as a moan of desire escaped him. She slid from his arms, and he moved with her, pushing her into the soft sand while he kissed her over and over, his mouth moving from her lips to her chin to the velvet mounds of her breasts. He eased the straps of her dress off her shoulders, baring her to the moonlight.

Her breasts were small and in proportion to her slim

body, but when he touched them, they seemed to blossom in his hand like wild, exotic, hothouse flowers suddenly transplanted back into their native soil. Pat arched her back, her nipples tight and erect. She moved toward him, filling the spaces between them like a form made of sand, shifting her shape to meet her love and become one with him.

He tugged at the waistband and pulled her dress off before stripping himself fully. Then he leaned back, crying out, "How beautiful you are!" He ran his hands down the length of her legs, and each finger left its burning mark on her flesh. She couldn't stand to be so far from him, and she pulled him back, offering her breasts for his caress. His lips were moist and firm, and they seemed to tantalize her with their sometimes insistent, sometimes delicate exploration. He licked her nipples, then buried his face in the hollow of her throat. At last, when she could stand it no longer, he finally took her mouth again, moving over her as he did so. She opened herself to him, and he entered her swiftly. She moaned in ecstasy. This was what she had longed for; this was the dream now made real.

They moved together for what seemed an eternity, and yet, when they both cried out, one after the other, and lay limp in each other's arms, it seemed too soon. Body on body, they remained very still, listening to the sound of the surf.

Pat finally opened her eyes to look at her lover. He had given her so much pleasure, and the emptiness she had known before was receding like the waves on the beach.

"You are very warm now," he teased, raising himself up on one elbow. "Come for a swim with me." Laughing, he pulled her up and they ran together to the water. The feel of it was wonderful on her limbs, and she dove into an oncoming wave, almost daring it to break before she came out on the other side.

As she began to swim, she felt herself lifted again. Santos's strong hands came around her waist and slid up to cover her breasts. He pressed her back against him and murmured in her ear, "We are not finished yet." He spun her to face him, and she wrapped her legs around him, gripping him tightly. Entwined together, they shared a salty kiss and their bodies merged once again. Even when Pat thought she could give no more, Santos challenged her to new heights. He held her steady as she thrashed against him, making her enjoy each second to the fullest.

When they finally splashed out of the waves and huddled together on the sand to let the breeze dry them, Pat was completely happy. She was about to tell Santos what she was feeling when something occurred to her.

"Oh, my God!" she exclaimed, sitting up abruptly and nearly knocking her lover sideways.

"What is it?"

"It's just . . . well, it's perfectly ridiculous, but it's true. It came true!"

"What are you talking about, you madwoman?" He laughingly brushed sand onto her bare legs.

"I was in Mexico City just before I came here, and this little gypsy boy told my fortune. I thought he was making it up!" Suddenly, she threw back her head and roared with laughter. "He said he saw me on a beach with a dark, handsome man who looked like Burt Reynolds. He said we were swimming!"

"Yes?" Santos peered at her skeptically. "And what happens next?"

She grinned and got up, starting back toward their

clothes. "That's for me to know, and you to find out," she teased.

As they dressed, helping each other on with their garments so that they could touch again, Pat decided against telling Santos the end of her fortune. It seemed a little premature to mention marriage, even after tonight.

Chapter Ten

"Oh, Pat, there you are! I've been looking for you." Ted had just finished his breakfast and was rushing from the poolside buffet back toward the elevator. Orlando trailed behind him. "I need to see you about something. Could you come upstairs to my office in, say, fifteen minutes?"

"Sure, Ted." Pat nodded hello to Orlando. Although it was barely eight-thirty she'd been up for several hours, drawing up roughs of her new ad campaign for the Ixtapa hotel owners. Part of her felt guilty for going ahead with this after the evening she had just spent with Santos, but the other part of her acknowledged that it was simply part of her job.

"Orlando, get the blueprints out of the safe for me," Ted instructed his assistant as he rushed off. There was a gleam in his eye Pat hadn't seen there in a while. Wonder what he's up to, she mused.

But she was only mildly curious because she was still airborne, floating on a cloud and unwilling to come down. All she could think of were the waves on La Ropa Beach covering her body and that of her lover. All she could feel was the impression of his hands and mouth on her, stimulating her to heights she had never imagined she would scale. Santos was so extraordinary, so tender and yet so powerful. His lovemaking was not simply physical, but was a manifestation of the way he truly felt. He had awakened her to her own potential last night, and her limbs still throbbed and pulsed as they had when he caressed them. No man would ever be able to fulfill her the way he had; she was sure of that.

Dreamily, she took a glass of orange juice off the sideboard and found herself a secluded table overlooking the beach far below. But the waves here were almost violent in comparison to the gentle swells on Zihuatanejo's placid bay. The contrast between the two places reminded her of the contradictions of Santos's temperament. He could be tempestuous, arrogant, fearless, and then turn right around and be soulful and compassionate. And yet he was the same man, mysterious, elusive and as multifaceted as the countless moods of the Pacific.

What would he be like when they saw each other again? She never knew, and perhaps this was partly what attracted her to Santos. Her last experience with a man had been so predictable, so completely routine, that she almost enjoyed the tension Santos provoked in her. Although she did wish he wouldn't be quite so pigheaded about what she did for a living and the person she worked for. After all, she didn't think of him as the mayor, nor did she think of herself as the employee of his enemy. The only important thing between them was their electric relationship, as man and woman together.

"Pat? Excuse me." Orlando appeared at her side, disturbing her reverie. "Mr. Beckman wanted me to let you know he's ready whenever you are." He pointed to his watch.

"Has it been fifteen minutes already?" she asked, embarrassed. "I wasn't watching."

"You are on Mexican time now, Pat," Orlando joked. "Do one thing slowly and well—this is our motto."

"Well, it's sweet of you to make excuses for me," Pat grinned as they walked toward the entrance of the Paradiso together. "But our boss is on business time, and we work for him." Ted Beckman, as she so poignantly recalled, was too involved with business to express sympathy for her sick father. If he was indicative of exploitative entrepreneurs, was it any wonder that Santos hated him so? Unlike Santos's buddy Kurt over at the Pelicanos, Ted hadn't bothered to study the Mexican customs before going ahead with the Paradiso.

As the elevator slowly made its way to his rooftop office, she told herself to stop thinking this way. It was plain old disloyalty. Now that she had learned so much from Santos, how could she ever be happy working at the Paradiso for a person who basically didn't give a damn about anything but money? Suddenly Pat felt split down the middle. She had wanted this job so badly, and now, almost overnight, she had grave doubts.

But as she walked toward Ted's office, she put on an even, calm demeanor. He would sense her resentment immediately, and she'd never be able to make any significant decisions at this hotel if he didn't trust her.

Telling herself to play it by ear, she knocked and let herself in.

"What's going on?" she asked. Ted's normally meticulous office looked like a cyclone had just struck it.

"Come here, come on," he urged her. He was standing at his desk examining a set of blueprints, and dozens of mailing tubes lay on chairs and on the floor near him. "This is so fantastic, I can't tell you how pleased I am." He grabbed her by the hand and led her around to his side of the desk, smiling at her puzzled expression. "This, Pat, is the *new* Paradiso."

"The new Paradiso?"

"Yes, indeed. A little surprise—I didn't want to tell you until the architect had the plans ready. While you were conducting that meeting here a couple of weeks ago, I was up in Mexico City negotiating with FONATUR for the rights to put up a hotel in Mazatlán. Nice little place on the ocean north of here. Oh, they've already got their Camino Real and some other expensive places, and Andersons has restaurants all over the city, so we wouldn't have the same problem drawing tourists the way we do in Ixtapa. Everything's there already, and all we have to do is collect it. See, some British investors started to build on this site I've got about three years ago, but they ran out of money. I bought them out for a song, practically. And my architects have adapted their original idea for a smallish place so we can build a real palace on the site—outdo everything else in the area. You should see it, Pat. It's right on the bay—simply beautiful! We're going to build right into the side of the cliff. It'll make the Camino Real look like subsidized housing."

"Well, that's . . . great, Ted." Pat forced a smile, even more confused than she had been when she walked in the door. It was hard to give him her total approval, although the idea did sound like it had possibilities—*if* he didn't ruin it.

"I can see I'm making your head spin," he chuckled, "but I'm showing you these plans for a reason. Hang onto your hat, sweetheart, because you're going to run this place when it's ready."

"What!?"

"That's right, Pat. I think you're an enormously capable woman, and I'm making you manager of the Mazatlán Paradiso. You're the only one for the job."

Pat was speechless, trying to absorb what he had just told her and trying, at the same time, to see how she felt about it. Ted was offering her an unbelievable career opportunity on a silver platter, and it was clear that once she was in charge, she could do whatever she wanted with the hotel. Of course, it was being built to look like an American extravaganza, but maybe she could learn to run it the way Kurt ran the Pelicanos in Zihuatanejo.

Stop kidding yourself, girl, she thought. When you have a palace, as Ted calls it, complete with golf course, disco, three pools and hundreds of servants, you can't turn around and run it like a charming little inn. That was the first rule of hotel management—exploit your facilities.

Pat stared at the plans blankly, wondering if she really wanted to ally herself so completely with Ted Beckman. She could just imagine Santos's reaction when she told him. Not to mention the geographical problem. She wondered how far north Mazatlán was. Would they continue to see each other if she moved away? But more important, would Santos even consider loving a woman who was devoted to running yet another exploitive hotel for foreigners?

Wait a second, Pat, she told herself firmly. Don't let your imagination get the best of you. She had no idea whether Santos loved her or not. It was certainly clear that he enjoyed making love to her, but that was only part of the larger picture. He was such a strange, changeable man; how could she be sure that he felt for her what she did for him? She had always made her own decisions; she had left Steve because he could never have shared the sorts of things she believed to be crucial and vital. It would be totally hypocritical for her to turn around now and change her life for Santos, a man with so little respect for women. Much as she wanted to turn him into the man of her dreams, she wouldn't allow herself to do it. Her father had urged her to listen to her heart, but her heart now prompted her in two directions. She craved love, but she also craved her freedom and her growing capabilities.

"That's quite an offer," she stammered at last.

"I can see your mind is running a mile a minute, sweetheart," Ted chuckled. "I don't want you to make up your mind this instant. Give it time; think it over. I just wanted to show you the plans and whet your appetite, okay? When you're ready, just let me know, and we'll talk details then." He began rolling up the plans, slowly removing temptation from her path. But he saw the look in her eye—he knew he'd thrown out the right bait, and given the right amount of time, his fish would bite.

"Fine, Ted, thanks," Pat murmured. She walked to the door in a daze and was unaware of Ted's self-satisfied chuckle as she closed the door behind her. She wished she could call her father and ask his advice about this, but the idea of suggesting she might stay in Mexico for good seemed unwise. He was recovering, but he was still vulnerable to a setback. Her mother, evidently, would be in no frame of mind to be objective about Pat's career—all she wanted was her daughter all neatly wrapped up like a package, signed, sealed and delivered to Dr. Steve Elman. So she would just have to keep this to herself for a while.

She worked doubly hard that day, coordinating staff schedules, looking over the talent lists for the night-club, settling a dispute about a checkout time with an angry French guest. By seven-thirty, all Pat wanted was a cool glass of freshly squeezed orange juice and a hot shower to ease away the day's tensions. She hadn't even gotten around to looking at the day's mail, which included a note from her father.

She slipped out of her embroidered Mexican peasant blouse and tailored white slacks, and stood under the hot shower until billows of steam wrapped the bathroom and outer dressing room in a thick fog. She was already spoiled by the luxury of her Paradiso apartment, and she had to admit that the huge plush towels, which were changed daily, gave her a special sense of delight in her job. The perks of living this way made up for the long hours and the variety of unpleasant clients she had to deal with.

When she emerged from the shower, freshly scrubbed and rosy from the water, she wrapped herself in her silk kimono, took another towel, along with her letters and writing pad, and went out to sit on her private patio. The evening breeze lifted her damp mane of blond hair and ruffled it dry. Days of walking in the hot sun had turned her honey strands almost wheat-colored, and she liked the change.

She sat in one of her wicker chairs, put her feet up on the low table, and opened her father's letter. It read:

Patricia dearest,

When you read this, I'll probably be stuck in some big chair or lying out on the porch, doing nothing. Or else I'll be eating that mess your mother tells me she has to cook up for me. No spices, no fats, none of those brimming mugs of coffee I used to down one after the other. In short, Pat, none of the good things of life. I hate to sound like a complainer, but this day in, day out taking care of myself is getting me down. I feel generally okay, but still not well enough to go out in the boat, so I won't do anything foolhardy. But I would like a change, you know, just a little something to liven up my days. All right then, I'm going to give it time. But not *too much* time!

Now write me a letter, girl. And make it long enough to tell all.

Your loving father

Pat sighed and put the letter down. It was depressing to hear how bored he was, despite his little jokes about it. What could she suggest that might "liven up his days"?

She was just about to sit down and answer with a long, newsy letter, when there was a soft knock on her door. "Just a second," she called as she got up to answer it. She just hoped it wasn't Orlando with a message from Ted—she had enough on her mind right now.

But when she opened the door, she was startled to see Santos's face smiling down at her. He gave her an appraising glance as he walked past her into her room.

"*Buenas tardes, querida,*" he said in a low voice. "And how are you this evening?"

155

"I'm . . . just fine," she answered shortly, backing away. She was so confused about him right now, and she wanted more time to think before confronting him with her news about the job. And despite their passionate encounter the previous night, she felt somewhat vulnerable, dressed only in a skimpy robe. For him to see her this way implied a kind of intimacy she had never known with a man.

"All day long, my mind has been unable to function properly," he confessed, dropping into a large upholstered chair near the bed. "And so I knew I would come here after work and take you out to dinner. But my mother is entertaining some old friends from Mexico City tonight, and she has asked me to come. It's impossible for me to get through an entire day without you, though. I look at reports, and I see your face, your hair. I have a meeting with my staff and I can only hear your cries of pleasure echoing in my ears. Come to me, *querida.*" He stretched out his muscular arms for her, and the look on his face was impossible to deny. His eyes clearly invited her to another tryst, and his body moved suggestively in the chair, accommodating a place for her on his lap.

"Santos, I'm not sure that I—" She tugged the belt on her robe tighter and wrapped her arms around her shoulders. "I really have to get dressed.

"Then go ahead," he smiled. "I'll watch."

She laughed nervously before turning away. "Give me a little time to digest last night, will you? There's a lot on my mind right now."

"And on mine." Suddenly he was walking across the room toward her. His tall, masculine form loomed before her, and she was powerless to evade his crushing embrace. His arms enveloped her slender body and his mouth was everywhere at once—in her hair, on her throat, parting the fabric over her breasts. She moaned and her head lolled back, giving him freer access. Now her limbs were taking on that wonderful loose sensation, as though she were swimming in a warm pool.

Deftly, his knee parted the edges of her robe and she was aware of the strength of his thigh, covered in soft cotton material, leaning on her bare flesh. Her naked body burned under the robe, and she longed to be free of it. She knew now that it would only be a matter of time before he removed it from her languid, unprotesting limbs.

"Patricia," he murmured in her ear as his hand cupped her breast through the thin fabric of her robe. "You have captured my heart, and now you must be gentle with it. Never say no to me again."

When he kissed her this time, she could not respond in the same way. If he knew about her ambitions, her interest in the new job, he would be furious. And certainly, going off on her own would be tantamount to saying no to him. Wouldn't it be better to be honest with him tonight, instead of letting it fester between them? How could she make love to him with this on her mind?

"Please," she begged him as he slowly untied the belt of her kimono and ran his thumb along the inside of the robe to edge it off her body. "I have to tell you something, Santos. It's really important."

"Nothing is as important as this moment," he corrected her, backing her toward the bed. The robe fell to the floor and she stood naked before him, her mantle of blond hair flowing around her shoulders and framing her small, uplifted breasts. "You have told me all I need to know," he went on, stroking each of her nipples in turn while his other hand moved lower over her stomach. "Even now your body yearns for mine."

He conquered her resistance with one deep kiss, parting her lips and allowing his tongue to explore the inside of her mouth. Her tongue circled his, and the ache within her grew deeper and wilder. She allowed him to push her backward on the bed, and he swiftly undressed while she watched, mesmerized. His sun-tanned limbs rippled with each motion, and as he threw off his final piece of clothing, she drew her breath in sharply, marveling at the perfection of his masculine form. His torso was finely etched with muscles, and covered with dark curly hair. It ended in a narrow waist that curved down slightly toward slim hips. No thought could enter her head now; she was so filled with his presence and her own longing.

He lay beside her, slowly stroking her. When she could bear it no longer, she rose up on one elbow, and he pulled her over on top of him, letting one breast drop into his mouth so that they could be even closer. Her body was covered with a damp sheen of perspiration, as was his, but neither noticed. The heat of their passion consumed them, but sparked a new flame that would not be extinguished. They moved together softly at first, and then with an uncontrolled abandon, learning the lesson of their two bodies' needs. When she neared a peak, he would subtly change position or stimulate her differently, challenging her on to new heights. His own body was a sensitive instrument that brought forth the music of her inner yearnings. He told her, before she knew it herself, where to travel on this wonderful voyage, and at the end, she understood that the destination was not even as important as how they had arrived there, together.

Later, they sprawled diagonally across the bed and allowed their ragged breathing to subside to normal. She must have dozed, because when she next opened her eyes, he was standing above her, dressed. He smiled down at her and took an edge of the sheet to wipe her damp brow.

"I took the liberty of using your shower. I've got to go now, although I don't want to. Tomorrow, I promise you, we will talk, and you will tell me what you find so important." He bent down and brushed the lightest of kisses along her top and then her bottom lip. *"Hasta la próxima vez, querida. Buenas noches."*

He was gone before she had a chance to say good night. But she wondered, as she stumbled out of bed toward the shower, if the next time, after she had told him her news, he would even be speaking to her.

The man's going to turn me into a raving maniac, Pat thought as she moved up on the luncheon line the following afternoon. Or else I'll blow the whole thing by not coming clean with him. She vowed to go into Zihuatanejo the instant her work was finished for the day and tell him about Mazatlán. But now, she was starving from having skipped dinner the previous night, and needed something in her stomach. The poolside buffet looked really spectacular today, and she selected the cold crab and avocado salad.

Two bronzed Californians invited Pat over to their table and she accepted graciously. She didn't usually eat with the guests, but she was interested in doing as much informal survey work as possible these days. After all, if she was considering taking a job as manager of a new resort, she wanted to go in functioning on all cylinders. If she could correct some of the mistakes Ted had made in the Ixtapa Paradiso, she'd have even more going for her. That was, *if* she took the job.

"You know, we've been all over Mexico," the young

woman from L.A. was saying as she dug into her salad, "but we wanted to pick someplace special for our first anniversary." She smiled playfully at her husband, who was staring at some teenage girls lounging by the pool.

"Then you're pleased with the Paradiso?" Pat asked.

"Oh, we adore it!" the woman gushed. "The only thing it doesn't have is casinos, like Las Vegas."

Pat smiled politely, but her heart sank. This was evidently not the clientele she would have envisaged for her small, romantic honeymoon hotel. The husband was busy watching other bikinis and the wife wanted slot machines! Was this going to be typical of Mazatlán as well? And would Ted encourage all the things Pat hated? Maybe the new job would be more of a disappointment than a challenge. And if Santos wasn't around. . . . Suddenly Pat was more confused than ever.

"Can I steal you away?"

Pat squinted up into the bright afternoon sun to see Ted standing at her elbow holding a glass of iced tea.

"How are you folks? Enjoying your stay?" Ted asked the couple as Pat made her excuses and got up.

"Oh, we adore it," the woman repeated. "You people sure know how to run a hotel!"

"Pat, I'm awfully sorry to barge in here, but I wanted to talk over a couple of things with you."

"Fine. See you later," she waved to the couple. Actually she was overjoyed to get away from them.

"Why don't we settle down over here?" Ted led her to the quiet pool behind the main one, used basically by mothers with small children. Since most people were at lunch, the area was practically deserted. Ted and Pat took two lounge chairs and made themselves comfortable.

"I don't mean to rush you," Ted said, "but it just so

happens I got a call from Bill Higgins, my architect over at Mazatlán. Funny he should ring me the day after we discussed it, but anyway . . ." He moved his chair closer to Pat's and began gesticulating in his typical enthusiastic manner. "He's ready to show off the site, find out if we have any input at this point before he goes too far in one direction. I thought maybe you and I could drive up there tonight. There's not a lot to see, but it might be fun, you know, to get away for a while."

"Oh, well, I've just sunk my teeth into that ad campaign here, Ted. I was going to take some stuff to the printer tomorrow."

"It can wait! Say, it's a lovely drive up there, and if you're going to move to Mazatlán, you ought to get acquainted with the area."

"Ted," Pat laughed, noticing suddenly that he had placed his hand over hers. "I haven't actually made up my mind about the job yet."

"You know, we never discussed money. I see you want to pin this down, so I better make you an offer. I intend to make you a vice-president of Paradiso Enterprises, sweetheart."

The words rang a bell. Hadn't Ruth said he'd made his ex-wife vice-president? And what about the last assistant manager who'd left because of "personal differences" with Ted? Pat was suddenly very uneasy about the whole thing.

"You go up to Mazatlán without me this time, Ted. I don't want to commit myself to something I can't follow up on. I promise I'll give you an answer within the week." She smiled at him, but her heart simply wasn't in it.

"I don't get you." He shook his head and his green eyes questioned her. "I offer you the moon and you say

you have to think about it. Pat, I think you're tops—
I've never met a woman like you. When our two brains
get together on something, no one can stop us. Do you
hear what I'm saying?"

He pulled her up out of her seat and held her by both
shoulders. Then, before she knew what was happening,
he was kissing her.

"Please, Ted!" She pulled away abruptly. "This is a
business decision. Let's not confuse the issue." When
she saw the hurt-little-boy expression on his face, she
reached over to pat his hand. The gesture felt phony
and awkward. "I need some more time, and I honestly
think it's better for both of us if we get through the
business part of it before we even consider discussing
anything else. Don't you agree?"

He shrugged and picked up his iced tea glass.
"You're right as usual. Mazatlán can wait—a short
while. But I'm afraid I have to have your answer by
next Monday, Pat. Things are moving fast, and if you
don't want the job, I'm going to have to scour the earth
for a replacement."

He grinned and backed away, evidently too embarrassed about his lapse of professionalism to push her
any further. "So give it some thought, okay? See you
tonight, Pat."

She didn't bother to tell him she wouldn't be in
Ixtapa that evening. No sense in mentioning her split
allegiance—at least not yet, before she'd made up her
mind.

She drove into Zihuatanejo early and went past the
town hall, where she knew Santos would be working.
They'd agreed to meet at the Pelicanos for a drink
before dinner, but she wanted a little time for herself.
She drove slowly into the Zona Hotelería, making way
for the men coming home from work on their burros. It

was odd how she never saw this sight in Ixtapa, nor did she awake to the sounds of cocks crowing as she had at Santos's house on the beach. It was as if every natural thing had been stripped from the environment in Ixtapa, leaving it cold and sterile. Yes, she decided as she pulled into the courtyard of the Pelicanos, this place was the more beautiful—Santos was right. She parked and walked past the line of stucco dwellings, making a beeline for the beach, nodding to the owner, Kurt, as she went. It was a very warm evening, although it was already past seven, and she was glad of her light seersucker sundress and the broad straw hat she had bought at the *mercado*.

Kicking off her sandals, she walked the length of La Ropa alone, smiling at the kids on their way home for dinner and gawking at a young man who was walking a tiny alligator on a leash. What a wonderful place this was, she marveled as she strolled back toward the Pelicanos. As for Mazatlán, well, she had no idea. She had searched long and hard for a place and a job that felt right to her. She had longed for a man who would make her feel the way Santos did. Now she had both, but she wondered, could they survive if she joined them together? It was a very hard question.

It was about eight when she settled herself at a small table under the Pelicanos *palapa* and ordered a glass of white wine. Several of the hotel's guests, chatting in German, French or Italian, were just beginning to emerge from their apartments to begin the evening.

"Would you like to order now, miss?" asked a young waitress in rather halting English.

Pat answered her in Spanish, which brought a smile to the girl's face. "No thanks, I'm waiting for someone."

The girl nodded with a smile that implied she was

163

well aware who Pat was waiting for. And where was he, anyway? Pat glanced at her watch. Fifteen minutes late! How could she expect commitment from a man who couldn't be on time for dinner?

Aren't you being a bit unreasonable? she asked herself as she took a sip of wine. Don't look for problems.

At that very moment, Santos appeared, walking briskly down the path and under the *palapa*. He came toward her with outstretched arms and Pat was thankful that only the bartender and four other guests were around to see the kiss he gave her. Had she been standing, it would have knocked her off her feet.

"You were not waiting long, *querida?*" he asked in a concerned tone.

"Not too," she said noncommittally.

"Excellent, because I cannot stay long. As it happens, I must meet tonight with the chief of police and his deputies. I am so sorry—"

"Wait a minute. I thought you and I were having dinner tonight. We were going to talk." She tried to keep herself under control, but he had pressed that button again, and she could feel an argument brewing.

"Pat, I have apologized—but this is a man's work, you know. As a servant of the people, I must go where they call me."

"Don't give me that," she said in a slightly louder voice. "Last night you wanted to see me, but you had to go to your mother's house. Tonight you can meet me for a drink, but then you have an important meeting. I suppose you planned to drag me over to your house for a quickie before you go out tonight?" She could feel the hot flush of her anger rising fast.

"What are you saying?" he asked angrily. "If you

164

think the only reason I wish to see you is to satisfy my lust, you are entirely mistaken."

"Am I? Then why is it so convenient to see me near a bed just before you have to go off and do something else more important?" She was really livid now, but her fury was nothing compared to the rage in his face.

"You malign me! I have never in my life heard such an accusation from a woman!"

"A woman! What's that got to do with it? Santos, I'm a person, and I'd like to be treated with a little respect. That means you don't just jump into bed with me and then run off to do . . . to do 'man's work!'" she sputtered.

"I see; I understand." He grasped her wrists and shook her, hard. "Patricia, you are never ever to suggest that I have no respect for you—*ever* again! Last night was unavoidable, and tonight, there is nothing I can do now. You misjudge me." His anger was dissipated now and in its place was genuine disappointment. She had failed him in some vital way by not trusting him.

"May I ask how long you have?" she asked evenly.

"I am due to meet my colleagues at nine-thirty," he said.

"Oh, well, great. That gives me plenty of time."

They sat across the table, glaring at each other, neither willing to give an inch. The silence was broken only when the young waitress sidled over and asked Santos if he wanted a beer.

"*Grácias, un frío, por favor.*" As she walked away, he laughed and took Pat's hand again, this time gently. "What have I told you about how much Mexicans love a good argument? And you match me point for point, Patricia."

165

"I suppose," she sighed, looking into his piercing eyes and realizing that, angry as she was, it was hard to deny him anything he wanted.

"Now tell me, *querida,* what is this important matter you wish to discuss?"

She licked her lips and swallowed hard. This seemed like the worst time in the world to tell him. But they were there together, and she didn't really see any point in postponing it.

"Santos," she began, looking him directly in the eye, "I'd like to lay this all out in front of you, okay? I'm not really asking advice—I just want to talk it out."

"Yes?" he prompted.

"Well, Ted Beckman has offered me a terrific job running the new Paradiso he's building in Mazatlán. It's a great offer, but I just don't know if I want to accept it."

"How could you go to Mazatlán and leave me?" he laughed.

She picked her head up, suddenly angry again. "Can't you be serious for a second?" she burst out. "Why do you insist on playing big man with me? I'm not impressed, honestly."

Santos was silent for a moment, but his eyes spoke for him. In a grim tone, he finally muttered, "Is this the price I must pay for two nights of love? Now you feel you own me, is that it?"

She let her breath out slowly. "God, how can you be so dense! I think you owe me your honesty, your sincerity. That's all. I wasn't trying to push you into begging me to stay here, for heaven's sake."

"How could you speak of honesty and sincerity? You're nothing but the mechanical doll of that exploiter Beckman! He winds you up, fills you with promises of wealth and position and *basta!* you jump. What do you want? My blessings for his marvelous plans to make Mexico into another Las Vegas? Do you want me to congratulate you for helping him to ruin Mazatlán, as he and his kind have ruined Ixtapa?"

He pushed back his chair abruptly and stood up. He towered over her, his jaw working with rage and disillusionment.

"It's incredible to me that a man of your experience could be so shortsighted, so simple!" she spat back. "The hotels bring money into the area, Santos, and provide honest labor for those people whose servant you claim to be. But I don't think you really give a hoot about them—or about anyone for that matter. This is your personal vendetta against Ted and the other hotel owners, isn't it? And getting back at them is more important to you than your people's welfare! It really infuriates me." She got up and rushed away toward the stone steps and the beach. But he was right on top of her. He grabbed her and pinned her arms to her side. Struggle as she might, she could not budge an inch and was a helpless target for his wrath.

"You Americans are all alike," he insisted. "All you know is money, money, money. The land and tradition and history mean nothing to you."

She faced him down, unwilling to let him turn her into something she despised. "You know that isn't true. You know I feel the same way you do about preserving Mexico's culture. That's the only reason I'd consider the Mazatlán job, by the way. To make sure it's done right! But you don't want to hear that. You just want me to fit into your little pigeonhole. Good in bed, but lousy for Mexico."

"You are—" He raked her with a cruel glance and for

a moment she thought he was going to leave her right there. She would never see him again. And part of her rejoiced, although the other part cried out to him.

"As long as you work for Beckman," he muttered, "you are an enemy to my people and to me. I cannot celebrate the expansion of your employer's empire, because despite your good intentions, he will soon have you dancing to his tune. I hope you find happiness in your new Paradiso!" With that, he let her go and bolted away.

She tried to stifle a sob as she watched him storm down the path. Her chest was heaving with anger and desolation. To have been so exquisitely happy with this man only to have him turn on her! He was unnecessarily cruel, and in one brief tirade he had ruined everything they had shared together. And this was the man who had the audacity to say that their souls spoke to one another! He had no more idea of what made her tick than Ted Beckman did! How could he have made love so tenderly, so wonderfully to her and then destroyed every shred of affection?

The sound of couples walking down into the sunken pit of the dining room roused her. Naturally they had attracted a lot of attention with their argument, and the people who were still sitting at the bar met her glance with uncomfortable smiles of sympathy.

She walked stolidly back to her table, left a hundred-peso note for the wine, and started for the car. There was nothing to keep her here now—she might as well return to the Paradiso and start planning her ideas for Mazatlán.

Yes, she thought as she gunned the accelerator, getting out of Ixtapa, away from both Ted and Santos, would be good for her. She'd buckle down to the new job, throw herself headlong into her work and forget she ever had a romantic bone in her body.

But it was impossible to forget those two precious nights with him. How could he have faked that? He'd been so tender, so loving, so real then. He'd allowed his armor to dissolve when he took her in his arms and made passionate, exuberant love to her. Why can't he be like that all the time? she wondered miserably. Why does he let his damn pride get in the way?

And then, like a shot, it struck her. He wasn't rejecting her because she worked for Ted Beckman, or because she had a dream of a career. He just couldn't admit in broad daylight that he cared for someone, that he wouldn't want her leaving him for a better job in another town. He could shout his passion for "his people" to the rooftops, but he couldn't deal with his feelings for a woman.

Pat felt little consolation that she had stumbled on this rationale, though. What difference did it make if she had him all figured out? He'd written her off as an enemy, and no amount of worrying over it was going to change that.

She pulled into the parking lot of the Paradiso and handed the keys to the attendant with a weary smile. There was nothing to do but erase him and the relationship from her mind. She was going to try her damnedest to forget him.

"Are you sure you want this one, Ruth? It's a little large." Pat eased the gigantic sombrero off the older woman's head, but Ruth grabbed onto it, feeling the brim for size.

"I love it," she assured Pat. They were standing at one of the small shops in the Ixtapa "mall," and Pat was itching to get back to work. The boards had come in from a fancy ad agency in Mexico City, and she was dying to get a look at them. Above all, she wanted to see them before Ted did—just in case anything needed fixing. She had been quite successful in being busy all the time for the past week, and she had managed to stay out of Zihuatanejo entirely.

"Here, sweetie, take my purse and pay the man," Ruth insisted. "I can't make out a peso from a dime these days." She shrugged hopelessly.

Pat bit her lip and fished around in Ruth's mammoth bag until she found the wallet. It was true. Ruth's eyesight was considerably worse, and even though her attitude toward it was amazingly realistic, it caused Pat a lot of distress to see her. She hadn't given it much thought before, but she knew she was going to miss Ruth when she went to Mazatlán. And thinking about Ruth generally led her to thoughts of her father. She'd called him late the previous night and had been as cheery as she could be, but it was hard in the face of his depression. The doctors all told him he was improving, but fishing was still out of the question. They couldn't say when they might give him the okay. And oddly enough, his formerly rebellious attitude had calmed to a mere ripple on the waters. He simply didn't feel up to it yet, he'd told Pat.

Still immersed in thought, she guided Ruth across the road and back up the circular drive to the Paradiso. When Ruth asked her for a compliment on her new purchase, Pat didn't even respond.

"I don't know," Ruth said, shaking her head. "You're in a bad state these days. Something wrong with your love life?"

"What?" Pat whirled around in shock.

"I haven't noticed that glow you had the last time we spoke," Ruth mused as they wandered through the lobby and toward the pool. "I don't mean to pry, sweetie, but I'm dying of curiosity."

"Ruth!" Pat forced a laugh. "For heaven's sake. I've just been busy, that's all. And thinking about my father. I guess the glow's just a bit dimmer, that's all."

"Well, leave me at the pool. I'm in no mood to be depressed by a girl who's supposed to be in love." She clucked in mock annoyance and selected a lounge chair near a very continental-looking couple playing backgammon beside the pool.

"Okay. I've really got to get back to work now," Pat said, nodding mechanically to the guests. "I'll talk to you later."

"Pat," Ruth patted the side of the chair and indicated that Pat was to sit beside her, "I'm just rattling off stuff that's sitting at the top of my head, of course, but why don't you fly your parents down here for a while? You said your father wanted a change, and you also said Zihuatanejo looked like your old hometown. What better way to get a couple of birds with one stone?"

"You mean," Pat began wonderingly, "move my father down here?"

"Well, he wouldn't have to rush into anything. He could just try it for a week or so, and if he liked it, they could stick around. I tell you, the Paradiso is heaven on earth, but I could use a few friends who don't run off when their vacation's over."

Pat stared at the older woman, thinking for a brief moment that Ruth might have been leveling that criticism directly at her. But if she did intend to stay in Mexico, what better solution could there be than to move her parents down to Ixtapa? For a brief moment, it occurred to her that it would be marvelous to see her father and Santos hit it off, but she erased that thought the instant after it entered her mind.

"Ruth," she said, "I think you're a genius."

"Just call me Einstein," Ruth said, snapping her fingers and settling down lower in her chair.

"I'll write them tonight and propose the idea. And thank you for thinking of it." She bent over and gave Ruth a kiss on the cheek.

"Anything to cheer you up, for heaven's sake!" the older woman laughed, embarrassed at Pat's display of emotion.

"See you later, okay?" Pat got up to leave, and Ruth gave her a smile. In that short conversation, Pat's whole mood had changed. And in fact, the day would have been perfect if she hadn't overheard a couple of newly arrived guests talking quietly on her way back to her office.

The woman was short and blond, wearing an orange bathing suit and gigantic dark glasses. The man with her was bearded and very attractive. The two of them had a look of intelligence about them, as though they appreciated the finer things of life—things that didn't necessarily cost a lot of money.

"I had no idea it was going to be so ugly," the woman said to her husband. "I mean, I know we'll have a good time, but really—it looks like a gigantic, concrete-block prison."

"I know. I keep looking around for the barbed wire. Well, listen, it'll add spice to the book. And we can have dinner at that lovely place in Zihuatanejo."

Writers! Pat thought, totally horrified. Oh, boy, I hope Ted doesn't run into these two.

The thing was, she realized that somewhere, way back in her mind, she agreed with them. The Paradiso had a lot of marvelous qualities, but it did vaguely resemble a beautifully decorated jail.

As she made her way back to her office, it occurred to her that Santos's ideas and opinions had, despite her firm resolve, insinuated themselves into her way of seeing the world. And if the Paradiso was a prison, then being without the man she loved was like getting thrown into solitary confinement forever.

She forced herself to examine the advertising boards, willing Santos out of her mind and her heart. But try as she would, he was still there. Like a thorny but beautiful rose, he caused as much pain as he did pleasure.

Chapter Eleven

*P*at was closing her apartment door the next morning when she heard the sounds of an argument wafting toward her from down in the lobby. She ran down the short flight of stairs from the staff residence wing to the lobby, hoping to be able to take care of the problem quickly and efficiently. But what she saw at the front entrance of the hotel stopped her dead in her tracks.

A team of burly moving men were pushing seven grotesque statues into the lobby on rolling dollies. As Pat approached them her heart began beating wildly. The seven stone gargoyles from the Church of Santa Bárbara! What in the name of—?

Three of the huge forms were already leaning together on the floor while the men lugged in the next two. But Pat's vision blurred at the sight of Santos in a rage, standing toe-to-toe with Ted just outside the door. His face was a white mask of fury, and Pat didn't have to hear a word to know exactly what was going on. She could read the scene as clearly as if it had been printed before her.

"Beckman, you are a snake!" Santos yelled. "Nothing is sacred to you!"

"This is no concern of yours, Ribera. Father Luis sold them to me, plain and simple," Ted sneered. "I gave him a damn good price, and he was very grateful."

"They were not his to sell!" Santos countered. "Those gargoyles belong to the people of the parish."

"Right," Ted nodded. "The people, the people! You're always going on about the people. Well, *señor*, Father Luis is a lot more aware of their needs than you are. Those people are hungry, and they need that money I gave them for necessities. Food, medicine and shelter. I suppose you'd rather have them starve so your precious tradition can be preserved. What kind of mayor are you, Ribera? You care about buildings more than you do about people."

Santos stared him down, his eyes two burning lances set to pierce his adversary. His fury made the anger he'd directed at Pat the other day seem mild by comparison. "It is useless to explain anything to you, Beckman, because all you know are profits and business deals. You could never be made to comprehend that depriving people of their heritage is worse by far than depriving them of food. Once you and your fellow thieves have robbed them of all their pride, they will not even want to eat."

"I don't know what the hell you're talking about, Ribera, and I'm not sure you do either."

Pat could see the cords at the back of Santos's neck tense, like those of an animal about to spring. "It is clear to me that God made you without a conscience. Even the lowest criminal spares the churches in Mexico. Evidently, you are lower than that."

Ted threw back his head and gave a laugh of derision, and Pat stood transfixed, seeing a new side of this man. She had known that he had a one-track mind, but she had never wanted to believe he could take people for granted like this. As Santos turned away from Ted in disgust, his gaze fell on Pat. She recoiled from those terrible accusing eyes. Did he really think she had anything to do with the purchase of these gargoyles? He couldn't!

"Everything is yours for the taking, isn't it, Beckman?" Santos said in a voice quieter than death. He included her in his declaration, and even the anguish in her face didn't move him. He turned on his heel and started down the front steps, the strong muscles of his back rigid with disapproval.

Without thinking what Ted's reaction might be, Pat ran after him, fighting to hold back the sobs. It had taken her a long time to figure out where her true loyalties lay, but this one incident had weighted the scale for her.

"Santos! Santos!" she called, racing after his departing form. "I have to talk to you!"

He reached his car and yanked open the door, flinging himself into the driver's seat. She could see the fierce determination in the set of his masculine jaw. "We have nothing to discuss," he spat at her, his eyes raking her body. "You and your vulgar plans are of no interest to me."

"For God's sake," she cried in exasperation. "Why don't you believe that I knew nothing about this? I would never have let him decorate his lobby with those gargoyles!"

"I don't want to hear it," he snapped. "As long as you work for him I hold you responsible as well!" He gunned the motor and the car shot out of the drive as she watched, helpless. After a long moment, the exhaust of his car vanished, and she had no alternative but to turn around and walk back into the entrance of the Paradiso.

The moving men were bringing in the seventh gargoyle as she entered the lobby. Ted was supervising their placement, trying out the statues in various locations until he was satisfied. Pat stood there gathering steam, finding it impossible to believe that he seemed so calm, so placid, as though nothing unusual had happened and as if the shouting match with Santos had never occurred. Guests were milling around, commenting on his new acquisitions, and Pat noticed the two writers shaking their heads in disbelief over in one corner. Evidently they felt the gargoyles were about as appropriate to a hotel lobby as she did.

"Well, what do you think, Pat?" Ted walked over and stood beside her, rocking back on his heels proudly. "They give the lobby some class, don't you agree?"

"I'd like to talk to you privately," she muttered, looking at the face of the closest gargoyle, a menacing eagle with mad, avenging eyes. The one beside it was a grotesque turtle with a man's head embossed into its shell. The third was a monkey with a devil's pointed ears and tail. Pat was simply dumbfounded that her employer considered these statues, taken from a church no less, as apt and fit for his lobby.

"Yeah, sure," he said, leading her out onto the patio. He turned back and gazed at his new possessions through the glass. "You probably have a better eye for this kind of thing than I do. Why don't you tell the guys where to put them, okay? Just scatter them around the lobby." He grinned at her, and she knew at that instant that he was perfectly well aware of what he was doing: involving her in something she wanted no part of.

"Why didn't you tell me you were buying these statues from Father Luis?" she asked evenly.

"Well, I guess I just didn't think about it," he answered innocently.

"You want to make me supervisor of a new hotel, and you don't even consult me on something as important as this?" She would put it on his level, because questions of power and authority were the only things he understood. He would never appreciate a plea about tradition and history.

"It didn't seem awfully important," he shrugged. "Listen, I'm expecting a call from FONATUR. You take care of these." He started to leave and then turned back, putting a hand on her shoulder. She felt tainted by his touch, and she pulled away. "Hey, I'm sorry if you feel undermined. I honestly didn't know you'd care about something like this." He nodded, and she was sure he was playing her for a fool. Either that or he was testing her loyalty, throwing up his victory to her. She was shocked and angry to think that Ted knew what she felt for Santos, and that he would go out of his way to sabotage their relationship.

"If you want my opinion, which you clearly don't, though I'll give it to you anyway, I don't think the gargoyles belong here. They belong on a church."

"Yes, well," Ted said slowly. "To each his own. That's what makes horse races, hon. See you later." He was grinning with smug satisfaction as he walked away.

Pat wandered back into the lobby and glared back at the seven snarling gargoyles. Her head was throbbing, and all she wanted to do was go after Santos. How could she stay here now? The man she loved would undoubtedly never speak to her again, and she'd lost all respect for the man who'd offered her the professional opportunity of a lifetime. If Ted made her manager of the Mazatlán Paradiso, would he actually allow her her head? Or would she be a puppet ruler, expected to do just as her boss told her?

She walked away quickly from the stone demons looming over the lobby. The place really did resemble a little hell now, Pat thought ruefully. Well, there was nothing she could do but get back to work. Even though she felt incapable of concentrating on anything, she knew it would be good for her. She started back to her office, stopping at the front desk to pick up the day's mail.

"Good morning, Pat," Orlando smiled and handed her a bundle of letters. "Have you seen the excitement?"

"Have I ever! What do you think of the new additions, Orlando?" she asked him, flipping through the stack.

Orlando bit his lip and didn't respond. Pat gave him an understanding look. This man was about the most loyal employee Ted Beckman had. A poor kid from Zihuatanejo, he'd started as a busboy at the Aristo years ago. Now with a wife and five children to support, he was not about to jeopardize his position. But Pat could see he was aching to say something, so she decided to help him out.

"Those gargoyles looked really great on the facade of the Church of Santa Bárbara. They look kind of out of place here. Of course, that's just my personal opinion."

"They have a long history, these statues," Orlando murmured.

"Yes, well," Pat gave the man's hand a squeeze, "they'll outlast us all, you know that?" She took the mail behind the desk to the reservations office and sat

down to sort it, thinking once again that Santos understood a lot more than she gave him credit for. Give the
people pride in their tradition, he said, and it will spur
them on to bigger and better things. It was clear
Orlando agreed that using these gargoyles like so many
potted palms was a travesty. Well, she wouldn't stand
for it. She was going to set it straight. What she'd do
about the money Ted had given Father Luis, she had no
idea, but something would occur to her. Even if Santos
never spoke to her again, she was going to work—in
her own way—to take care of the problem.

Pat followed the signs toward Zihuatanejo, wondering exactly where she thought she was going. Santos
might throw her bodily out of his office if she showed
up there. And what would he do if he found her waiting
for him at his house when he got home that night? He'd
have to listen and hear her side of it. But she couldn't
do that, she thought as she steered the car toward the
road that led to the church. She had her own pride, and
she wasn't going to destroy every shred of integrity she
still had left just to satisfy her need for him.

She parked opposite the Church of Santa Bárbara
and sat there for a moment, staring at the bare facade.
Pieces of stonework lay around the front wall, testimo-
ny to the destruction that had gone on. It was just a
simple stucco chapel now, no less beautiful, but to Pat
is looked stripped and hurt. There was no reason for
this sort of thing!

She got out of the car and walked around to the side
of the church, hesitating for a brief moment before
ringing the rectory bell. In a moment, a young priest
wearing rimless glasses came to the door.

"Buenos días," he murmured.

"Buenos días. Por favor, dónde está Padre Luis?"

"Aquí. Mire." He opened the door further to reveal the rotund priest seated behind an enormous desk. He smiled and stood up when he saw her.

"Ah! The young woman from Massachusetts, am I correct?"

"You have a very good memory, Father Luis."

"As do you. Please, my child, have a seat. How may I help you?"

"I'm Pat Jessup—I'm sorry, I should have introduced myself long ago. I don't think I mentioned when we met before that I work in Ixtapa. At the Paradiso," she added pointedly.

"Ah?" The priest looked shocked and embarrassed.

"Yes, I work for Mr. Beckman. But, Father Luis, I had no idea he'd approached you about buying those Spanish gargoyles."

The priest threw up his hands and looked heavenward. "I cannot say I am pleased about what has occurred, but I felt it was the least I could do for my parish before I left."

"You're leaving?" Pat sat forward in her chair and gripped the arms hard.

"I am retiring to America. I requested a transfer so that I might live near my brother in Texas, and by the grace of God, I have been granted my prayers. In only three weeks I shall be gone, and Father Francisco will take over." He nodded to the young priest who was sitting and reading by the window.

"But those gargoyles belong here. They were intended for this church, not a hotel lobby."

"Of course, you are right, Miss Jessup. I am not proud of what I have done. But Mr. Beckman, he has been offering me more and more pesos each month.

181

Every time before, I have said no. But this time," he shrugged, "I was leaving, you see, and my people can use the cash." He gave her a shy smile.

"If I could get you the gargoyles back again—" she began.

"I am sorry, the money is already in the bank. It is allotted for the children, for medicine. I don't know . . ." His words trailed off and he looked away.

"Maybe you can have the money and the gargoyles too," she said hopefully, getting up to leave. "I don't have any great ideas yet, but I will, I promise you. It's important that you get those statues back, Father," she finished.

"Yes, the mayor said as much to me this morning."

"Santos was here?" she asked, already at the door.

"He was angry, very much so. I told him to pray for the preservation of the church—and I tell you to do the same." His tone clearly said that he didn't believe anything could be done.

"I'll think of something—before you leave for America, Father Luis," she promised as she rushed from the rectory. She had to talk to Santos; that was all she could think of. Together they would solve this thing.

The plaza across from the town hall was already filling up with people leaving their offices for the lunch break. She started up the steps, her eyes fixed on the sign that read *Mayor*.

"Are you busy?" She stood at the open doorway, her heart racing.

Santos raised his dark head from his desk and stared at her, his expression cold and unreadable. "I'm always busy. You're here on business?" he scowled sarcastically.

"No, actually," she admitted staunchly. "I want to

talk about us, and about what we can do together if we put our energies behind it."

He put down his pen slowly, and she felt the heat of his gaze on her body. Even in his anger, he couldn't check his inclinations. Every flicker of his eyelids told her he had not been able to get her out of his system. "We have nothing to discuss. Your precious career and your affiliation with Beckman make it impossible for me to love you as I had hoped I could."

Pat was stunned by his forthright declaration. He had never spoken of love directly before, and his flat toneless statement that there was no chance for it now was like a cold wind blowing over her. The fact that he was being honest for once did nothing to alleviate the dreadful chill.

"Well, I only want to talk to you about the church— about those gargoyles. I think we can do something."

He sighed and tilted his chair back, appraising her real interest in something that meant so much to him. "Come with me. We can talk upstairs."

He led her through the archway to a staircase. As they mounted the five flights, Pat could see the various offices of the town hall, now deserted at siesta time. At last they reached the top floor, a sort of storage area, and Santos reached up to pull a trapdoor down from the ceiling. They climbed to the roof on a small rickety ladder.

"I have fixed this up only recently—a respite from the noonday sun and crowds. I enjoy being here alone when everyone else has gone."

Pat looked down over the teeming city. Although the town hall was a small building by American standards, it towered over the one-story stucco structures of Zihuatanejo, and the only thing of comparable height was the tower of the Church of Santa Bárbara several blocks away. The broad canopy strung over the roof afforded some shelter from the blazing heat, and Pat settled herself on a lawn chair in the shade before daring to look at him again. He was perched on the one large piece of furniture he had evidently dragged up there: an old upholstered green chaise longue with curved ball feet.

"Now, you wanted to discuss the church?" he said, scanning the landscape before him.

"I've just been to see Father Luis," she began in a businesslike manner. "I'd like to think of a way to get those gargoyles back before he leaves the parish."

"Even he wants to go to America to seek his fortune," Santos nodded. "Where you come from the streets are paved with gold!" He turned on her, his eyes blazing.

"Will you come off it!" She got up and stalked over to him, determined not to let him get the better of her this time. "For heaven's sake, you ought to know me well enough by now to realize I could never condone anything like that. Ted didn't tell me about buying the gargoyles on purpose, Santos, because he knew I'd oppose the move and come running to tell you."

"Yes," he said evenly. "The words sound very good, Patricia, but I still have my wits about me. You work for the man. Why should you contradict his actions? He's giving you a fine job, the opportunity of a lifetime, with which any woman would be thrilled."

Pat wanted to shake him, to reach out and pound some sense into his thick stubborn head. "That's the whole ball of wax to you, isn't it? I'm a woman and I should know my place! Just think of me as a person, Santos, a person who cares about tradition and culture just as much as you do. Don't think of me as a woman."

184

Suddenly his face changed, and it was he who reached for her. "You ask the impossible," he whispered, and then his hands gripped her tightly around the waist. "I've tried so hard to escape you, but you're in my blood now. No matter what you do, no matter how much I should hate you, I find myself unable to. There is no logic to it, Pat, but I can't deny my need for you. I think you feel the same."

All her good intentions vanished as he pressed her in his arms and they tumbled together onto the chaise. He bent over her, his hard body molding her soft one just as he wished it. She was pliable in his arms and lost in a world where they had no arguments, no differences. His mouth sealed each of her eyelids shut with a cool kiss, and then he turned his attention to her right ear, running his tongue along the small furled hollow and then traveling on until he reached her mouth.

She no longer had to breathe, because he was filling her mouth and her senses with his own warm breath. Once she murmured, "Santos, this can't happen—not now," but she knew that she didn't mean the words. His hands explored the shape of her breasts and hips under the thin fabric of her skirt and T-shirt. Pat cursed herself for her weakness. What good was it to love a man who didn't love her in return? The passion, the heightened awareness of her needs and emotions, that was all worth something, of course, but where would this dizzy, intoxicating adventure end?

As he slowly unzipped her skirt and eased it off her, she threw caution away and gave herself utterly to the moment. If this was to be their last time together, she would enjoy it to the fullest. Her hands flew to help him out of his clothes, and when they were both naked, glistening with sweat in the heat of the day, they joined together greedily, hungering for the closeness that would blot out everything else. She burrowed her lips deep into the hollow of his neck and wrapped her arms around his strong back, corded with muscles. She lost herself in him and allowed him to lead, to prod her onward when she hesitated and hung back. Even after she had cried out her joy, he would not let her go, but insisted on giving her even more pleasure, bringing her to the peak once again and pushing her over to the other side. This time he went with her gladly, and it seemed to Pat that if the world had ended at that very moment, she would have been content.

They lay in each other's arms afterward, their bodies spent and loose in postures of exhaustion. And although she might have expected him to get up and leave her abruptly, he was actually unable to take his hands off her. They teased and delighted her, absently stroking the moisture from her tired limbs. When she rolled over to look into his face, she saw that he was smiling.

"How can there be any bad feelings left between us?" he mused. His gaze traveled the length of her naked body in frank admiration and she blushed with the private knowledge that even that brief look had inflamed her. She was ready for him again.

But they both knew it was growing late, and eventually, reluctantly, they sat up, still holding hands. Santos reached for the towel that covered one of the lawn chairs, and rubbed Pat dry. Then he did the same for himself. Her body felt burnished and kissed by the sun and the heat as well as by her lover. While she dressed, she allowed herself the luxury of watching Santos do the same. He was absolutely the most extraordinary man she'd ever laid eyes on, and she had to restrain herself from rushing over and peeling his clothes off after he got them on.

"Are you ready?" he asked when they stood in front of the trapdoor, about to reenter the world.

"I suppose," she shrugged.

He planted another kiss firmly on her mouth before they descended the ladder, but somehow she felt the closeness slipping away already. They had shared something undeniable, something more powerful than the tides and the sun, and still, they were as far apart as they had been before.

Pat climbed down the ladder with a sad sigh. Nothing had changed; she was still in love, and a lot of good that did her.

She wasn't in a very good mood when she stalked into Ted's office the next morning. "I've gotten back one hundred questionnaires in the past week, Ted," Pat slammed the sheaf of papers down on her employer's desk, "and I want you to read every single one of them. We have kudos on room service, cleanliness, the food, the nightclub acts. Oh, a few grumbles here and there, but basically it's an A-rating. With one glaring exception." She sat on the edge of his desk and glowered at him.

"Oh? What's the problem?"

"Those seven ugly gargoyles in the lobby, that's what. Unanimous and unequivocal disapproval from the guests. I rest my case. You and your hotshot sense of taste."

Ted smiled and leaned back in his chair. "I've already paid the church for them, Pat. Now, where are they going to get that kind of money to buy them back? And you and I both decided a month ago that the lobby looked bare. You come up with an alternative and let me know." He turned back to the mountain of drawings and plans scattered over his desk.

"I've got one already," she said smugly, "and I'm astounded you didn't think of it first."

"Yes?"

"Ted, Zihuatanejo has more brilliant sculptors and artisans than you can shake a stick at. You can commission them to do whatever you want for your precious lobby, in exchange for putting the gargoyles back on the church facade. The pride they take in their parish will make it more than worth their while to do the job for you."

Ted batted a pencil playfully on top of her hand. "Pride, huh? You sound just like Mayor Ribera."

Pat gritted her teeth and forced herself to be calm. "Well, what about it?"

"I kind of like those statues; I don't know. Tell you what, I'll think about it." He grabbed the telephone receiver, clearly indicating that Pat was dismissed.

"You just want to keep the gargoyles out of spite, don't you?" she said. "Because it burns Santos up."

"I think you've lost your objectivity, Pat," he said in a condescending tone. "Just because he's giving you a little action—"

"Oh, for heaven's sake!" She stormed out of his office in shock, realizing, even as she hurried away, that by not answering him, she'd let him win.

She returned to her office to work on the staff schedules for the next week, but her mind wasn't on it. Ted's crass, rude comment was only half of it.

She acknowledged that her whole complaint before she'd come to Mexico was that her life was dull and predictable. Now it was the complete opposite. The trouble was, she was never ready for each new cog that slipped in between the wheels. They always caught her off guard.

But no amount of experience could have prepared her for the shock she got when she drove into Zihuatanejo that afternoon. She was on her way to the church to see Father Luis about hiring some artisans when, on impulse, she turned into the municipal plaza instead. She was drawn as if by a magnet to the door with the sign saying "Mayor" over it.

Santos was pacing his office like an angry tiger, raging at his assistant, a small young man with an uneven mustache and glasses. He was yelling so fast, it was difficult for Pat to make out the idiomatic Spanish. But when he saw her, he dismissed the man immediately.

"So good of you to drop by," he snarled, his white teeth bared in a grimace. She had never seen him like this before. It wasn't at all like the day he'd come to scream at Ted. Now his anger was fueled by bitterness and scorn, and it was devastating.

"What in God's name is going on?" Pat asked, keeping her distance.

"I have just learned that you and I are on opposite sides of the battlefield. You have lied to me with your body and your heart."

"Oh, don't be so dramatic. Tell me what you're talking about," she demanded.

"You are no better than one of the first conquistadors who came here bent on raping Zihuatanejo and robbing her of her beauty."

"Look, I have the whole thing under control, Santos. The gargoyles will be back on the Church of Santa Bárbara within a week. If you'd give me half a chance, I'd explain—"

"The church! You think that is my main concern now? How naive do you expect me to be, Patricia?"

She threw up her hands in exasperation. "All right, now what *is* your main concern?"

"Ah, the classic woman's ploy: play innocent!"

"I'm not playing innocent, damn you. I honestly don't know—"

"You don't know that Mr. Beckman is planning to build a new Paradiso here in Zihuatanejo? Is *that* what you don't know?" He came to her and loomed over her. For a moment, she was genuinely frightened.

"Are you mad? He's building in Mazatlán, Santos. I told you that."

"You told me *wrong!*" He grabbed her hand and squeezed it until the knuckles were white. "The Royale, madam. He's made an offer to finish the Royale, the hotel that no one else was ever able to complete."

"You mean," Pat stammered, "you mean the place you showed me in between La Ropa and Las Gatas? The one the Europeans abandoned?"

"Exactly. He let it be known around that his plans were for Mazatlán, so as not to raise any hackles unnecessarily before his deal was signed and sealed. That German Dorfmann is the backer, and he has money to burn on this hotel. Twenty-five stories, three restaurants, two pools—it will take up that entire stretch of land between the beaches. He even plans to put a huge dock there with tennis courts out over the water. Beautiful, no?" he sneered, finally releasing her hand. "The new Paradiso will be a tremendous scar on the bay!"

Pat swallowed hard and rubbed her bruised hand. "How do you know all this?" she breathed.

"I have a friend at FONATUR. Naturally Beckman must submit all plans to them to get clearance, and when my friend received them, she sent me copies.

Here, look for yourself." He tossed a manila envelope at Pat. Not daring to hope that this was all a terrible mistake, she pried open the clip and took out a sheaf of architect's drawings.

This was no mistake. The renderings and reduced blueprints clearly stated their intention to build a new Paradiso in Zihuatanejo, a huge glass monolith stuck into the cliff with blocklike auxiliary buildings scattered around it. Pat was appalled as she examined the drawings, but something looked oddly familiar about them. The floor plan, the hotel built into the cliff— these were the plans Ted had shown her in his office, the ones he'd said were for Mazatlán. No wonder he had lied to her about his new hotel!

"Why, that lousy con!" Pat was infuriated. "He was lying through his teeth. Santos, for God's sake, you've got to believe that I knew nothing about this. It was just like with the gargoyles. He lied to me by not saying a thing!"

Santos stood before her, breathing heavily, his eyes trying to pierce her soul to divine the truth. When he didn't answer her, she went on softly, "If you ever felt anything for me, if our lovemaking meant something other than simple animal attraction, you will listen to me now. We've got to stop this thing—and we have to do it together." She was practically begging, but her pride meant nothing now. All that was important was that she convince him.

"I no longer know what to believe, or what is right," he said finally, turning to the window with a sigh. His normally erect frame was bent, and despair registered in his whole body. "You can never appreciate what that man has done to me or to my people."

"No," she admitted, coming over to stand beside

him. "That's very true, I can't. But it doesn't stop me from wanting to help. Santos, I'm on your side—all the way."

"A lot of good it will do," he muttered. She had never seen him this vulnerable, and it cut her to the quick. Her heart went out to him, and she longed to embrace him, to hold him in her arms and assure him that everything would be all right. But how could she make such a wild promise?

"If FONATUR stands behind Beckman, there is nothing you or I can do to stop him. The man has money and power, and a kind of determination that moves mountains." He gave a scornful laugh. "You have to admire him for that."

Pat touched his sleeve hesitantly and when he didn't pull away, she let her hand lie there, trying to transmit her love and concern through the thin barrier of his shirt. "We have determination too. His entrepreneurial spirit has gone too far this time. We can fight, I know we can."

Santos turned and gave her a look of disbelief. "I want to believe you, but I've lived in Mexico too long to think that I can stop the encroachment of the developers. They've always won, and they'll continue to do so. You're naive to think otherwise."

"Listen," she suggested quickly, feeling guilty by association with her employer and his kind. "Why don't we take a ride out to the Royale? I want to see it up close. I have a lot of influence with Ted," she went on, grabbing at straws. "Maybe I can change his mind about going ahead with this. And if I can't," she added when Santos looked at her skeptically, "then I want to get a bead on where to lay the detonator as soon as he's finished building."

She'd wanted to make him laugh, but she only

succeeded in deepening his anguish. "It seems hopeless to me," he shrugged. "But if you want, I'll take you there. It may be the last time to see it as it is."

"Santos—" she began, but he cut her off.

"Your attitude is so American," he said sorrowfully. "You aren't the villain, Pat—I don't think I ever believed that you were—but you have such dreams! None of them can ever come true."

She followed him out the door of his office, choking back the tears that threatened to overcome her. He was right, of course. She had come to Mexico dreaming of a new life, a new job, a wonderful man, and each triumph had only led to disillusionment. Her dreams were foolish and counted for nothing. The only thing remaining now was her love for Santos Ribera, and even that seemed shattered, gone for good.

They drove out to Las Gatas in silence, and after they parked, they got out and walked down the long flight of steps to the beach. But this time, he made no move toward her. The touch of his hands as he bent to take off her sandals came back to her in a flood of memory, and she was even sadder than she'd been before.

Santos greeted an old man, who was sitting in the shade by the docks, watching the moored boats, and asked him if he could borrow his dinghy for an hour. The old man agreed readily, so they climbed into the small motorboat, and Santos pulled the cord to start the engine.

"You can get a better view of the Royale from the water, and if Beckman's people are there now, we'll just speed away without stopping." He pulled away from the dock, and soon the little craft was skipping and bouncing over the turbulent waves. Pat held onto the gunwales for dear life as the spray hit her in the face

193

and soaked her hair and clothes. On any other day, on any other occasion, Pat would have thoroughly enjoyed this outing with Santos, but today everything had changed. She couldn't quell her feelings of dread as they drove toward the Royale site.

It was a short ride. The unfinished hotel was exactly halfway between Las Gatas and La Ropa. There was a modest concrete dock, and beyond that, the skeletal Royale set up on huge pylons. What was to be the lobby was nearly completed and actually looked quite attractive, with high arches that sculpted the front of the building and overlooked the bay. A multilevel fieldstone deck caressed the side of the cliff from the lobby down to the dock. As they putted up alongside, Pat could see that the original plan for the Royale had been an excellent one. Nothing seemed outlandish or out of character with the natural beauty of the place. Ted's monolith, however, would be more than an eyesore. It would be a constant reminder to the people of Zihuatanejo that their town was no longer their own.

"I don't see anyone around. Want to get out and walk?" Pat asked. The surf tossed their boat gently as Santos stood up and reached for the post with their tie line. Without a word, he got out of the boat and helped her up. Their hands touched only briefly, but it was as though an electric spark had jumped between them.

"This could be a beautiful little resort," Pat commented. "Someone with brains and creativity could do a hotel something like the Pelicanos, actually. Do you know what the original developers had in mind?"

He strolled past her along the dock. "A restaurant was going to sit on top of the structure that's here now. Not too high up. The rooms were to be in three two-story buildings set into the cliff."

"Sounds very nice. And sensible," Pat nodded, walking beside him.

"Yes. I opposed the project at the time because the developers were foreigners. But I'd welcome them back with open arms now." Santos spoke wistfully, his sad eyes never leaving the unfinished Royale.

"But you never fought Kurt. He's a foreigner," she pointed out.

"Well, whether you believe it or not, I've learned a thing or two in the past few years. Yes, I was wary of him, but he proved himself a true friend and a member of the community. Nationality does not always matter. It's what's inside a man that counts for me."

Pat bit back the angry words she longed to hurl at him. He'd just castigated her for being "so American," and now he was saying that nationality wasn't the deciding factor when he chose his friends. "I take it this spot holds memories for you," she said, starting up the deck leading toward the lobby.

"As a boy, I used to swim over here from La Ropa."

"From La Ropa! That's a long way in a strong current," she marveled.

"Almost a mile. I did it to build stamina, to make myself a man," he laughed. "Then, I'd hurl myself into a wave about to break on the rock so that I could climb up. I was nearly killed several times, but I kept coming back for more. Try to tell a fifteen-year-old boy that something is dangerous!" He sat on the side of the deck and she squatted beside him on her heels.

"You were an idiot," she said softly and tenderly.

He turned on her for making fun of him, but then a more important thought struck him, wiping the frown from his face. He gripped her by both arms and forced her down beside him.

195

"Beckman evidently wants you to manage this new hotel. His offer for the Mazatlán job, I am sure, still holds here."

"Ted Beckman can go to hell," she said flatly, looking out toward the pounding waves.

"Are you saying you will not accept the position if it is offered? All that money, Patricia. And the position! Once you have managed a hotel down here, you can go back to America and name your salary. You can start a hotel of your own and create it exactly as you want it. Some lovely spot on Cape Cod, perhaps, or in the mountains of Vermont, or by the water in California. You'll forget all about this."

She listened to him, dumbfounded. "You really don't know anything about me, do you? You persist in believing that I'm just an ambitious American woman, set on conquering the world."

He shook his head. "That's not all of you."

"That's not any of me," she practically shouted. "Listen to me and get this straight because I'm not going to repeat it. If Beckman thinks he can keep me here after he tricked me, he's as mistaken about me as you are. I could never work for a liar and a con man, nor could I go along with his notion about destroying the bay. He's undermined the authority he gave me in my present position, Santos. Why should he behave any differently in the future?"

"Then what will you do?" He looked at her almost pleadingly, hoping she would have some solution to the problem. She racked her brain for an answer, an alternative plan she could submit to Ted and to FONATUR, but she came up blank. Ted would never want any part of a tasteful little resort. It wasn't his style, and it would be small potatoes compared to the business he could take in at a huge hotel. It would also take him that much longer to get a return on his investment, and it was doubtful that Herr Dorfmann would wait indefinitely for his money.

And what was she going to do about her own situation? If she resigned from the Paradiso and severed all connections with Ted, as she wanted to, she'd probably have to leave the area. Beckman's influence was considerable in Ixtapa, and in most of the Pacific coast resort towns. If anyone would be vindictive about her leaving and going on to another job, it would be Ted Beckman. Loyalty in his employees was practically a requirement, and his feelings for her weren't all professional either. The fact that he knew about her relationship with Santos ate at him. Undoubtedly if she quit, the first words out of his mouth would be, "I'll see to it that you'll never work again."

And then the final blow: moving away from Santos. It didn't matter that he had told her he couldn't love her, because the bond between them now, forged of passion and anger, could not be broken. How could she ever live without him? He might drive her away, but she could never leave of her own accord.

Pat looked over at the man she felt so much for. He was waiting for an answer, and she had none to offer. "I don't know what I'll do," she finally told him. "The only thing I'm certain of is that I'll fight Beckman every step of the way."

Santos shrugged and got to his feet. "What if we both fight him? It's still a losing battle, Patricia."

"It doesn't mean we should give up." She couldn't believe Santos was going to knuckle under without a fight. But he looked so defeated, as though he realized he had just met his match, and it was useless to go on. This was not the man she had fallen in love with, and she longed to do something that would restore his fire.

197

"Let's get out of here," she urged him. "It's depressing sitting around looking at it."

"I could do with some coffee," he said shortly as he marched down to the dock and the moored dinghy. "Do you mind stopping at my house after we return the boat?"

"Of course not." She followed him down and let him help her into the small craft. The tide had changed in that brief time, and now they had to fight the current. The waves swelled and crashed behind them on the jagged rocks under the Royale. Even the ocean seemed to be angry at the proposed resort, and it matched the mood of the two tortured souls tossed about in the little boat.

Chapter Twelve

Santos drove at breakneck speed to his house, but Pat didn't complain. She liked the reckless feeling, the impulsive careening around corners and up hills. The ride was over too soon, and they climbed out of the car in silence.

Santos walked up the path ahead of her, immersed in his own thoughts, and when she caught up to him, he was routing El Presidente from a cluster of flowering bushes.

"*Caramba!* I cannot keep you from bringing home these lizards!"

El Presidente was crowing in triumph at his latest catch, and Pat couldn't help but laugh at the nasty old cat holding a squirming chameleon in his mouth.

"Do not bite down, for heaven's sake!" Santos bent down and tried to pry the lizard from his mouth.

"He's a real terror," Pat commented. "I think we should sic him on Ted."

Santos gave El Presidente a smack on the rump, and the cat finally dropped his prey with a growl of defeat. The poor lizard scurried off into the brush. El Presidente looked up at his master in annoyance.

"You're a menace to the neighborhood," Santos stormed, and the cat grunted back as though he understood.

"We used to have a mouser like him at home," Pat laughed. "My father used to complain that it ate more fish than he could catch in a week."

Santos glanced over at her, and a fleeting smile crossed his face. He opened the door of his house and ushered her inside. The place smelled fresh and woodsy, as though sage were growing in every room.

"How is your father?" Santos asked gently, leading her to the raised kitchen area and offering her a seat at the counter.

Pat gave him a rueful smile. "You'll never believe this, but I just invited him and my mom down here. It was Ruth's idea, actually, and it seemed great at the time. Oh, he's physically okay, but his spirits were really low, and we both thought maybe a vacation would be good for him. I even had some crazy idea about finding him a house in Zihuatanejo. It looks a lot like Gloucester, you know, and I figured if he couldn't ever go back to work, and if I was going to stay down here . . ." She let the sentence trail off.

Stantos put a handful of beans in his hand-cranked coffee grinder and started turning, meeting the resistance they offered with powerful strokes. "But now you may not stay," he murmured.

She looked into his face, trying to read the expression. But it was cold, unfeeling. Did he care at all whether she left Mexico? When he'd finished the beans and went to put the kettle on, she decided it was unfair to expect emotional reactions from him today on any subject other than the Royale.

"How's your mother?" she asked him suddenly.

"Oh, she is well, busy as usual. Tucked away in the hills as she is, she rarely sees what is happening to the little village where she grew up. And I am glad for that. I would not wish to have her share my disillusionment. That is something I must keep to myself."

She let her breath out slowly, totally exasperated with his martyr-like attitude. "You can share it with somebody who's on your side, you know. It's not only *your* pain, Santos. It belongs to all your people—your whole constituency. And believe it or not, it even belongs to some of us who have grown to love Zihuatanejo."

"What do you know about it?" he asked angrily, turning his back on her to set out mugs and a pitcher of cold milk.

"I know what I feel, damn it. Don't shut me out." She slipped off the bar stool and came around to his side of the counter. Still, she was nervous about how he would react, so she didn't touch him, although she longed to.

"I'm so confused, Pat," he admitted, leaning heavily on the counter top. "So much has changed in my life."

"And in mine," she assured him. "Which only goes to show that neither of us can turn back now. Something new and different is sure to happen tomorrow and things will change again."

She placed a hand lightly on his shoulder, but he didn't turn around. Then she brought her other hand up and, at a total loss as to what might make him feel better, she began to massage his back and shoulder blades. At first he was rigid and unresponsive, but after a few minutes he sighed and moved his head around in a circle.

"Yes, yes, that is good," he told her. "There is so much tension in my body. I feel close to exploding."

"Then lie down—I'll give you a real rubdown. Good for what ails you," she added gaily when he looked doubtful.

"Perhaps." He turned back toward her, and together they walked down into the living room. He sprawled on the thick woven rug on his stomach, and she knelt beside him, her hands already working on the knitted muscles of his neck. At her touch, he relaxed slightly, and his strong masculine body accepted her ministrations.

"You'll get more out of this if you take off your shirt," she suggested hesitantly. He did as she asked and lay down again.

The sight of his bare back and torso was enormously exciting to her. It brought back memories of those other times when they lay together in each other's arms. The touch of his warm, tanned skin was like an aphrodisiac, inflaming her heart and her senses. But now, all she wanted to do was give him solace, to ease away some of the pain.

The sound of the kettle whistling brought her back to reality. She got to her feet to silence it. "You want coffee now?" she asked.

"No," he answered in a muffled voice. "Come back here."

She turned off the light under the burner and walked back to him. He was propped up on one elbow, stroking El Presidente, who was evidently jealous of all the attention his master was getting. The cat did a little dance in a circle, arching his back and rubbing his head against Santos's hand. When Pat approached them, Santos reached for her and pulled her down.

"Now you," he commanded. "Lie down."

She settled herself on her stomach and closed her eyes as his hands lightly caressed her back. It was torture to submit calmly to this without being able to do anything or touch him in return.

"You will get more out of this if you take off your shirt," he breathed, repeating her words.

Before she could respond, he was tugging her T-shirt out of her jeans and stripping it off over her head. When she lay down again, he undid the hooks of her brassiere and slipped the straps from her shoulders.

"Better," he whispered thickly, his hands working her flesh as a sculptor does clay. Pat's breath came in short gasps as she realized where this would inevitably lead. It was clear that the two of them needed one another now. This was different from the other times they had made love. It lacked the wild passion of their earlier sessions, but that heat had been replaced by a deep intensity, a desire to soothe all the hurt that the world had inflicted.

He rolled her over on her back and covered her body with his own, and she moaned as her breasts received the pressure of his muscular chest. Her nipples were hard and sensitive to each subtle brush of the mixed black and copper hair on his torso. His fingers grasped at her long hair, which lay tousled around her like an open fan.

"Pat," he sighed before he kissed her.

She was lost in that kiss, as was he. It seemed to go on forever, and it carried them both away from the problems that had separated them only a few moments ago. His mouth was unyielding, his tongue exploring every private space. Wrapping his arms around her, he drew her up from the floor to meet his insistent demand. He asked everything from her and she gave willingly, somehow aware that, if this wasn't love, if he didn't really care about her, she would know it by his touch.

His hands went lower on her body, and she knew she didn't have the power to stop him as he unzipped her jeans and eased them off her slim form. Even as he laid her naked beneath him, he kissed her again, reassuring her with his force and his passion.

Only a kernel of doubt remained in her, but she couldn't seem to rid herself of the nagging sensation. Why *did* she give in so easily, why was she his for the asking? Of course, he was attractive, but so were many other men. It had to do with the challenge, with the immediate friction that sparked between them even when they so much as glanced at one another.

His kisses traveled from her mouth in a burning path, past the hollow of her throat to her breasts, which arched up to meet him. Slowly and languorously, he let his tongue inscribe the circle of one rose-colored nipple, and then it trailed across to perform the same delicious service for the other.

Her mind clouded with desire, she was barely able to think straight. And yet, she wondered whether she wasn't doing exactly the same thing she had done once before. With Steve. Oh, it was easier to deny him, because sex never really entered into the scenario. But she had allowed herself just so much freedom with one man before and realized that she had nearly jeopardized her integrity, her sense of herself as a whole woman.

And in a way, wasn't it the same with Ted? He admired her, treated her as an equal in business, but still he would never give up until he had molded her into his vision of a professional. She'd only recently started fighting, and she was pleased with herself for standing up to him.

But if she was to have any kind of pride in herself, she finally decided, she was going to have to stand up to Santos as well. She couldn't simply bend to his will every time he gave her the devastating glance that turned her blood to fire and her limbs to jelly. If there really was more than lust between them, she would have to end this now, before it went too far.

"No," she gasped finally, pulling herself reluctantly from his grasp.

Santos looked at her as though she must be out of her mind. He was breathing heavily, and she could feel the unmistakable evidence of his excitement about to take over.

"Not this way." She shook her head sadly and pulled herself up to a sitting position. But she made no attempt to cover herself or do more than move her body so that it was not in direct contact with his.

"I don't understand you. Not at all." His look was stern and there was more than a hint of disappointment in his eyes. She could see she'd hurt him deeply by pulling away.

"We can't always lose ourselves in wild abandon every time something goes wrong, Santos," she explained, getting up to walk away from him—as far away as she could get. "There's got to be more to it than this."

"You can't deny that you enjoy my kisses, my touch," he said in a demanding tone. "Every fiber of your body cries out for me. You're like a small candle igniting into a bonfire." He walked up behind her, about to touch her again.

"Listen to me," she insisted, turning to ward him off

with her outstretched hands. "If we don't get a few things cleared up between us, then sex won't mean anything, don't you see? I'm serious about this," she added when he seemed about to protest.

At last, he nodded. Even though he had no idea what was going on with her, he respected her enough to listen. He reached down and picked up his shirt, which he then thrust at her. "At least put this on," he said. "I can't hear your words when I look at your body."

She smiled and did as he asked, buttoning the shirt all the way up. He was so tall, the long blue chambray tail flapped beneath Pat's bare thighs.

"I'd like some coffee—I don't know about you," she muttered, walking back to the kitchen to turn up the heat under the kettle. He dressed and took a seat on the sofa, while she went about arranging the pitcher of milk and two mugs on a tray, and not a word was said until the kettle whistled loudly and broke the silence.

"Okay." Pat poured the water through the filter and set the coffeepot on the tray beside the other items. "Let's talk."

She settled herself far away from him on the couch, and while she poured them each a cup, El Presidente hopped up between them, lying down, with a loud *"Meow,"* beside his master, who scratched the old cat's head obligingly.

"What I want to say is that I've been wracking my brain about those gargoyles, and I figured out what to do about them. Now you tell me Ted's about to ruin your town, and I'm just as broken up about it as you are, but you won't grant me that. I feel like I'm getting a bum rap, Santos."

"Bum rap?" he repeated. "This is an idiom I never learned at school."

"You're giving me a raw deal. You lump me with all

the other Americans, all the other foreigners who've ever walked into Zihuatanejo. Can't you see that it's possible for me to want to work in the hotel business and *also* to preserve the beauty of a lovely place? Hotels and beauty are not mutually exclusive, you know. Look at the Pelicanos."

"That is the only example you can give," Santos scoffed, pouring himself a second cup of coffee. "Nobody understands."

"Oh, you're such a . . ." She threw up her hands in exasperation. "You think that if you don't solve the world's problems all by yourself, it's something to be ashamed of. You haven't even asked me what I intend to do about the gargoyles."

"Yes?" he asked rather reluctantly.

"I'm going to get Ted to request that the artisans of Zihuatanejo design something original for his stupid lobby. Those statues were intended for the church, and they're going back to the church."

"So you say," he muttered.

"Santos, I've done a guest survey. They all hate the gargoyles in the lobby! Do you think Ted would stand in the way of public opinion?"

He shrugged, then looked at her intently. "That's not a bad idea, actually. It might be an excellent forum for the artists. They could sell their work right at the Paradiso if there was a demand."

"See?" she laughed, relaxing back against the cushions. "So you give me some credit for having a brain—and a heart?"

He grimaced and suddenly got very busy scratching El Presidente's ears. He was embarrassed; he wasn't used to being proved wrong. "And about the Royale?" he asked without looking at her.

"No idea yet, but give me time," she shrugged. "Do

207

you know the proverb, 'Where there's a will, there's a way'?"

"This I do know," he admitted, getting up and walking over to the window. But she could tell by the slump of his shoulders that the problem was weighing on him.

"You better not give up," she challenged him. "What would your father do if he were alive? Just imagine you're fighting him instead of Ted Beckman, and I bet the solution will pop into your mind."

He turned around and looked at her curiously. "How did you know I was thinking about him?" he asked gravely.

"Because," she said, coming to stand beside him, "I'm getting to know you a little bit, Santos. You're still a mystery a lot of the time, but the big things about you are becoming a little clearer."

He smiled faintly, and she saw that he had a new appreciation for her. In fact, he saw her as a person now, and he never had before. She had succeeded.

"Are you rushing back to the office?" she asked. "Or could I persuade you to take the afternoon off?" She placed her hand on his shoulder and slowly, tentatively, stood on her toes so that she could reach his mouth. To his astonishment, she kissed him long and hard.

"But you said—?" He looked at her questioningly.

"That was before. It's different now."

He gave her a quizzical look, but he drew her close, into the warm circle of his bare arms. "Women," he muttered as he buried his face in her hair.

She undid his belt buckle and tugged at the zipper of his pants. They fell to the floor and he sighed with pleasure as he reached under the big shirt to feel her naked body once again.

"I may remove this now?" he asked tenderly, and

when she nodded, he simply drew the garment over her head.

He lifted her in his arms and carried her to the bedroom, shutting the door just before El Presidente could bound ahead of them. He sat down and looked into her face deeply and intently. "I have never felt this way before," he murmured, poised on one knee over her.

"I haven't either," she confessed, reaching for him. Together they tumbled over and over on the bed, hugging like two children who have just discovered one another's friendship. But then the touches grew less innocent and more passionate. She moved to accommodate him, their limbs all tangled. Still kissing her, he entered her swiftly, and she gave a small cry of delight. He was so dear to her now, so precious. She tightened her grip around him and he smiled, responding to her every subtle suggestion.

They rocked together and then, because neither wanted the experience to end, they lay very still, counting one another's heartbeats. She could feel him pulse within her, a constant reminder of his potent desire for her. When finally neither could stand it another moment, they began to move again, slowly at first, and then with increasing tempo and furious insistence. Together they drove toward the brink, then paused and went further. All she could feel was the love shining inside her, a love she would never again try to vanquish. It was as much a part of her as her arm or hand, and so firmly fixed throughout her life that she could no longer tell when it had entered her and made its home in her heart.

When she cried out, he smiled with satisfaction and only allowed her a moment's respite before starting the dance again. It was all a blur when he joined her in that wild dive into oblivion. Even when she opened her eyes moments later to see her lover, flushed and exhausted, gasping beside her, she had no idea how she'd arrived at this point.

But she had arrived, and he had come with her. United as they were, nothing could stop them now.

Pat prepared herself mentally and emotionally before walking into Ted's office the next morning. She was dying to throw something at him, scream at the top of her lungs at him, but she realized that neither of these tactics would get her anywhere. So she'd confront him with his lies, she'd rail at him about the lousy thing he wanted to do; he'd only shrug in his charming boyish way and apologize with some lame excuse about preparing her properly for the job of her lifetime. He'd be ingratiating and effusive, and he wouldn't listen to a damn thing she said.

After much debate with herself, she picked the approach that usually worked with him. Logic and rationality would see her through the meeting. She would point out all the reasons why a big hotel in Zihuatanejo would be sure to fail; she would mention marketing surveys and FONATUR's computer studies. As for his lure of the nonexistent job in Mazatlán, she wouldn't even mention it. She would also be prepared for him to drag Santos into the conversation. Why should she try to hide it now? Her feelings were clear, and there was no sense even pretending anymore.

Just as she had hoped, she found Ted sipping his morning coffee beside the pool at one of the wrought iron tables. He was wearing white shorts and a white knit shirt, and a tennis racquet was lying on the table next to his coffee cup. Perfect, Pat thought as she approached him. He wasn't in a working mood if he was about to play a set of tennis, so maybe she could catch him off guard.

Pouring herself a cup of coffee for sustenance, she strolled over to his table, a rather insincere smile plastered on her face.

"Morning, Ted. Mind if I join you?" The sounds of giggling kids pushing one another in the pool distracted her momentarily. "That bunch from Woonsocket got an early start," she commented.

"Me too," he nodded. "I wanted to get in a few games before buckling down this morning, and now my partner appears to have stood me up."

"I hardly ever see you play tennis," she said.

"I'm not very good, I admit. I used to be better, but work got in the way, and I'm pretty rusty now. But I like to get out on the court every once in a while and smash a few balls. Nothing like it for getting out the aggressions, you know."

"Um, I know," Pat commented, thinking to herself that she'd like nothing better than to smash a few balls on her employer's thick head. She wondered if his aggressions stemmed from anything in particular. Actually, he seemed awfully relaxed and self-confident this morning.

Enough waffling, Pat. Let him have it, she told herself as he drained his cup. "Ted, I'd like you to know that I heard about your plans to build on the Royale site in Zihuatanejo," she stated flatly.

He didn't flinch, nor did a flicker of surprise show in his broad, handsome face. "Word certainly does get around," he said evenly. "May I ask who told you?"

She thought carefully about her answer. If she told him the truth, he'd undoubtedly accuse her of fraternizing with the enemy, and that wouldn't gain her any points with Ted Beckman. But if she lied, then she was just playing his game. Sooner or later he'd probably find out, because there weren't too many other people who would have known. Besides, she was tired of concealing her true sentiments about the man she loved. It was about time she just came out and admitted her feelings. If she hid them any longer, Ted would only decide that it had been a conspiracy later, when he put all the pieces together.

"Protecting your source?" Ted asked sarcastically.

"No." Pat looked directly at him. "Santos told me."

"Oh . . . I see." He nodded, and a strange gleam came into his eyes. He gave her a wry grin, as if to say, "All's fair in love and war—and the war has just begun."

But Pat would not be intimidated by him. "Don't you think Zihuatanejo is the wrong place for a big hotel?"

"Did he put you up to this?" Ted countered. His voice was very calm, almost methodical.

"Certainly not," she snapped back. "And I'm insulted that you would even ask. Listen, Ted, I've been in Mexico a little while now, and thanks to you, I've had an opportunity to get really good at my job. When you tell me about a project, I think I generally come up with useful input. What does FONATUR say about all this anyway? It doesn't sound like their kind of deal. An isolated resort in a small town—"

"Not isolated. Ixtapa is only three miles away. And the Royale is just the beginning, Pat. That hotel is the tip of the iceberg. My long-term plans involve extending the Ixtapa strip all the way over there."

"Amazing," she stated flatly, so that he could not miss her disapproval.

"Come on, level with me. You don't have to play games. Santos sent his girlfriend to do his dirty work, right?"

Pat kept her rage under control. She knew he was only doing this to get the upper hand. "My feelings for him, or anyone for that matter, have nothing to do with my professional assessment."

"You're absolutely right," he agreed readily, leaning across the table. "And professionally, I don't believe you know the score yet. The Royale is a great place for a second Paradiso."

"Ted, Zihuatanejo is an entirely different kind of resort. It attracts a different clientele. If you extend Ixtapa over there, you're losing one whole market."

"Small potatoes," he scoffed. "Frankly, Pat, I'm not interested in the kind of tourist who wants to get away from it all. There's no money to be made on people who aren't into nightlife, shopping, etc. And small hotels make small profits. They're hardly worth the effort, Pat," he smiled sympathetically. "I'm surprised at you. That's one of the first lessons they should have taught you at Cornell. Maybe you need a refresher course."

She stood up, gathering all her resources. "School only teaches you the fundamentals, Ted. There's nothing like life experience to give you an appreciation for how it really works. And I see Zihuatanejo very differently from you. Honestly, I think tourists will too. Big spenders will find it boring."

"Not so, sweetheart." He tilted his chair back and locked his fingers behind his head, squinting at her. "Once I pioneer the area, the ground will be broken for other developers. In ten years these two towns will comprise the biggest resort area in Mexico, with fatter revenues than Cozumel and Cancún put together. We'll have shuttle boats running twenty-four hours a day between the towns. There'll be restaurants and all kinds of diversions—shops and games—on every beach and cove between here and there. I figure eventually we'll have to lobby to change the name to eliminate the confusion of the two places. I was thinking about Zixtapo as a catchy hybrid."

Pat grabbed the back of the chair and held onto it for dear life, willing herself not to explode. "I wish you'd leveled with me before, Ted. Your dream is quite extraordinary. I didn't know you'd gone this far. To turn an unspoiled paradise into Las Vegas!" She shook her head in wonder and disgust.

"I'm beginning to hear the good mayor's words spouting out of you, Pat. You wouldn't have come here to work if you'd felt that way yourself."

"Well, he's taught me a lot, and I took it from there. And it is now my firm belief that Zihuatanejo should be preserved."

He looked extremely disappointed, as though up to this point he'd been certain he could sway her opinion. "You're cutting your own throat, of course."

"What do you mean?" Pat asked defensively. Here it comes, she thought. I'm fired.

"I still think you're the best person for the job. I want you to manage my new Paradiso. Not in Mazatlán, as I originally thought of it, but right around the corner in Zihuatanejo."

"You never had any intention of building in Mazatlán, did you? How fortunate for you that I didn't agree when you offered to take me up there to see the site."

Ted shrugged, rather pleased with his own ruse. "I didn't think there was much chance of your going anywhere overnight with me, but I felt it was the right thing to ask, at least. You see, Ruth told me you were spending a lot of your free time in Zihuatanejo, so I didn't want to spring anything on you before you were ready. And it was obvious to me as far back as that dinner party for Dorfmann that you and Ribera had eyes for each other." He said this with some regret, and Pat realized suddenly that Ted had always felt more for her than a boss should for an employee. At any other time, she might have felt sorry for him.

"Well, that's the reason I lied. You would have turned my offer down flat if you'd known where I wanted to build."

"And what makes you think I won't turn it down now?" she asked angrily.

"Because, sweetheart," Ted said, rising from his chair and coming around to her side of the table, "because you're a real smart girl. When you look at the bottom line, your personal life is going to take a backseat to your career. I know you." He grasped her by both arms and whirled her around to face him. She pulled away, but he was too strong for her. "No, I'm sure you'll come around. I figured I'd make it easy on you and keep you from making a rash decision you'd regret later. Once you have a chance to give my offer some serious thought, I know you won't refuse it."

"You seem pretty sure of that."

"Well, am I wrong?" His green eyes were searching, trying to get behind her real emotions.

She stood there, aching to tell him to go to hell. Why didn't she just quit right now? she asked herself. She opened her mouth to speak, but then she thought of her father. "Never be a quitter, Patricia," he'd often said to her when she'd told him she wanted to leave the Magnolia Breakers. "It boots you naught to quit. Let 'em throw you out on your ear, if they've a mind to. Then it's *their* fault."

Of course, he was right. It would be much easier for her to fight Ted's expansion into Zihuatanejo from inside his empire, where she could keep an eye on him. And she realized now that he had no intention of firing her; he wanted her for his own. She was a prize, a conquest, something else that he could win from Santos if he worked at it, if he planned it and fussed over it as he had the architectural drawings for the new Paradiso.

As much as the notion of being his pawn in this game aggravated her, she would use it to her advantage. The only thing that saddened her, as she looked right back into Ted's eyes, was that Santos didn't want or need her the way this man did.

"Yes," she said as easily as she could. "You're probably right, Ted." She forced a deliberate calm that she did not feel. "When all is said and done, I suppose you have me pegged correctly. I'm a career woman above everything else."

The look of triumph in his face galled her, but at last he let go of her arms. "I thought so," he said smugly.

Pat swept her empty coffee cup off the table and turned away from him. "I'm glad we cleared the air about this, Ted. I think a little friendly disagreement is healthy—good for both of us." She was acting now, and she knew it better be good or else he'd simply start lying to her again. "Maybe we can come to some middle ground on the new hotel if we mull it over together. I'm sure we'll never see each other's perspective exactly, but we can probably each add input that'll be valuable."

"Maybe that's so," he said, picking up his tennis racquet and the can of balls. "You may have a few insights about the area that have escaped me. Just . . ." he casually slipped one arm around her shoulders, and she tried not to cringe. ". . . I wish you wouldn't get so emotional about things, sweetheart. It wastes a lot of productive time, and all it does is get you upset."

"Uh-huh," she smiled. "I'll work on it. Listen, I've got a stack of inventories to sort through this morning. I better go."

"Catch you later. Guess I didn't deserve that tennis game today," he shrugged as she started back into the lobby. She could feel his keen appraising stare always on her as she walked away, but she didn't quite catch his muttered words.

"I hope you're playing it straight with me, sweetheart," he said grimly. "For your sake, I hope you are."

The day seemed endless to Pat. She was nervous and jittery, jumping when anyone entered her office and even when the phone rang. Her new role as "hotel spy" was not at all to her liking, and she started wondering whether it would have been better to quit after all.

But she'd have no clout whatsoever once she was out of the Paradiso. How could she possibly jam the works of this rotten lousy project if she wasn't insinuating herself into Ted's good graces? Of course, she hadn't a clue as to how to sabotage his plans, and as Santos had plainly stated, Beckman was a very powerful man in these parts. With Herr Dorfmann's money and FONATUR's approval, he would be on his way. And what influence did she have? Who did she know? Would Dorfmann believe her if she tried to malign Ted in some way? No, he wouldn't. Would the deal be off if she stole the blueprints and threw them into the Pacific? No, the architect would have another set of copies.

That's just great, Pat, she scolded herself, pacing her office. Ted will prosecute you in a second if you try anything drastic. Is all this worth the end of your reputation?

All of this. The beautiful bay and the smooth stretch

of La Ropa Beach. The terns running gaily along Las Gatas. The cows lazing in the sun under a *palapa*. The burros braying at dawn. The wonder of the place struck her, and for a moment, she could see it through Santos's eyes. To deface such a paradise with a big hotel would be criminal. Zixtapo, indeed!

The whole problem, she had to admit, always came back to Santos. Much as he said he understood, part of him resented her as a foreigner, and undoubtedly always would. She couldn't seem to break through that last barrier. Once she started meddling, sticking her fingers into the preservation of his town, he was liable to flare up at her again. And much as she hated to think about it, there was a distinct possibility that he felt the same way that Ted did about her. She was useful as a go-between in his ongoing war with Beckman. She was the catalyst who kept things humming.

No, she protested silently. He couldn't make love to me the way he does and feel nothing. Santos is a man of deep passions—one of them his town.

As the afternoon wore on, and very little of her work got done, she came to the conclusion that she would have to act on her own, because of her own convictions. It was a waste of time worrying about what Santos would think, and if he disapproved, then at least she could say she had "listened to her heart."

As her father did. Oh, if only he were here, if only she could ask him for advice. He always had such an uncanny ability for cutting through the confusion and getting straight to the root of the problem. He would look at the thing squarely, without becoming wildly irrational. Because, much as she tried to be logical, Pat was a woman in love, and every thought she had, every decision she made, seemed to hinge on that excruciating, but magnificent, romantic bond.

What would my father do, if he were me? she asked herself. What simple wisdom would he offer? It vaguely occurred to her that she should call him and explain that this wouldn't be an awfully good time for him to come to Mexico, but that might muddy the waters even more. He was counting on her now, as she so often had on him, because she had offered him a lift from the doldrums of his temporary retirement. No, calling him would be a mistake—he might even ask if she was wiring him the plane tickets!

"All right, Pat," she said aloud. "Don't get trapped in all the rigamarole that sprouts up all around a problem. Go to the root of this thing, as your dear father used to say, and the rest will wither away with the devilish weed."

The problem was not Ted's job offer, nor was it Santos's feelings for her. It was that obnoxious hotel, and that was what she vowed she would concentrate on.

"Hello, Pat?" Orlando's face appeared at the door.

"What?" She bolted away from the window and clutched at her throat. "I'm sorry—you startled me."

"No, it is *I* who am sorry." The little man looked very worried and confused. "I did not knock first."

"That's okay," she smiled. "What is it, Orlando? A summons from our boss?"

"Ah, no, Pat. May I come in?"

"Sure, of course." What was all this about? she wondered.

He practically tiptoed in and closed the door quietly behind him. He stood before her silently; she watched his face change. For a moment, she thought he was going to burst into tears.

"The gargoyles," he began. "Father Luis, he is leaving."

"I know that, Orlando. I'm really working on it. I'm

going to get those gargoyles back to the church, I
promise."

"But Mr. Beckman, he has already spoken with
Father Francisco."

"The new young priest who's taking over?"

"Yes, yes," Orlando hurried on. "Mr. Beckman told
him, and he told Father Luis, who told me."

"What did he tell you?"

"Mr. Beckman will only return the gargoyles if the
money he paid for them is first deposited in his account.
Only afterward will he consider hiring the Zihuatanejo
artisans to create some sculpture for our lobby. But the
money is gone—spent!" Orlando wailed.

"Why, that no good . . ." Pat muttered, coming over
to grasp Orlando's hand. "He can't get away with it,
honestly. Don't give up hope, Orlando. We've got to
keep thinking. Damn it," she stamped her foot in
frustration. "If I had the money, I'd pay him back
myself."

"I know you would, Pat. My wife, the little *niños*,
they always made up stories about those statues. The
turtle with the man's face on his back, that is the
favorite of my son, Juan." He shook his head sadly,
and tears welled up in Pat's eyes.

"Just give me some time," she begged Orlando as
she saw him to the door. He nodded, but she knew he
didn't believe it was possible.

She marched back to her desk, totally determined
now. No tactic was too low, mean or underhanded in
her battle against Ted. The course of action was
completely clear to her now, and she no longer considered what Santos might think of her.

She did have one influential friend in Mexico, one
man who might be on her side if she played her cards
right. Hadn't he said to her at that party for Dorf-

mann that he would do anything for a student of his old buddy, James Travis? She picked up the phone and asked for long distance. When the operator came on the line, she gave her the number of FONATUR headquarters in Mexico City.

"*Buenos dìas. Me llamo Pat Jessup, del hotel Paradiso, Ixtapa. Señor Costilla, por favor.*"

If the head of the commission couldn't help her, no one could.

Chapter Thirteen

$\mathcal{S}$antos sat with his arms crossed over his chest, a deep scowl creasing his handsome face. The music playing under the big *palapa* at the Pelicanos that night was a gay, light Mozart sonata, but it didn't register with either of them. Pat could feel his mood within her own soul, and it increased the sense of trepidation she'd had about telling him in the first place.

Eventually, he broke the silence. Staring down into his untouched glass of red wine, he spat the word out. "Impossible!"

"But it isn't!" Pat insisted in exasperation. Naturally, she had expected this reaction, but that didn't make it any easier. "This is no time to let your foolish pride get in the way. It's the only chance we have to stop Ted putting a big, ugly Paradiso here. Just think of those poor people who live in those shacks on La Ropa Beach. The *rentas* offices in town are crowded enough as it is. Where are they going to go when they're displaced?"

He shook his head adamantly. "There are too many problems with your plan."

"Such as making a woman the head of a newly created town commission?" Pat asked pointedly.

He gave her a withering look. "Once again you accuse me where you have no right to do so. I've already told you I respect your competence; I see you know how to run meetings and such, how to organize groups."

"Well, then?" she demanded, leaning over to grasp his hand. "Come on, Santos, we haven't got that much time—"

"There are other considerations," he cut in.

"Let's deal with them, one at a time." She gave him a look that said she could answer any question he threw in her path. This was her mission now, and she was damned if she'd let him stand in her way. "What are they?"

"How do I justify a—what did you call it?—a Zihuatanejo Resorts Commission when I can barely run the town with the budget I have?"

She made a face. He was obviously looking for a way out. "Don't pay me right away; that's simple enough. Don't pay me at all, I don't care! The important thing is that we get the Royale away from Ted. As soon as we do that, the commission can be disbanded."

He leaned back in his chair, weighing the possibilities. "All right, suppose I do appoint you to this commission. I still don't see how you can outbid him. With Dorfmann behind him, he undoubtedly has limitless funds. He wouldn't even need a financial boost from FONATUR. And if you think that Zihuatanejo has the money to start developing hotels for itself, you are more naive than I suspected. The idea would be laughable if it were not so sad."

"This will not cost the town one red peso, Santos. I told you that," she said calmly, refusing to let him rattle her.

But he shook his head and downed half his glass of wine in one swallow. "Ridiculous. I can't believe that."

"Why must you be so stubborn! Why can't you give me a little credit—just a little—for knowing something about the hotel trade in Mexico? FONATUR wants to build up this country, not tear it down. I'm telling you that we *do* have a chance if we can convince them that we have a better plan than Beckman."

"The first thing I learned in business school is that only a fool begins a project without cash on hand—"

"Santos, please. FONATUR has money. FONATUR is the key, don't you understand? They finance half of every new resort project, except in unusual circumstances. But we have the advantage over Ted."

"What are you talking about?" he asked suspiciously.

"Remember what you told me about your friend Kurt?" She looked over at the attractive owner of the Pelicanos, who was having a drink with two South American businessmen.

"What about him?"

"His wife, Santos. She's Mexican, right? Why would FONATUR want an American-German partnership when they could have a Mexican-owned and -operated resort at the Royale site? And I'll bet my pal Señor Costilla could come up with a Mexican investor for us."

Santos shook his head doubtfully. "I'm still not convinced that this will work."

"Why? Because a woman thought it up? Because a woman would be implementing it?"

He glared at her. "That doesn't matter to me anymore. It's the plan. There's something missing, something I cannot put my finger on. It doesn't sound right to me."

She threw up her hands. "Because you didn't think of it. Santos, you have to stop treating Zihuatanejo like your crippled child. You can't do everything all by yourself. If this town is going to prosper on its own and fend off foreign developers, you are simply going to have to start accepting help. Let me help you. Please."

Santos did not respond, but instead, he searched her face, looking for some sign. Pat could see that he wanted to believe, but a part of him hung back, unable to acknowledge her trust and sincerity.

"Santos," she whispered, "I love Zihuatanejo. It's become home to me, don't you see that? I didn't grow up here as you did, but now it's in my blood. I don't want to see the beaches scarred by big hotels; I don't want to see your position as mayor undermined by a lot of foreign investors who think they can throw their weight around—as they do in Ixtapa with poor old Mayor Sánchez. But that is exactly what will happen unless you let me help you."

He turned away from her, letting his gaze wander off to the moonlight shimmering over the waves. She could see the beauty of the place reflected in his eyes, and she could sense the terrible pain welling up in him. It would kill Santos to have to let go of his dream for this town. He stared out at the water for a long time before he answered, and when he began to speak, it was so low that she didn't hear his first words.

"You're right, I suppose. Your plan is our only hope.

Tomorrow I'll set up the Zihuatanejo Resorts Commis sion and put it through the town council. They'l accept, I'm certain. The day after, I can appoint yo head of the commission."

"Santos . . . I'm speechless . . . it's, that's wonder ful." Tears shone in her eyes as she smiled at him deeply moved by his declaration. It was the sign sh needed from him, the indication that he trusted her.

"Now. I'm starved. Shall we order?" He looke vaguely embarrassed that he had fought her so ada mantly.

"Are you kidding?" she grinned. "We don't hav time for dinner. We have to get our proposal t FONATUR, *pronto.* Now," she started ticking of items on her fingers. "We'll need an architect to dra up some preliminary plans. They'll reject the propos out of hand without a set of professional blueprints And they've got to be really special, showing just wha kind of tasteful, beautiful inn we're going to erect o that site. The kind of hideaway that would be perfec for a honeymoon," she went on, realizing that she ha been describing her own dream all along. "Then we'l need to write up a convincing proposal, a stron statement that will encompass a description of th character of Zihuatanejo and towns like it all through out Mexico. We have to make a case for the future o small inns and hotels in Mexico, how they must blend i with their natural surroundings and how retaining th flavor of an old village can be vital to the economi development of a new Mexico. Then—"

"Basta! Hold on, stop!" He was looking at her, hal in amusement, half in horror as she rattled off he position paper on his country. He reached over an teasingly put a hand over her mouth. "You are actin crazy, *querida.* Please, slow down."

"But, Santos." She was already starting to get up. "There's so much to do."

"Listen, Patricia. I have copies of the blueprints that the former Royale developers used. They had to submit them to my office before construction got under way. We can submit these to FONATUR initially with the proposal, and later, we can make changes and additions. I know the architect well. He is working in Mazatlán now, as a matter of fact. But I'm sure he will be overjoyed to hear his design will be used at last."

"Oh, that's fantastic!" Spontaneously, she flung herself across the table and kissed Santos hard on the mouth. He recovered from his surprise quickly and held her there, letting the kiss deepen, oblivious to the two couples at the next table who were watching them.

"Now," he murmured, finally letting her ease back into her chair. "We can start work on the proposal at my place, right after dinner. But I cannot work on an empty stomach, nor can you." He gave her a smile that promised he was with her, completely and earnestly, at long last. She took the hand he held out to her, her heart overflowing with joy and anticipation.

"Por favor." He waved at the young waitress who was standing near them, and she came over to take their order with a shy smile on her face. She had evidently seen what had just gone on between them.

"Have you decided?" he asked Pat.

With a knowing chuckle, she turned to the waitress. "Oysters," she grinned. *"Ostras,"* she repeated loudly. *"Muchas ostras!"*

"Sí, muchas ostras para mí también," Santos declared with a mischievous sparkle in his eye.

"Buenos días," Santos whispered, his eyes sleepy and languorous as they gazed at her.

"Morning," Pat said hoarsely, forcing her lids apart and smiling at him.

They drew closer, their lips meeting in a tender kiss. Santos pulled Pat over on top of him, squeezing El Presidente out from between them and off the bed. The cat growled, announcing his presence, but they didn't notice.

"I'm glad we finished up the proposal last night," Pat purred in Santos's ear, nuzzling the soft hair at the side of his neck.

"Fast workers, both of us," he agreed, stroking her back and hips fondly and firmly.

"I think it's because we're both so smart," she giggled.

"I think it's because we had something better to do afterward," he murmured before he covered her mouth with his own. They knew each other's responses so well by now, that it was easy to lead or follow at will. She opened her lips, and their tongues met playfully for a moment.

With a sigh, she drew away. "What's the fastest way to get the stuff to Mexico City?"

"We can send it by courier later this morning. That'll get it to FONATUR right after lunch."

"When does the plane leave for Mexico City?"

"Not until eleven. We have plenty of time." Santos smiled lasciviously and rolled her over onto her back. He bent down to take one rounded breast in his mouth, and he teased the nipple until it stood up proudly to meet him.

"Santos," Pat gasped, holding his head while his mouth moved to encompass the other breast. "You've got to get the town council together and tell them about the resorts commission."

"Of course, *mi amante, mi prometida*," he breathed

228

in her ear. "But I need strength and sustenance for the day ahead. You are forgetting all those *ostras* we consumed last night."

"No, I—"

He stopped her mouth with a fierce kiss, and he put his hand under the sheet, reaching lower with tender, light strokes until she was panting. Her hands wrapped around his neck, she abandoned herself to his embraces with a carefree laugh. The work could wait. It would have to.

Chapter Fourteen

At about two o'clock the next afternoon, Pat was sitting in her office reading over her letter of resignation to Ted. It was calm, well-stated, not overly emotional. But as head of the Zihuatanejo Resorts Commission, she couldn't possibly continue as the Paradiso's assistant manager. How odd, she mused as she signed the letter with a flourish, two days ago, she'd been all torn up inside as to how to handle this conflict in her life. Now it seemed clear as glass. Her father would approve of this, she was certain. She wasn't quitting out of hostility and frustration now; she was quitting because she had something else, something much better to do.

"Afternoon. Can I talk to you a sec?"

Pat looked up, startled, to see Ted standing at the door of her office. His face was set and determined. He didn't look like he wanted to woo her at this moment.

"Sure, Ted. Come on in." She would have preferred to give him the letter at the end of the day, but so be it.

"I just got a call from FONATUR, Pat," he said as he placed his large frame in the chair opposite her. "I heard all about your bid for the Royale site." His voice was surprisingly calm, and there wasn't a shred of anger in his expression, which made Pat uneasy. She would have preferred a blowup; it would have made quitting simple.

"I'm not at all pleased to see you collaborating with Ribera behind my back, Pat. I'm very disappointed in you. It makes me wonder just how much was going on before now."

"Ted, I won't apologize. I felt it was not in the best interests of this community for your plan to be put into effect, and I—"

"Let me finish, please," he interrupted. "It seems you're more clever than I ever gave you credit for. You have a modest plan, one that'll cost FONATUR a lot less if they select it. It's not my style, of course, but what the hell, I can make a concession every once in a while—as long as the outcome is to my liking."

"What are you talking about?" She looked at him, suspicious and troubled.

"You may be right, is what I'm saying. Maybe Zihuatanejo is too special for a big hotel. Maybe you're right about moving out the other tourist market. I don't know."

He shrugged and got up to come around to her side of the desk. He picked up a rubber band and fingered it. "I have to tell you, Pat. I want you. I need you here. And if building a hotel in paradise for you was what I had to do to have you, that's what I was prepared to do." Almost shyly, he laid a hand on her shoulder.

She flinched and he, noticing it, drew his hand away quickly. Was she hearing this correctly? Suddenly Ruth's warning came back to her. Ted always fell in love with a woman as soon as she attained a position of power and influence. In his own clumsy way, this was what he wanted to do with Pat. He would actually have put up an entire resort so that she would want to run it and never leave the area. And eventually, he'd figured, she'd be so grateful that she'd just fall into his arms.

"Ted, you and I have got to get one thing straight," she began.

"The only thing we have to clear up is the money."

"What?" Here he was, talking business again, when she'd thought he was about to declare undying love!

"FONATUR will only put up fifty percent of any financing. How about my chipping in the other half? You'll be vice-president and operating manager, exactly as I promised you before. We'll give Ribera some bogus title to get our Mexican partner problem taken care of. After a while, I'll buy out his share in the company. Actually, Pat, I'm delighted this has happened. Because your plan is so much more modest than mine, I can go into the deal without Dorfmann's help. The little Paradiso will be all ours."

Now Pat was really burned. The man was insufferable! He wanted to take over the whole world! "You don't understand," she said evenly.

"What's to understand? Sweetheart . . ." He took her hands in his. "I love you, and this is our opportunity to be happy together. I mean, didn't you pull this whole scheme just to get me to come around to your style? I'm willing to do anything to make you happy."

She pulled away abruptly. "That's not why I did it at all, Ted. I submitted that bid because I wanted to save the bay from the big eyesore you want to build there. I wanted the people of Zihuatanejo to be proud of their town. But there's something else. I did it for Santos, Ted, because I love him."

Ted's face darkened, and he took a step backward as if he'd been hit. This was far worse treachery than going behind his back with a business deal. "How stupid can you be?" he snarled, his laid-back facade dropping off like a stone into water. "I offer you everything you ever wanted, on a silver platter, and you have the gall to throw it away!"

"Get out of my office. I'd like to pack my things now." She felt a white-hot rage suffuse her entire body, making her stronger than she'd ever been. "I'll leave my letter of resignation on your desk."

"I assume you're moving in with your Latin lover. Well, you better keep your eyes on him every minute, baby, because everyone knows the good mayor is about as faithful as a tomcat."

Pat didn't answer him. Very calmly, she began taking her manila folders out of the drawer and stacking them.

"You're a fool if you think he's going to accept you as you are. He'll have you making babies within a year."

She took several more cards out of her address file and put them in the pile. His words meant nothing to her, and her love for Santos burned like a steady, true flame, warming her heart and soul.

"Santos certainly can't stomach the notion of a woman with a career. You know it's true. It's just a conquest for him, Pat, to get a luscious American blonde for his very own. And if you don't obey his every command, I predict he'll throw you out on your ear. Then you'll be running back to Boston to work the night desk at some highway motel. If you're lucky, that is."

She swept the contents of her top drawer into her

tote bag and zipped up her attaché case. Then she swept past him, her back as straight as it had ever been in her life.

"You think about it, Pat," he said in a shaking voice. "Consider your future with him. And consider the fact that I've got a lot of influence at FONATUR. They haven't accepted your bid yet. My door is always open for an apology. You think about it."

She turned and gave him a withering look. "You can't beat me, Ted, because you don't know a thing about people. And I do. And that's what life is all about, you know." She stepped through the doorway and walked briskly down the corridor, feeling the icy wind of her fury propelling her forward.

She went immediately to her room and closed the door behind her. But once in that safe haven, she was struck by everything that he had said to her, and it suddenly hit her hard. She slumped on her bed, struggling to keep up her brave front. As much as she fought it, she found herself repeating Ted's assessment of her relationship with Santos. Oh, Ted was an idiot, and he had his own reasons for being so disgusting and hateful, but something vital gnawed at her and filled her with doubt.

Of course, she and Santos shared something very special. They had spent miraculous times together, days and nights of great pleasure and tenderness, of passion so deep and moving that Pat had lost herself entirely in it. But the crucial fact was that Santos had never declared his love to her. In fact, he had told her all the reasons he could not love her. She had wanted to believe that things had changed between them, but now she wasn't so sure. He remained a mystery to her, keeping his most important cards close to his chest. He was the master of vague, equivocal answers.

Well, she'd burned her last bridge, so she'd better get cracking. She had to pack, go see Ruth, say good-bye to Orlando, and finally, call her father. That would be the worst of it. He'd been looking to her to bring him a new reason for getting better. Now, she might be crawling home with her tail between her legs if FON-ATUR didn't give the okay on their plan. It was clear she'd never work in Mexico again if she wasn't running the show. Ted Beckman would see to that.

She walked around her little apartment, picking things up and packing. She'd grown really fond of the place in the months she'd lived there. She walked to the window and gazed out at the open sea. Just like Gloucester. Like home.

But where was home now? She'd told Santos that she had a commitment to this town, and that was no lie. She couldn't turn into a Mexican in a puff of magic smoke, but she had found something in this country that she'd never known in America. The rolling waves outside her window calmed and hypnotized her. There was a small fishing boat on the horizon, becoming larger as it approached. Like her father's boat, she thought with a smile. It was incredible how her two lives had meshed so completely. Hadn't he told her that if she listened to her heart, she would never go wrong?

But what was her heart telling her? She turned away from the window, torn by self-doubt and ambivalence. Did she want to stay with Santos if he refused to make a true commitment to her? Was her sense of herself as a professional woman so important that Ted's offer might become appealing if she considered it long enough? But she loathed his values, detested the way he exploited people and ideas. And aside from all this, the final problem loomed larger than any of the others. How was she going to get FONATUR to accept her bid instead of Ted's?

She flopped into an armchair beside a stack of magazines she was going to leave for Rosa and Orlando. On top of the pile was an old copy of an old news magazine with a picture of a jet fighter plane on the cover. Absently, her mind still on her problems, she began to flip through the pages. The world was in an awful state, she mused. She was so protected from everything in this exotic paradise. There was fighting, terrorism, the plight of the economy, all of it just hopeless. At least she'd had a little peace here. For her, Zihuatanejo was the world the way it might once have been, a reminder that life still could be beautiful.

Suddenly, her eye lit on a picture that looked familiar. She stared at the page, at the masts of fishing boats lined up at an old port.

What was this? She began to read, and as she did, a new spark of excitement flared inside her. This was it! This was the answer! There was not a sliver of doubt in her mind anymore. The Royale site was theirs, and what was even better, the gargoyles would be back in the Church of Santa Bárbara!

With a whoop of triumph, she tucked the magazine into her purse and dashed out of her room. She fairly flew to the parking lot and, for the final time as a Paradiso employee, she borrowed the keys to one of the staff cars.

She zoomed to the entrance and slowed as she saw the approach of one of the minibuses coming in from town. Ruth Beckman climbed out of the van and Pat honked the horn to attract her attention.

"Ruth," she yelled. "It's me, Pat."

"Why didn't you tell me you were driving in?" Ruth grumbled as she approached the car.

"I'm sorry. I'd have been happy to take you. Ruth, something's happened. I've got to see Santos right away or I'd stop to tell you about it."

"True love, I know, how can I compete?" shrugged the tiny woman. "But I just want to tell you that if you don't have dinner with me and my son pretty soon, he's going to fall into the doldrums and never recover. He's got it bad, I'm afraid to say. Didn't I warn you?"

"Oh, Ruth," Pat sighed. She opened her door and got out. She might as well tell her.

"What? What's going on?"

"I quit this afternoon. Ted and I had an enormous blowup."

"Oh, that louse," Ruth muttered. "He can never let a good woman be. He has to get his little petty emotions all mixed up in it. So I suppose you've got a job in Zihuatanejo now?" She sounded so forlorn, as though she'd lost her best friend.

"Santos and I," Pat began, "we're going to start a little inn over on the Royale site. We'll start it, but it'll be run by Zihuatanejans."

"Sounds great. When can I move in?" Ruth asked eagerly.

Pat laughed and took her friend's hand. "I don't want to jinx it by giving you a date. See, FONATUR hasn't actually agreed to it yet, but they will. And as soon as it's done, you get the honeymoon suite, I promise."

"Are you kidding?" Ruth chortled as Pat climbed back into the car and started the engine. "That's for you and the mayor, and don't tell me different!"

Pat smiled nervously. "I'll be back for my things. I'll see you later, Ruth." She drove off, mulling over the idea Ruth had planted in her roiling brain.

I love him, but maybe that's not enough. In Pat's

mind, Santos's respect for her professional ability was intimately linked to having his love in return. He would have to accept her for what she was now, she was certain. As soon as he heard about her foolproof plan, he would . . .

Would what? Throw his arms around her and declare that he would never love any other woman but her? Ask her to marry him and promise to be true forever?

Hogwash, Pat, she told herself sternly. Love doesn't work that way. It's not tied to conditions and details. Only somebody like Steve Elman thinks that you can present a work contract and mortgage on a house along with a marriage proposal. If Santos doesn't love you, he just doesn't. That doesn't mean you shouldn't go ahead and save his town with him. It'll just be a different kind of relationship, that's all.

She was very calm when she got to his office. Her expectations were for one thing, and one thing only.

"Read this," she said, as soon as the police chief and several local bankers had left Santos's office and he was alone.

He looked curiously at the magazine, then glanced at the article she opened to.

"'A New Life for Old Collioure.' What's this? Where is this place?"

"It's a tiny town at the southern tip of France. I'd heard of it before, but I never thought of it until I started throwing out old magazines."

"*Querida,* this is no time for you and me to be taking vacations in the south of France," he smiled distantly. "We have much to do here." He pushed the magazine aside.

"Santos, for God's sake! Read it, don't fool around!"

He frowned at her insistent tone, but did as she

asked. He shook his head at first, and then the light began to dawn.

"You mean—" he began.

"Exactly," she smiled triumphantly. "Collioure is just the same as Zihuatanejo. We'd qualify in a minute!"

"I don't know. The Mexican government is not the same as the French government." He knit his brows and continued reading.

"But they are! Remember when they built the subway in Mexico City? They engineered the whole thing around that shrine to Ehecatl, the god of the wind that they found when they were excavating. It was a ruin; it was a national monument, for heaven's sake! They preserved it. Piño Suárez is the only subway station in the world with a pyramid in it! How can you say the Mexican government doesn't have a sense of tradition?"

"But a whole town, Pat! It would be a first," Santos pointed out.

"So what?" She faced him down with a broad grin.

"Well, then, what are we waiting for? It was *your* idea—you get on the phone and talk to the Cultural Affairs Department."

"You trust me to do this?" she asked, astonished.

"As long as you will let me help," he nodded, getting up to take her in his arms.

They met Señor Costilla at the airport the next afternoon. He brought with him the director of the Cultural Commission of Mexico, Señor Ruiz del Rey, a tall, rather stern-looking man with a pointed white goatee.

"I am delighted to see you again, my dear." Señor

Costilla took Pat's arm as he shook Santos's hand warmly. "And you, sir. May I present my colleague and friend, Señor del Rey."

"We have not much time," the older man said. "May we see the site now, please?"

"Of course. My car is just over there." Santos pointed to the old Rabbit, and the two men gave him a quizzical look. As they walked over to it, Costilla whispered to Pat, "I should have thought of this myself when we spoke on the phone the other day. But perhaps it takes an eye less accustomed to our country to see its beauty in the right perspective."

"I'm so happy to hear you say this," Pat grinned.

"But it is del Rey you must convince," he cautioned her as they got into the car.

Santos started the engine and drove directly to the Royale site. The afternoon sun glinted on the high beams, illuminating the unfinished hotel with a brilliant gleam. The waves were pounding hard on the dock when they got out of the car to look around.

"Señor del Rey," Santos said, leading the man toward the site. "Miss Jessup and I would like to give you a complete tour of Zihuatànejo when we leave here. Only then will you understand the motive behind our request."

"I would be delighted to see what you have to show me," the man nodded, his keen gaze riveted on the landscape and the hotel. "Quite frankly, I am intrigued by your idea, Miss Jessup. I have heard of Collioure myself, although I have never visited France."

Pat gave Santos an anxious look and thought carefully before she spoke. "There aren't many lovely old towns left unspoiled anymore in Mexico. The tourist trade is enormously important to the economic health of your country, but too often the developers wipe away everything of historic value in their attempt to create a luxury environment for their clientele. That's why we're asking you to declare Zihuatanejo—the entire town and all its buildings—a national landmark. We feel we have a good case," she added hopefully.

Señor del Rey nodded. "You may be right. May I see the town now?"

"Of course, sir." Santos gave Pat's hand a quick squeeze as he led them back to the car. He drove slowly, pointing out the various areas of the town as they approached the *centro*. Easily, and with enormous confidence, he answered every question del Rey threw at him. Pat was quiet, listening to the man she loved describing the place that meant so much to him. Her heart was filled with deep tenderness for him, and over the hour they spent driving around, her worries were somehow dissipated as she saw the changing expression on del Rey's face. Señor Costilla, she knew, was already on their side.

At last they reached the Church of Santa Bárbara, and Santos pulled up on the opposite side of the street. He didn't say a word.

"But, what is this?" Costilla leaned over the back of the seat, craning his neck. "This is the chapel that used to have the gargoyles, is it not? The ones brought from Spain many centuries ago?"

"That is correct," Santos answered.

"And where are the gargoyles?" he insisted.

"I'm afraid they've been temporarily removed," Pat said quietly. "Right now they're in the lobby of the Paradiso in Ixtapa."

"They are where? In Beckman's hotel!" Costilla was outraged, and del Rey looked very concerned.

"He paid the church for them, and they did need the money for the parish. But when I suggested an exchange of some modern sculptures, designed by the artists of Zihuatanejo, Mr. Beckman refused. He won't let the gargoyles go now."

"He will if this town is given landmark status," del Rey cut in. "There will be funds for the complete restoration of this church, and of all local buildings of historic import." He got a notepad out of his pocket and began jotting things down. "Señor Ribera, what you have in this town is very precious. It must be preserved."

A wide smile broke out on Santos's face, and it lit up Pat's very soul. This was the answer they'd been praying for!

"Then you'll do it?" Santos asked eagerly.

"It will be my honor to declare Zihuatanejo a national monument, as Collioure is in France. This designation, you understand, means that no modern buildings may be erected within the city limits or in the surrounding countryside. Construction will be restricted to buildings that blend in with the landscape, in the same style as the old buildings."

"FONATUR likes the plans for the small hotel on the Royale site," Señor Costilla added. "And they are delighted that there will be Mexican participation in the ownership and management. I must warn you, though," he shook his finger at Pat. "You may have to tone down some of the elements in accordance with Señor del Rey's new designation for Zihuatanejo. The hotel perhaps must be a bit more intimate."

"We'd be delighted to have our architect work with you," Pat nodded.

"Mr. Beckman, of course, will be sent a formal rejection of his plans and notification that the gargoyles must be returned to the Church of Santa Bárbara within two weeks."

Pat wanted to shout for joy, but she was determined to act professional. "I'm pleased to hear that," she said calmly.

"Now, Mr. Mayor, if you will be so kind as to take us back to the airport, we will get started on the official papers as soon as we return to Mexico City," del Rey told him. "I wonder if you might send me all of the historical information you have told me about today that pertains to the church and the town, as well as a sheaf of photos of your most precious buildings and town squares. We wish to determine what sort of restoration will have to be done."

"I'll put together a whole package for you," Pat nodded as they drove along. She could have sung for joy, but she managed to contain herself until they had the two men safely at the airport, their return tickets in hand.

"Thank you so much for coming," Santos said before they left.

"I am pleased, most happy, to have visited your charming town. I will be back for the dedication ceremony," del Rey smiled.

"And I," Costilla added, giving Pat's arm a squeeze of congratulations as they walked off toward the waiting room for their flight.

Pat turned to Santos with a mischievous grin. "We did it!" she laughed. "We did it!" She threw her arms around his neck, and with a whoop of triumph, he picked her up and spun her around, much to the amusement of several tourists on their way to a parked minibus.

"Let's go home and celebrate," he whispered in her ear.

"Wait a second! You forgot the best part," she said, still held tightly in the circle of his strong arms.

"And what is better than going home to celebrate?"

"We have to tell Ted!" she laughed. "I can't wait to see his face."

"Later." Santos steered her to the car over her vehement protests. "He is not as important as what I have to discuss with you. He is not important at all."

She looked into his eyes, and solemnly, she nodded her agreement.

El Presidente was waiting for them at the door, his fur decorated with blossoms from a nearby tree. Santos bent, laughing, to dust him off, and the cat zoomed inside the house with a yowl.

"Now, *querida,* somewhere here I have a bottle of California champagne." He began rummaging in the kitchen cabinets while Pat eased herself onto a bar stool. Everything was perfect now, wasn't it? She should feel delirious, happy, on top of the world.

But as she watched him puttering around, putting the bottle and two glasses into the freezer, recapping their grand success half in English, half in Spanish, she felt her spirits dropping lower. What had changed really, between them? He had accepted her idea for saving his town and was enthralled with her. She had proven herself competent, capable, enormously valuable. But she longed to be something else to him.

"I will begin by calling Kurt at the Pelicanos to share the news with him. Then we must get in touch with the architect and find out what his time schedule looks like. You'll make a tour of the town tomorrow, and take those photos Señor del Rey requested and write up something for the restoration project. Oh yes, and when you collect your things from the Paradiso, you

244

can, of course, drop in to Mr. Beckman's office and tell him to his face what has occurred."

"Poor Ruth," Pat smiled sadly. "She has a certain interest here. Do you know, when I told her about the Royale, she asked when she could move in? I told her we'd give her the honeymoon suite."

She watched for a reaction, but none came. Santos was busy writing things down. "I will spend tomorrow at the four largest banks of Zihuatanejo. I have spent hours with the men who run these local offices, suggesting until I am blue in the face how they should best invest their money. I know that together, they will be able to match FONATUR's fifty percent."

"That'll take care of the Mexican partnership, I guess," she murmured.

"You have some plans, I am certain, for the operation of the hotel?" Santos asked her, evidently oblivious to her mood.

"Well, I've thought about it, sure." Pat looked at him quizzically.

"Since you will be manager, I think you had better start hiring a staff by the beginning of June, what do you say? Perhaps we will put in an ad for an assistant manager immediately."

"Me, as manager?"

"But who else?"

She bit her lip, wondering what he meant by all this. He seemed totally comfortable with allowing her the power and position.

"I thought you might have a Mexican friend in the business, that's all."

"Pat, Pat!" He came over and gripped her by both shoulders. "I am going to be very busy. A new political campaign must be mounted as there are elections next fall. There have been a few contenders for the throne,

245

you see, and you must admit, I have been busy with many other things lately. I must have someone in charge I can trust implicitly."

"Santos, after rescuing Zihuatanejo from the developers, they'll probably elect you emperor for life," she grinned, still in the dark as to what was going on in his elusive mind. The notion of running the hotel and furthering her career was enormously exciting, and at any other time, she would have been bounding from one room to the next with joy, but not today.

"Let me make a phone call, please. Would you see if the wine is chilled?" Whistling, he went into the bedroom and closed the door behind him. He was still keeping secrets from her, then. Pat sighed and wandered toward the kitchen.

Well, Pat, she told herself. Two out of three's not bad. She had finally discovered the three things in life that would make her happy: first, an unspoiled Zihuatanejo; second, a career that fulfilled her. The third now seemed hopeless, impossible, and yet she didn't see how she could live without it. Santos's love was like the brass ring on the merry-go-round, always just an inch or two out of reach.

She was mulling all this over when she heard a car pull up outside. The door slammed. She went to the window to look out, but was nearly knocked down when the door was pushed open. Ted Beckman stood glaring down at her.

"I thought I'd find you two here, in your little love nest," he sneered.

"Ted, I—"

"Costilla called me from the airport. Said we'd known each other so long, he felt it wouldn't be right to just send me a rejection letter. I bet you feel real smug, Pat. To go behind my back, do everything in your power to discredit me, it's unbelievable!" He stood in the doorway, looming over her, but she wasn't afraid.

"I can't say I'm sorry," she shrugged. "And nothing I've done will in any way hurt your Ixtapa business."

"I don't believe you were invited here," said a deep voice behind her. Santos walked out of the bedroom and to the door.

"I just wanted to tell you two that I've got my people behind me," Ted rushed on. "We're going to mount the biggest ad campaign in the States you ever saw for Ixtapa. Your little podunk restoration town won't have a chance."

"I don't know about that, Ted," Pat smiled. "You know the old expression, 'We try harder'?" Suddenly she was up again, determined that she was going to do the best job of her life.

"You're going to have to work day and night, the two of you," Ted said grimly. "And I don't think I need add that I'm only paying your salary through the day you put that phone call in to FONATUR."

"That sounds fair," Pat nodded.

"I'll see that the check is mailed to the mayor's office," he threw over his shoulder as he whirled around and stalked down the path to his car.

Pat shook her head and went over to sit on the sofa. "I have to admit," she sighed, "I ought to have quit first and put all my cards on the table."

Santos came around to sit beside her. "You did what you had to. Thank God," he added softly.

"Well, what about that champagne?" She was about to get up, but he held her firmly where she was.

"Not yet. Here, take a look at this first."

He had written down the times and flight numbers of planes from Boston. She stared at the piece of paper, uncomprehending.

"What's this?"

"I have a good travel agent in town. She's wired some tickets for me." He smiled mysteriously and his hand crept around her shoulders.

"What are you talking about?"

"Did I hear you wrong? Did you not tell me that you wished to bring your parents here for a vacation? If I am wrong, I will call my friend back and cancel the reservations."

"You mean you—"

"Surely you would want your parents to attend our wedding?" He raised his eyebrows in mock concern.

"What—?" she began, but he sealed her lips with a warm kiss.

When he broke away briefly, he murmured, "That night I saw you at the party for Dorfmann, you were wearing the loveliest Mexican wedding dress I'd ever seen. Will you wear it again?"

"Oh, Santos!" Her eyes filled with tears, but she wanted to laugh at the same time.

"Marry me, Pat. I love you more than I can say; my heart is yours. And as we say here, *mi casa es su casa.*"

"Oh, my darling." She threw her arms around his neck, so happy she thought she would burst with joy. Then something occurred to her, and she pulled back to look at him.

"But you want me to be manager of the Royale?"

"You cannot be manager and my wife as well?" He looked shocked.

"I didn't think you'd want it."

He ran a hand through her tousled blond hair, and slowly it traveled down her cheek to the place where her blouse parted. "You have taught me much about what a woman can do. And this is why I love you so fondly, so deeply, so passionately." He began to unbutton her blouse, and her heart started pounding around her chest.

"But why didn't you ever tell me how you felt? Sometimes I thought you were furious with me."

"Sometimes I was," he chuckled. "But an argument never lasts long, and love lasts an eternity." He smoothed the hair back from her forehead and looked down at her with an expression of sublime happiness and total peace of mind.

"Once you said you could never love me as you wished to, though. Do you remember?"

"Clearly," he nodded. "But I still had much to learn at that point—about you and about myself."

"Are you sure now?" she persisted.

He answered with a lingering kiss.

"I love you, Santos," she whispered when their lips parted. "I have for such a long time."

"And I, you." He bent to kiss her golden hair, and she hugged him to her.

"Well, in that case," she smiled. "I have to go call my father. And Ruth, too. They'll be so happy."

"What are we waiting for?" he grinned. "The phone, as you know, is in the bedroom, beside the bed."

Hand in hand, they got up and went into the other room. Santos steered her to the bed, but before he could nudge her down onto it, he noticed it was occupied. El Presidente was sprawled in a posture of total exhaustion, right in the middle of it.

"My fine friend!" Santos laughed. "You will be my best man at the wedding. I will fit you out in a top hat and tails."

The old cat lifted his head and looked at the embracing couple. Before they could catch him, he escaped, jumping up onto the sill of the open window and then out to the woods, to freedom.

"You're so mean to him," Pat chided Santos as he pressed her back in the warm hollow the cat had left.

"Not intentionally." His firm body molded itself to the curve of her soft one. "Now tell me, *mi novia*, where would you like to be married?"

"Do you have to ask? In the Church of Santa Bárbara, of course, after the gargoyles are returned."

He kissed her, and his hands began to work their wonderful magic on her pliant body. "I love you, Patricia, but you must promise me one thing."

"What's that?" she asked, wrapping her legs around his.

"You must be the one to tell Ruth she cannot have the honeymoon suite, not for a long while, anyway. We are going to have it occupied, and very busy, too."

"I was hoping you'd say that," she smiled happily, snuggling down into his arms. "I just didn't want to seem pushy."

His mouth came down on hers, and she met his kiss with fire and tenderness. Her dream had come true; now she did have everything: a wonderful career in a beautiful place where she could create a honeymoon hideaway for people like herself and her lover. Except that there was no one else like him, nor was there any love equal to theirs. The pounding of their two hearts meshed to one strong, steady beat, and soon, neither they nor the noisy birds outside their open window could have distinguished that sound from the lapping of the waves on La Ropa Beach. They were part of the landscape now, and it was theirs forever.

If you enjoyed
this book...

you will enjoy a Special Edition Book Club membership
en more.

will bring you each new title, as soon as it is published
ery month, delivered right to your door.

15-Day Free Trial Offer

e will send you 6 new Silhouette Special Editions to keep
r 15 days absolutely free! If you decide not to keep them,
nd them back to us, you pay nothing. But if you enjoy
em as much as we think you will, keep them and pay the
voice enclosed with your trial shipment. You will then
tomatically become a member of the Special Edition
ook Club and receive 6 more romances every month.
here is no minimum number of books to buy and you can
ncel at any time.

MORE ROMANCE FOR
A SPECIAL WAY TO RELAX
$1.95 each

2 ☐ Hastings	21 ☐ Hastings	41 ☐ Halston	60 ☐ Thorne
3 ☐ Dixon	22 ☐ Howard	42 ☐ Drummond	61 ☐ Beckman
4 ☐ Vitek	23 ☐ Charles	43 ☐ Shaw	62 ☐ Bright
5 ☐ Converse	24 ☐ Dixon	44 ☐ Eden	63 ☐ Wallace
6 ☐ Douglass	25 ☐ Hardy	45 ☐ Charles	64 ☐ Converse
7 ☐ Stanford	26 ☐ Scott	46 ☐ Howard	65 ☐ Cates
8 ☐ Halston	27 ☐ Wisdom	47 ☐ Stephens	66 ☐ Mikels
9 ☐ Baxter	28 ☐ Ripy	48 ☐ Ferrell	67 ☐ Shaw
10 ☐ Thiels	29 ☐ Bergen	49 ☐ Hastings	68 ☐ Sinclair
11 ☐ Thornton	30 ☐ Stephens	50 ☐ Browning	69 ☐ Dalton
12 ☐ Sinclair	31 ☐ Baxter	51 ☐ Trent	70 ☐ Clare
13 ☐ Beckman	32 ☐ Douglass	52 ☐ Sinclair	71 ☐ Skillern
14 ☐ Keene	33 ☐ Palmer	53 ☐ Thomas	72 ☐ Belmont
15 ☐ James	35 ☐ James	54 ☐ Hohl	73 ☐ Taylor
16 ☐ Carr	36 ☐ Dailey	55 ☐ Stanford	74 ☐ Wisdom
17 ☐ John	37 ☐ Stanford	56 ☐ Wallace	75 ☐ John
18 ☐ Hamilton	38 ☐ John	57 ☐ Thornton	76 ☐ Ripy
19 ☐ Shaw	39 ☐ Milan	58 ☐ Douglass	77 ☐ Bergen
20 ☐ Musgrave	40 ☐ Converse	59 ☐ Roberts	78 ☐ Gladstone

MORE ROMANCE FOR
A SPECIAL WAY TO RELAX

$2.25 each

79 ☐ Hastings	82 ☐ McKenna	85 ☐ Beckman	88 ☐ Saxon
80 ☐ Douglass	83 ☐ Major	86 ☐ Halston	89 ☐ Meriwether
81 ☐ Thornton	84 ☐ Stephens	87 ☐ Dixon	90 ☐ Justin

LOOK FOR *WAY OF THE WILLOW*
BY LINDA SHAW

Silhouette Intimate Moments

Coming Soon

Dreams Of Evening by Kristin James

Tonio Cruz was a part of Erica Logan's past and she hated him for betraying her. Then he walked back into her life and Erica's fear of loving him again was nothing compared to her fear that he would discover the one secret link that still bound them together.

Once More With Feeling by Nora Roberts

Raven and Brand—charismatic, temperamental, talented. Their songs had once electrified the world. Now, after a separation of five years, they were to be reunited to create their special music again. The old magic was still there, but would it be enough to mend two broken hearts?

Emeralds In The Dark by Beverly Bird

Courtney Winston's sight was fading, but she didn't need her eyes to know that Joshua Knight was well worth loving. If only her stubborn pride would let her compromise, but she refused to tie any man to her when she knew that someday he would have to be her eyes.

Sweetheart Contract by Pat Wallace

Wynn Carson, trucking company executive, and Duke Bellini, union president, were on opposite sides of the bargaining table. But once they got together in private, they were very much on the same side.

Love, passion and adventure will be yours FREE for 15 days... with Tapestry™ historical romances!

"Long before women could read and write, tapestries were used to record events and stories . . . especially the exploits of courageous knights and their ladies."

And now there's a new kind of tapestry...

In the pages of Tapestry™ romance novels, you'll find love, intrigue, and historical touches that really make the stories come alive!

You'll meet brave Guyon d'Arcy, a Norman knight . . . handsome Comte Andre de Crillon, a Huguenot royalist . . . rugged Branch Taggart, a feuding American rancher . . . and more. And on each journey back in time, you'll experience tender romance and searing passion . . . and learn about the way people lived and loved in earlier times than ours.

We think you'll be so delighted with Tapestry romances, you won't want to miss a single one! We'd like to send you 2 books each month, as soon as they are published, through our Tapestry Home Subscription Service℠ Look them over for 15 days, free. If not delighted, simply return them and owe nothing. But if you enjoy them as much as we think you will, pay the invoice enclosed. There's never any additional charge for this convenient service — we pay all postage and handling costs.

To receive your Tapestry historical romances, fill out the coupon below and mail it to us today. You're on your way to all the love, passion, and adventure of times gone by!

HISTORICAL *Tapestry* ROMANCES

Silhouette Special Edition

Coming Next Month

Love's Gentle Chains by Sondra Stanford

Lynn had fled from Drew believing she didn't belong in his world. Then she discovered she was bound to him by her love and the child he had unknowingly fathered.

All's Fair by Lucy Hamilton

Automotive engineer Kitty Gordon had been in love with race driver Steve Duncan when she was sixteen. But this time, she would find the inside track to his heart.

Love Feud by Anne Lacey

Carole returned to the hills of North Carolina and rediscovered Jon. His family was still an anathema to hers, but he drew her to him with a sensuous spell she was unable to resist.

Cry Mercy, Cry Love by Monica Barrie

Heather Strand, although blind since birth, saw more clearly than Reid Hunter until love sharpened his vision and he realized that Heather was the only woman for him—forever.

A Matter Of Trust by Emily Doyle

After being used by one man, Victoria Van Straaten wanted to keep Andreas at arm's length. However, on a cruise to Crete she found Andreas determined to close the distance.

Dreams Lost, Dreams Found by Pamela Wallace

It was as though Brynne was reliving a Scottish legend with Ross Fleming—descendant of the Lord of the Isles. Only this time the legend would have a happy ending.